THE INVESTIGATION OFFICER'S FILE

The Investigation Officer's File

A WOODY WHITE LEGAL THRILLER

Dallas Clark

Charleston, SC
www.PalmettoPublishing.com

The Investigation Officer's File
Copyright © 2021 by Dallas Clark

Hardcover ISBN: 978-1-68515-910-8
Paperback ISBN: 978-1-68515-253-6
eBook ISBN: 978-1-68515-254-3

Thank you to my friends who supported this endeavor by me. It could not have been completed without your help.

With all my heart, I dedicate this novel to my daughter Katie; her husband, Keith; and their children Andrew, Thomas, and Jake; to my daughter Joanna, her husband, Jeff; and their children Frances and Dallas; and my daughter Hannah and her mom, Melanie. Their support has been helpful beyond measure.

Candidate White

1315 Hours, Mon, 30 Sep 68
Officer Candidate School
United States Marine Corps Base
Quantico, Virginia

"Maggot, in the one hundred ninety-three year history of *my* Marine Corps, that is the worst push-up ever. You ain't got the chance of a snowball in hell of being a second lieutenant in *my* Corps. I'll see to that. Get your fat ass up and haul it over to the candidate reporting station right over there, if you can find it, and tell them you won't be here long, and you tell them that Sergeant Gonzalez said you ain't got what it takes to lead Marines to the chow hall, much less on a mission to kill the Cong. Now get outta here."

As Woody White struggled to his feet, exhausted by the push-ups he had attempted and scared as he had never been from the tirade of Sergeant Gonzalez, he was thinking he made a big mistake when he enlisted in the Marines during his second year of law school at Wake Forest University.

He had parked his car in the "Candidates Park Here" lot and was heading to the "Candidates Report Here" building when he first met Sergeant Andros Gonzalez. The meeting started pleasantly enough.

"Good morning," Sergeant Gonzalez asked, "Do you have the time, please?" He was dressed in utilities with the three stripes of an E-5 sergeant pinned on the collars and on his barracks cap, and the name "Gonzalez" was printed over the right breast pocket of his utility shirt.

Woody put his suitcase down and looked at the Hamilton watch he had inherited from his father. "Yes, sir, it is one thirty-five."

Sergeant Gonzalez rushed to Woody, standing so close to him that his nose almost touched Woody's. He was yelling so loudly that Woody thought he could be heard in Washington, D.C., twenty-five miles to the north. "Why did you call me 'sir'? I'm not an officer 'cause I *work* for a living. And what do you mean 'one thirty-five'? Do you know you are on a military base?"

"Yes. Yes, sir, I know…"

"What did I tell you five seconds ago, you maggot. I am not an officer. I'm giving you a direct order. Don't call me 'sir' again, or I'll have your ass. Understood?"

"Yes, sergeant."

"That's not right either, you worm. You address me, 'Sergeant, yes Sergeant,' or 'Sergeant, no Sergeant.' Understood? What is your name, candidate?"

"Woody White, sergeant. I mean, Sergeant, Woody White, Sergeant."

"Did you cut your engine off when you parked your car, Candidate White?" Sergeant Gonzalez continued to have his face in Woody's. His eyes bulged, and he looked as mad as anyone Woody had ever seen.

"Sergeant, yes Sergeant."

"Why did you do that, White?"

"Sergeant, because I am reporting to Officer Candidate School, Sergeant, to become a Marine Corps second lieutenant, Sergeant."

"Well, White, you shoulda left the motor running 'cause I can already tell you ain't gonna be in *my* Marine Corps. You don't even know how to tell time. I'll bet you tell time by seeing where Mickey's hands are at, don't you? Well, let me tell you, as long as you are trying to become a Marine in *my* Marine Corps, your clock is a twenty-four-hour clock, so what you have known up to now as 1:00 p.m. is now and forever after known as 1300 hours, understood?"

"Sergeant, yes Sergeant."

"How much do you weigh, White?"

"Sergeant, about 196 pounds, Sergeant."

"White, do you know what an order is?"

"Yes, sir, an order is…"

The decibel of Sergeant Gonzalez's voice somehow reached a new high, and he was so close to Woody's face that his spittle hit Woody's nose.

"Numnuts, I gave you a *direct order* to address me as 'sergeant' when addressing me. And you violated my order, didn't you, maggot?"

"Sergeant, yes Sergeant."

"And I asked you what an order was, and that only requires a yes or no answer, correct?"

"Sergeant, yes Sergeant."

And then Sergeant Gonzalez's voice dropped almost to a whisper. "Well, maggot, if I asked you if you knew what an order was, and your answer had to be either a yes or no, then why did you start to tell me *what* an order was. I didn't ask you *what* an order was, now did I?"

Woody felt like his brain was turning to oatmeal. "Sergeant, no Sergeant."

"What are you going to do if you are leading my Marines in the jungle, and your company commander orders you to move your platoon one hundred meters east, but you move west, and the F-4 Phantom jet drops napalm on you and your men, burning you and some of my Marines to a crisp, like bacon, 'cause you didn't follow orders. What are you going to do?"

Woody had taken about two seconds to try to think of an answer when the sergeant was again yelling at him. "Maggot, drop and give me ten."

As Woody finished the ten push-ups and stumbled toward the reporting office, he knew two things for sure: OCS was going to be ten weeks of pure hell, and he hoped he could make it through and be commissioned a second lieutenant in the United States Marine Corps.

What Woody did not know was that the United States Senate would pass a law within two weeks of Woody reporting to OCS that would have a life-or-death impact on his Marine Corps career.

And Woody also did not know that the murder of an officer in Vietnam, a Marine's following an order about that murder, and the investigation of that murder would result in Woody's most important case as a Marine.

"Listen Up"

0935 Hours, Tue, 31 Dec 68
First Platoon, Alpha Company
First Battalion, Ninth Marine Regiment
Third Marine Division
Vandergrift Combat Base
I Corps
Republic of South Vietnam

"Listen up!" Sergeant Maurice Smith didn't need to give orders a second time. The thirty-nine men of First Platoon, Alpha Company, First Battalion, Ninth Marine Regiment, Third Marine Division (Alpha 1/9), directed their attention to him because he was their platoon sergeant. He was a six-foot-three-inch Black man from Dothan, Alabama, strong as an ox and fearless. He was midway through his second consecutive tour in South Vietnam, both with Alpha 1/9. He knew what to do in a firefight, and first platoon Alpha 1/9 had been in many firefights. The men of the five squads of the first platoon not only respected Sergeant Smith, they feared him and looked to him to lead them in combat.

"Well, here we are at beautiful Vandergrift Combat Base, aka VCB, within spitting distance of the DMZ, in beautiful South Vietnam, on this beautiful New Year's Eve." The men chuckled because there was nothing beautiful about VCB, previously named LZ Stud.

4

VCB sat in a valley, part of which was flat as an IHOP pancake. It had military value because it served as a landing/takeoff place for the many choppers supporting the Marines fighting in I Corps, the most northern of the four combat sectors of South Vietnam and the sector closest to North Vietnam. Men and supplies constantly came in and out of VCB either by chopper or a road, Route 9. Steel Marston matting had been placed on the floor of the valley and offered a foundation for the choppers to land and take on or off-load supplies or wounded or killed in action. There were more landings and take-offs than you could count. One began to not even notice the choppers, except when the larger CH-53 Sea Stallions lifted heavily with the bodies of KIA Marines in body bags, bundled in a large tarp, which was swinging slowly below the chopper on the way to the division morgue, wherever it was.

Sergeant Smith continued, "The word has come from on high! Since we ain't got a lieutenant platoon leader until Lt. Williams's replacement gets here, and that should be in a day or two, I was ordered to join the lieutenants of the other platoons of Alpha and meet with the company commander. That was when he told me our new platoon leader would be checking in soon. But the main reason for meeting was for him to tell us that our mission, it be changing. General Davis, the CG of the Third Division—you remember hearing about him; he was on the Canal in WW2, won The Medal in Korea don't think we's doing what Marines are supposed to do by just holding the line—if that's what we're doin'. He wants us to kick ass and take names. The NVA been moving supplies down the Ho Chi Minh Trail, scooting into Laos where they've been safe 'cause our tactical area of operations don't go into Laos. Our mission is called Operation Dewey Canyon if that matters. The brass comes up with these names, but for us, we just go out and do the grunt work. Don't know when this starts, but it will be soon.

"Now, about our new lieutenant. Name's Speight. He ain't gonna be able to hold Lieutenant Williams's jock strap. Lieutenant Williams was a Naval Academy grad who opted for the Corps, and the Corps don't take every Academy grad who wants into the Corps, we take only the best. The next lieutenant is gonna come straight from The Basic School, so we'll have to take it slow with him until he gets his sea legs. Be on the lookout on ways to help him through your squad leaders to me.

"One other point—important point. Somewhere, maybe south of I Corps, don't know, an Army unit was on patrol. One of the guys had to take a dump, so they held up while he went behind some bushes. Next thing they heard was the roar of probably a tiger, and one scream from the soldier. All they found was his rifle and helmet. They looked for him. No luck. The lesson is to take a dump before you go on patrol, and if you gotta pee or take a dump while on patrol, the whole platoon stops and forms a perimeter around the guy taking care of bidness until he's done. That is one hellava way to go. OK, dismissed."

For the first time since arriving in South Vietnam 110 days ago, Lance Corporal Ricardo Jackson felt he would not make it back home alive. He had basically been forced to join the Corps. He and five of his Philadelphia buddies had broken into a home in their neighborhood when that family was on vacation. He was the only one caught. After the judge heard the evidence from the arresting cop—that he heard noise from the home, saw a broken window, went to the front door, knocked, chased after the five kids who ran out the back door, and caught only Jackson, the judge gave Ricardo a choice, right there in the courtroom: Take a year in county jail, or join the Marines

Ricardo, who was only eighteen years old, had only the vaguest idea that there was a war in South Vietnam or that Marines, and other US servicemen and women, were getting killed in Vietnam. Since he didn't want to spend a year in jail, he agreed to enlist. When he brought a copy of the enlistment papers to the courtroom clerk two weeks later, the charges were dismissed.

Two weeks after the case was dismissed, Jackson was on a Greyhound bus, heading from Philadelphia to Parris Island, South Carolina, the boot camp for the Corps on the East Coast.

Ricardo thrived in boot camp. He was small but athletic, strong and aggressive, and he kept his mouth shut and his eyes and ears open. He was the top recruit in his class and in the ninth week of boot camp, he was asked if he wanted to go to Officer Candidate School in Quantico, Virginia. He was told there was no guarantee he could pass OCS and be commissioned, but if he went and succeeded, a year would be added to his two-year enlistment. Ricardo declined, and after boot camp he was sent to Advanced Infantry Training at Camp Lejeune in Jacksonville, North Carolina. His next stop was First Platoon, Alpha, 1/9, Third Marine Division, at VCB.

Ricardo had taken an instant liking to Lieutenant Williams, his platoon leader, who seemed to have a sixth sense of what was going to happen in combat. Their platoon had some troops wounded and killed in action while Williams was the platoon leader, but not because the lieutenant made stupid decisions. Ricardo had followed Lieutenant Williams's orders to the letter and was rewarded with more responsibility and more rank when he was promoted to lance corporal and made assistant squad leader.

But Lieutenant Williams had rotated back home, and he was going to be replaced by a lieutenant who was fresh out of The Basic School. Ricardo had heard that Basic School was a five- or six-month school with both classroom and tactical exercises. He knew there was just no way a new second lieutenant could learn all he needed to know about leading men in combat by shooting blanks and running around Marine Corps Base, Quantico, Virginia. Now with this new directive by the CG of the Third Marine Division to seek and destroy the enemy in Operation Dewey Canyon, the war took on a different feel for Lance Corporal Ricardo Jackson.

He had the feeling there was a body bag with his name on it.

It never crossed his mind that he could leave Vietnam in handcuffs and leg irons as a prisoner convicted of first-degree murder.

Lieutenant Speight
1100 Hours, Thurs, 2 Jan 69
Da Nang Airbase
Republic of South Vietnam

Second Lieutenant Alvin Speight, USMC (Reserves), service number 0108920, was scared shitless. He hoped no one could tell because Marine officers in combat zones were not supposed to be scared shitless.

Three days before arriving at Da Nang Air Base in Vietnam, he boarded a commercial jet at Norton Air Force Base in Southern California for a flight to Okinawa, where he was given shots—one of which felt like a one-pronged pitchfork shooting maple syrup into his ass, and other shots to ward off diseases endemic to South Vietnam. He wished they had a shot to ward off any bullets with his name on them. He was well aware of the old saying, "You can't do anything about the bullet or rocket with your name on it, but you do worry about those addressed 'To whom it may concern.'"

His body clock was all screwed up too because he had flown through the international date line and more time zones than he could count. The flights, both from Norton to Okinawa and from Okinawa to Da Nang, had stewardesses who served meals and flirted with the enlisted men. It was surreal as hell and only added to his confusion.

His orders read: "Report to the company commander of Alpha Company, First Battalion, Ninth Marine Regiment, Third Marine Division, Vandergrift Combat Base, I Corps, Republic of South Vietnam, for assignment as an infantry officer." He placed them in the left pocket of his utility jacket. As he moved through the busy terminal at Da Nang, it was easy to distinguish those who were starting their tour—all wearing stateside utilities—from those lucky guys going home, who wore jungle utilities and jungle boots. There were a few catcalls from those going home to "The Land of the Big PX," but for the most part, those coming into the country and those leaving were respectful of each other.

As he waited in the terminal for someone to tell him where to go, Alvin felt out of place. He not only was scared; he also didn't even look like a Marine. He was five feet, seven inches tall and weighed only 150 pounds. He had sandy hair and a fair complexion, and he wasn't very well coordinated or strong and had problems with the obstacle course at OCS.

He had been in the seating area of the airport for about forty-five minutes when a sergeant came out and announced, "All enlisted and officers with orders to report to any unit in the Third Marine Division, follow me." Alvin joined forty or so other Marines and followed the sergeant to another waiting area. As an officer, he moved to the front of the line and gave the sergeant his orders. After reviewing the orders, the sergeant took the top copy and placed it in a pile of other orders and told Lt. Speight to go through a passageway to the left, which led to the tarmac.

It was oppressively hot as Alvin walked to the aircraft that would transport him and other Marines to Quang Tri, the headquarters of the Third Division. Alvin had misgivings about the flight when he saw their aircraft, which appeared to be vintage World War II.

There was no talking by the men on the aircraft. The seats faced the rear, something Alvin had never seen. He was seated near the cockpit, which was then unoccupied. His sea bag—issued by the Corps as the only permitted luggage—was propped next to him. There were no overhead storage areas, or stewardesses.

His concern about this flight was exacerbated when the pilots came on board. They looked like two guys just barely old enough to ask cheerleaders for a date. Alvin was thinking he didn't have to worry about dying in combat—the plane crash would take care of that. He heard the pilots go through their checklist, after which they started the engine and taxied away from the hanger. Alvin looked out the window and saw an F-4 Phantom jet taking off and wondered if any of them would ever fly a combat mission in support of his platoon. The plane taxied and then stopped for about five minutes. Then it turned and the pilots gunned the engines. The aircraft started down the runway and was shortly airborne.

As the aircraft climbed, Alvin could see how huge Da Nang Air Base was. It banked to the left and continued to climb. Alvin had no way of knowing the cruising altitude, but he could see a hilly green countryside with red clay splotched here and there. As the plane continued its flight, Alvin saw they were over water, which he correctly guessed was the Gulf of Tonkin, but they never got out of sight of land.

Alvin had no idea how long they had been airborne but could tell the pilots were beginning their landing pattern. He could see what appeared to be a village here and there as well as what he guessed were rice paddies because the water reflected the sun. He became concerned as the descending plane veered left and then right. He wondered if they were under fire or if the plane was just lining up on the runway for its landing. But then they made the smoothest landing Alvin had ever experienced, so while these flyboys may have been young, they were good.

After the aircraft came to a stop, Alvin took his sea bag and stepped from the plane. The building, which served as the terminal for the Quang Tri airfield, had signs for the units in I Corps, and Alvin headed for the door with the sign which read "1/9." He was met by a gunnery sergeant, commonly referred to as a "gunny," which meant two things: he was an E-7, and since the highest enlisted rank was E-9, he'd been around the block a few times; and it also meant that he knew how to get things done. Since Alvin and the gunny met inside the building, the gunny didn't salute as neither of them was wearing their cover—Marine for "hat."

The gunny stood on a bench and spoke. "Everyone going to 1/9 needs to wait here for a few until the cattle cars get here. There's not enough choppers available to get everyone there, so you're going to VCB by vehicle. Just so you know, we go north on Route 1 and then hang a Louie onto Route 9, going west, to VCB. Don't know how long it will take. I know you have not been issued firearms, but all the personnel who are driving the cattle cars are armed, and each vehicle has a Marine with an M-60. There ain't been a lot of attacks on traffic on these roads in some time, so we should be good to go. Once you get to VCB, find the company HQ for your unit and report in. They'll take over then. If you're smart, you'll take a dump or pee before you get on the trucks 'cause this is a nonstop trip."

Alvin hated cattle cars. These large trunks were frequently used to transport Marines at OCS and TBS to various duty stations, such as the rifle range and the area where they were taught how to toss grenades. They had benches to sit on, and if they had shock absorbers, they didn't work worth a damn. But the thing Alvin hated most about the cattle car he was getting on was that it was taking him to a duty station within miles of the DMZ between North and South Vietnam, an area full of the North Vietnamese Army and Viet Cong and an area in which he would lead men in combat. Alvin was not full of confidence.

Alvin lost track of time as they headed to Quang Tri. There was no talking during the trip, not because there was a rule against it; there just was no point. The vehicles were so loud no one could hear anything being said. Alvin could tell when the vehicle turned left and headed west to VCB.

The cattle car finally reached VCB. Each Marine jumped out, and someone in the truck threw down the sea bags. Alvin looked around at this sprawling combat base. The buildings had sandbags—what appeared to be two deep—stacked up to the window areas around all four sides. Alvin guessed the buildings, with tin roofs, couldn't withstand a direct hit of a rocket or mortar, but the sandbags could perhaps protect Marines on the inside when shrapnel from rockets or mortars landed close to a building.

Alvin walked to the headquarters for his company, Alpha 1/9, and knocked on the screen door. After being told to enter, he stood before a desk being manned by a PFC. "I'm Lieutenant Alvin Speight, and I'm reporting for duty. Can you tell me where the company CO is?"

"I'm right here, Lieutenant. I'm Captain Jason Aldridge. This is Lieutenant Rip Bernhardt, my XO. Welcome to Alpha 1/9." Both officers extended their hands. Captain Aldridge continued. "Welcome. Here's what's gonna happen. I'll get the sergeant to get you to a bunk. Then he'll take you to supply, where you will get your jungle utilities and boots, and then to the armory to get your M16 and some rounds. We have perimeter security, which is damn good, and lately there's been no effort by the bad guys to probe the line, but you need to be prepared.

"I've arranged for Sergeant Maurice Smith to be your platoon sergeant. He's very good. This is his second tour, both with Alpha 1/9. He can help you get your bearings out in the bush. It would be smart to listen to what he says and do what he what he says, particularly when things get hot. Any questions so far?"

Alvin shook his head "no" and Captain Aldridge continued. "We've recently received orders to conduct an operation named Dewey Canyon. We'll have a conference about it at 0900 hours here tomorrow. You'll need to be there. Sit tight, and I'll get the sergeant to take you to supply and then show you our lovely base."

After dropping off his sea bag in his hooch—his living quarters—Alvin and the sergeant went to supply, where Alvin got three sets of jungle utilities. He also tried on three pairs of jungle boots until he got a pair that fit him. The sergeant advised him to always pack at least two extra pairs of socks for switching out when the feet got wet in the bush. Alvin asked the supply sergeant for some skivvies. "Sir, we don't issue many skivvies over here, 'cause they ride up. You can get the red ass real quick with all the humping you do, so it's a bad idea."

Alvin responded, "Give me three sets of skivvies, Sergeant. I wear underwear."

"Whatever you say, Lieutenant. Here you are. And here's your 782 gear too." The sergeant handed Alvin his canteen, web belt, ammo pouch, poncho liner, and the rest and then handed Alvin a form with the number "782" and a pen. Alvin wondered if 782 gear got its name from the form you had to sign to have it issued.

Alvin asked for a Marine Corps watch, which had a gray- green band and a luminous dial. The supply sergeant said, "Here you go, Lieutenant. You'll need to get some tape, like adhesive tape to cover the face. Those dials show up at night in the bush. Makes a excellent target for a sniper."

Alvin and the sergeant both had a load of gear when they returned to Alvin 's hooch, all of which they dumped on his rack—Marine for "bed." Alvin met the other three Alpha 1/9 platoon commanders and the platoon CO for putrid iced tea. Alvin was wiped out, so he hit the rack and did his best to get a good night's sleep his first night in a combat zone.

The next day, Alvin's first Friday in 'Nam, all platoon commanders for Alpha 1/9 and their platoon sergeants met with company commanding officer Captain Aldridge and Lieutenant Bernhardt in the CO's office, where maps of the area were displayed.

Aldridge addressed the group. "Most of you know about the change in our mission, but Lieutenant Speight is the rookie on this, so we're going over it again for him and all of you 'cause it won't hurt for all of us to review what's going to happen. The Division CG, General Davis, believes we should go looking for the PAVN, not sit on a hilltop and wait for them to come to us. This change in approach to the mission of the Corps in I Corps is consistent with Marines, who kick ass and take names."

Lieutenant Speight raised his hand. "What's PAVN?"

Aldridge replied. "That's the People's Army of Vietnam, the bad guys. We tangle with both the PAVN and the Viet Cong up here. What's happening is that while the outposts we have set up, the so-called McNamara Line, are supposed to stop the bad guys, it ain't working, and it ain't consistent with our mission to seek and destroy. The the CG has ordered us to leave our combat bases and engage and kill the enemy where we find them. It's called Operation Dewey Canyon. What these bad boys are doing is hitting our firebases and patrols, then scooting into Laos, and our tactical area of operation won't allow us to go into Laos after them. Also, they're coming down the Ho Chi Minh Trail with supplies and men, crossing into 'Nam, hitting us, and then going back across the border into Laos. What I hear is that we're gonna change that and go after them, and to hell with the border, so they won't have a place to hide."

As they were leaving the meeting, Alvin's platoon sergeant, Maurice Smith, spoke to Alvin. "Lieutenant, you ain't asked about the men in the platoon, who can do what, who has a hard time doing things, and it's a good idea for you to know about the men you're gonna lead. Here's what you outta know." When Sergeant Smith finished his rundown, Lieutenant Speight had no questions, and Sergeant Smith had misgivings about the lieutenant, which he kept to himself.

Operation Dewey Canyon
0835 Hours, Wed, 22 Jan 69
Alpha, 1/9
I Corps, South Vietnam

Alvin could not believe how fast time passed between 3 January and 22 January, when the unit started Operation Dewey Canyon. The four rifle platoons and the weapons platoon of Alpha 1/9 loaded onto nine CH-46 choppers for the trip to Firebase Jasper.

Alvin had flown in a 46 during a training exercise at TBS but didn't pay much attention to the chopper then. He did now. There were gunners on the port and starboard sides, right behind the cockpit area, and one at the rear of the chopper, each manning a 60-caliber machine gun. Each M-60 had a bandolier of rounds that snaked to the floor. They were loaded for bear. The choppers weren't too vulnerable flying to Jasper, but there was always concern when they were landing because they came in slowly and hovered so the men could disembark.

There was no such thing as a smooth chopper ride. A big chopper, like the 46, just moved around a lot, even when it was loaded with Marines. Alvin felt like he would get sick to his stomach, not so much because of the ride but because of the situation but he was able to keep his composure because he didn't want his men to know just how nervous he was.

When the choppers landed, Alvin had his first look at a combat firebase. The top of the hill had been leveled, and there were firing pits, a mortar pit, barbed wire topped with concertina barbed wire wound around the perimeter, some holes dug around which sandbags were positioned, a 106 recoilless rifle, lots of empty ammo boxes, and aiming stakes so that there were interlocking fields of fire covering the entire area around the firebase. The Marines of Alpha 1/9 hustled off the choppers and went to their previously assigned sectors on the perimeter where they got a "sit rep," a situation report, from the men of Charley 1/9 they were replacing. They then hunkered down, and the weapons platoon took its position. Captain Aldridge met with the CO of Charley to discuss what to expect. Then the men of Charley 1/9 boarded the choppers and flew back to VCB.

Captain Aldridge yelled an order. "Platoon leaders, check the wire and the claymores in your sector. We need to be sure the wire is tight as a tick and that our claymores are positioned to fire toward the bad buys, not us, 'cause they may sneak up and turn them around, so when they are detonated, it hits us, not them." Alvin crouched and quickly ran around first platoon's sector, checking the claymores.

As the company got in place, Lieutenant Speight found a big foxhole surrounded by sandbags and placed his gear in it. He dragged an ammo box into the foxhole to sleep on. This would be his living area as long as the company was on Jasper. His bunking area at VCB looked like a penthouse at The Plaza next to "Hotel Jasper."

When night fell, the company went on full alert because the PAVN could not have missed the choppers coming and going. It was their practice to probe the lines of a firebase when one company replaced another. And they did, starting with mortar fire. Everyone went to their firing places.

The PAVN came, and kept coming up the eastern side of the firebase, which Alvin's platoon was responsible for. The men of first platoon fired into the advancing PAVN, and as they neared the wire, Captain Aldridge yelled an order to the weapons platoon. "Willie Peter, Willie Peter," which was followed by the unmistakable hollow thump-like sound of mortar rounds being fired. In a few seconds, the night sky became brilliant as the white phosphorus in the mortar rounds ignited. The men of Alpha 1/9 could see the PAVN were in the wire, and with the light provided from the exploding willie peter rounds, they were able to kill many of them.

But the PAVN kept coming. Sergeant White, who was next to Alvin, yelled, "Lieutenant, they in the wire. We need to fire the claymores," which were positioned between the fighting positions and the wire. Alvin didn't react, so the sergeant gave the order to other members of the platoon to detonate the claymores. When detonated, the ball bearings in the claymores have a kill-zone distance of at least fifty yards. But two of the claymores in Alvin's sector were facing his own men, not the wire, and when detonated, the ball bearings hit the sandbags of some of the firing pits of Marines in the first platoon. Sergeant Smith hollered the order, "Cease firin' the claymores." The men of first platoon kept firing their M16s, and the machine gunner for the M60 machine gun from the weapons platoon kept firing. The PAVN finally retreated.

Once the firefight ended, Captain Aldridge and the company corpsman came over to Alvin's sector. "What the hell happened? Were the claymores turned around hit us?" Aldridge was livid. Alvin answered, "Captain, I checked them when we got here, but they must have snuck up and reversed them."

Captain Aldridge ordered Alvin to follow him to the center of the firebase, which the CO thought was out of the hearing of the company. "Lieutenant, you screwed up. I'm telling you this privately, so your men won't hear me, but it is your job to make sure you and your men protect your sector. You dropped the ball. Don't let that happen again. Lucky no one was hurt too bad. Get your head and ass wired together, got it?"

"Yes, sir, I got it."

But Alvin did *not* get it.

Captain Aldridge was *not* out of the earshot of every man in first platoon. Private Roosevelt Grant, in the first squad of the first platoon, heard the conversation and thought Lieutenant Speight couldn't hack it. That worried him.

The next day, at 1300 hours, Captain Aldridge led the first and second platoons on a patrol, moving down a path on the east side of the perimeter of Firebase Jasper. The executive officer, Lieutenant Bernhardt, and the third, fourth platoon and weapons platoons, stayed at the firebase. The patrol was no more than two klicks (a little over a mile) from the perimeter when the point man on the patrol held up his right hand, the signal to stop in position. He had seen something. Sergeant Smith was next to Alvin, and said, "Lieutenant, you needs to go up to the front of the platoon to see what he's got." After waiting a few seconds, Alvin moved from his crouch and ran to the front of the platoons.

The Marine pointed to the east, and Alvin saw several bunkers, a smoldering fire, and several boxes. Alvin called up Sergeant Smith, and Captain Aldridge came forward also. "What do we do with this stuff?" Alvin asked.

Captain Aldridge answered. "Lieutenant, we need to record what's here, get that info to S-2, battalion intelligence, destroy it, and move on. See that box over there, Lieutenant, the one with 'CCCP' on it, you know what that means?"

Alvin shook his head. Aldridge answered, "Well, Lieutenant, that means the gear in that box, whatever it was, came from the Russians. We're fighting them too." The order was given to set up a perimeter around the site and begin the inventory. The site contained bags of rice, some rounds for the AK-47 rifle—the Russian-made rifle of choice for the PAVN and Viet Cong—fuel drums full of diesel fuel, and a box with vehicle parts.

Sergeant Smith walked around the site and came back to Lieutenant Speight and Captain Aldridge. "Sir, they some vehicle tracks over that way, leading to Laos. This may be a place where they stop to work on vehicles, eat up, rest, and plan their next attack. They be back, so what you think about us setting up an ambush in that tree line over there?" Captain Aldridge agreed and gave the order to set up the ambush.

The first platoon set up at a trailhead to the left of the little roadway, and the second platoon set up on the right. Aldridge made sure the men had firing lines, which kept them from firing on each other, and gave a final order to his platoon leaders. "It's getting to be dusk. The best time for those guys to move is at night. We're staying here for the night. I'm radioing the XO to tell him what's going on. But—and listen up—we don't want to start firing until the main body of men and vehicles is in our kill zone, so we can kill as many as possible. There's enough moonlight for us to tell when that is. Don't fire until I give the order. Everyone understand?" Each platoon leader said they understood the order. The squads moved into their positions, hiding behind whatever they could find, and waited.

At 2300 hours, the Marines heard vehicles heading in their direction. Everyone took their safeties off and kept their eyes on the kill zone. One vehicle, which was surrounded by five men, came into the kill zone. The driver cut off the engine. The platoon heard more engines coming down the road.

Lieutenant Speight began firing and then all the platoons joined in. When the firing stopped, it was so quiet Sergeant Smith could hear the engines from the other vehicles quickly moving from the ambush site. Captain Aldridge ran up to Speight, and this time he didn't bother to speak privately. "Lieutenant, you screwed up. We got a few bad guys and their vehicle, but we weren't supposed to start firing until I started firing, and I wasn't doing that until we had as many vehicles and enemy in the kill zone as we could. You didn't follow my order, and we missed a great opportunity."

This time, the conversation between Aldridge and Speight could be heard by Private Roosevelt Grant and all other Marines in the first and second platoons. Grant was six feet, six inches tall and the strongest, meanest man in the first platoon. He had been in the Corps long enough to have obtained the rank of corporal but had been demoted twice for fighting and insubordination. Grant didn't care about rank; he just wanted to get back to the United States in one piece. All the men of Alpha 1/9 were afraid of Grant because of his quick temper and reputation as a gang member from Chicago, a reputation he fostered. He was one scary dude.

Grant realized that his odds of making it back home in one piece were dropping as long as Lieutenant Speight kept making mistakes. He had to do something about that but didn't yet know what to do or when to do it.

The platoons returned to Jasper at first light the next day. Alvin and Sergeant Smith were near the front of first platoon when they came to the same path they came down when they began the patrol. Alvin gave the order for the point man in the group, PFC Scully, to start up the path. Sergeant Smith spoke. "Lieutenant, we ain't supposed to go back the same way we left 'cause they can lay some mines on the path. Shouldn't we go 'round and come up the west side?"

Speight responded. "I got the red ass from wearing these skives and need to get back to Jasper the easiest way. Go up this way. It's the quickest and easiest way to get back. Get going." PFC Scully had taken about ten steps up the path when he stepped on a land mine placed in the pathway. The mine's detonation and Scully's scream occurred simultaneously. Lance Corporal Jackson was right behind Scully, and the force of the explosion knocked him down. When he looked up and opened his eyes, he saw Scully's right leg, severed from the knee down to the boot, bleeding like nothing Jackson had ever seen. The corpsman came forward and wrapped a tourniquet around Scully's right thigh as Captain Aldridge called HQ for a medevac chopper for Scully.

Grant was right behind Lance Corporal Jackson and had a clear view of what happened to Scully. His hatred of Speight, and his fear Speight would make a mistake again, intensified. He knew Speight had to go and that he had to make that happen.

When the patrol made it back to Jasper, Sergeant Smith spoke to the company commander. "Sir, Lieutenant Speight ain't cutting it. He made three big time mistakes, and he ain't been here a day. The men are grumbling about him. Have you thought about sending him back to HQ? If he stays out here, he may get a M16 round in his back. That's happened before."

Aldridge replied. "Sarge, I agree. I just got word that Lieutenant Colonel Brinson is coming out here to check on us. When he gets here, I'll ask him if the battalion has some place for Speight off the lines and if he has a replacement for Speight."

Within the hour, a Huey gunship was spotted in the sky north of Jasper. Captain Aldridge got on the horn to talk to the pilot. "We're popping our smoke grenade now. What smoke do you see?"

The chopper pilot answered, "Green."

"Roger green, Flyboy. It's windy down here as you can see from the smoke. You may want to come in from the west to get a headwind."

"Will do. See you in five."

The Huey made a perfect landing, and Lieutenant Colonel Brinson hopped out to meet Aldridge, who gave the battalion CO the written inventory and location of enemy gear and supplies they found and the body count of killed PAVN from the attack on the NVA basecamp and from the ambush. He also summed up the actions of Lieutenant Speight and told the colonel he hoped there was a spot somewhere—anywhere—off the line for Speight, so he wouldn't get men killed or be in danger from his own men. Both Aldridge and the battalion CO knew there had been cases in the Corps and the Army where officers had been fragged—killed when a live grenade tossed by one of their own men exploded near them. Colonel Brinson spoke. "Well, two intelligence officers just rotated out of S-2, and we need replacements. I'll take Speight back to VCB with me and tell the S-2 that he is being assigned to his unit. A lieutenant just reported for his second tour, so I'll get him out here today, so your company will be at full strength."

In five minutes, the Huey gunship, with Speight aboard, was on the way to VCB. No one explained why Speight was on the chopper.

Grant didn't need or want an explanation. He was glad Lt. Speight was leaving the company and that he did not have to kill him.

Grant was wrong.

S-2, the intelligence section of a unit is tasked with taking information from units, such as the size and location of enemy units, caches of enemy supplies, times of contact with the enemy unit, enemy movement, body count of killed enemy, and the like, and to make sense out of where the enemy is, where it came from and where it is going. On many occasions, that data sent up the chain of command led to B-52 strikes and artillery bombardment.

Lt. Speight fit in well with the intelligence unit of 1/9. He took the necessary time and gave the necessary attention to detail to be an effective S-2 officer and was given additional responsibility shortly being assigned to S-2. He had found a good niche for himself in the Corps and hoped he would finish his thirteen-month tour with S-2 instead of being in the bush fighting the NVA. But Speight was wrong.

Chow Time!

Woody had been commissioned a second lieutenant on 8 November '68, three days after Richard Nixon won the 1968 presidential race. Woody had no illusions that the president could bring the war to an end during Woody's three-year tour in the Marines.

Immediately after he was commissioned, Woody reported to The Basic School at Quantico to begin six months of training as a Marine combat officer, learning how to lead Marines fighting the North Vietnamese Army and the Viet Cong. The training was rigorous and challenging, so he and three of his fellow second lieutenants had taken a night off from TBS to dine at Blackie's House of Beef, one of the most famous restaurants in Washington, D.C.

Woody could tell by the way the maître d' looked at him, Ernie, Paul, and George that they really weren't welcome at this fine restaurant. He guessed, correctly it turned out, that they would be seated in the back in a corner near the kitchen—as out of sight as possible.

As soon as they were seated, their waiter, who was dressed in a tuxedo—all the waiters wore a tux—came to the table and asked what each wanted to drink. Ernie, Paul, and George each ordered Pabst Blue Ribbon beer. The waiter said—somewhat snootily, Woody thought—they didn't serve Blue Ribbons. They changed their orders to gin and tonics, and Woody ordered

Old Grouse scotch on the rocks. A server brought bread and whipped cinnamon butter and filled their water glasses.

Ernie said, "Damn, Woody, how did you know about this place?" The walls were paneled, the carpet was deep, the room had a muted sound, and the waitstaff moved with a quiet purpose. In a word, it was elegant.

"Well, when I was thirteen, that would have been 1956, my dad flew our family up here. First airplane flight. We stayed at the Willard Hotel, which is near the White House, and Dad and I went to the Major League Baseball All-Star Game at Griffith Stadium. Saw Mantle, Mays, Ted Williams—second time I saw him 'cause Dad, me, and some other dads and sons saw the Red Sox play the Senators one weekend.

"The players I remember most were Ted Kluszewski of the Cincinnati Reds—his shirt sleeves were cut off at the shoulders, so he could show off his huge biceps—and Nellie Fox of the White Sox, who looked like the smallest player out there. Fox went up to Ted and kinda messed with those huge biceps and everyone got a laugh. Don't remember who won the game, but after the game, Dad brought all of us here for dinner. It was the fanciest place I'd ever eaten—no place close to it back home, and I've never forgotten it. Thought we'd enjoy it. The food is better than the chow hall to be sure."

The waiter returned with their drinks and asked for their orders. They asked the waiter what he would recommend, and were told that the prime rib was Blackie's specialty. Each man gave his preference for rare, medium, or well-done, and the waiter left. The server brought some more bread and delicious whipped cinnamon butter.

Ernie, who was from Hershey, Pennsylvania, and a graduate of Temple, spoke up. "You know what happens next week? We get to give the Corps our three preferences for duty stations when we graduate TBS. I've looked around, and I'm gonna ask for Kolona Bay, in Hawaii. Girls dancing in grass skirts, sandy beaches—what a dream. How about you guys?"

Woody replied. "Ernie, first, the Corps' base on Hawaii is called Kaneoha Bay, not whatever you called it. Second, tell me how many Cong and NVA are attacking that base, and if the answer is 'none,' then you're probably wasting your time asking for that duty station. Besides, the very idea of the Corps wanting to know what *we* want just ain't happening. They haven't cared about our feelings—and shouldn't—since we reported for OCS. They care as much about our preference as I do in reading *The Iliad* and *The Odyssey* in the original Greek, and I can't read or speak Greek."

Ernie replied, "OK, smart-ass, what are you going to write as your three preferences?"

"Well, I'm putting 'Republic of South Vietnam' all three times."

George asked, "Woody, why in hell would you do that?"

"Well, I think—no, I know—all of us are going to 'Nam. They're teaching us how to fight, not push papers. Remember that captain who spoke to us about going into armor? He said the military was in the business of war and business was good, so we're going sooner or later.

"There are three bad things which can happen to me when I come back from 'Nam: First, I can get killed, in which event I don't care when I come back; second, I can come back maimed for life, and it won't matter much then; but third, if I come back healthy but at the end of my three years and get released from active duty in California or someplace other than North Carolina—with no job and no time to really look for one—I'm up the creek. I want to get it over with, and if I'm real lucky and come back alive without being seriously injured, I'm hoping to get assigned for the remainder of my time to Camp Lejeune or Cherry Point in North Carolina. I've passed the North Carolina bar exam and don't *ever* want to take another bar exam, so depending on when I leave for 'Nam and then rotate back home, I may have up to a year to find a job. Makes sense to me for my situation. But don't get fooled into thinking we're not going to 'Nam. It ain't 'if,' it's 'when.'"

All four men were lost in their own thoughts about their futures, drinking and eating the delicious bread and butter. Then Paul spoke up. "I wonder if we'd have gotten a better table—one away from the kitchen—if we'd worn our uniforms?"

George said, "Well, first, our buzz haircuts tell everyone who sees us that we are in the military. They may not know the branch but could guess we're Marines. But don't you remember what our company commander warned us about? There was a guy at TBS last year who went into either D.C. or Georgetown in his dress whites after their mess night, went to an all-night diner, got in an argument with someone about the war, and the other guy shot the Marine right in the heart, killing him. They told us to keep a low profile when we went into the 'civilian world.' There are a lot of folks who are against the war and don't think much of us who have signed up. We need to be careful."

Woody said, "I remember that warning. I am avoiding conflicts folks may try to start just because I look like I'm in the military. But look, our dinners are here. Boys, dig in. This prime rib will change your life. It's chow time!"

Naval Justice School
1300 Hours, Fri, 2 May 69
I-95 North
Northern Virginia

Woody never appreciated President Eisenhower as much as he did on Friday, 2 May 1969, when he took the overpass over I-95, turned left onto the on-ramp for I-95 North, put Quantico and The Basic School in his rearview mirror, and headed north to his next duty station at the Naval Justice School in Newport, Rhode Island. The NJS was established after World War II to teach military law and procedure to Marines, Navy and Coast Guard lawyers and legal personnel.

Woody appreciated Ike because he started the Interstate Highway System after seeing the autobahns in Germany as the Allies pushed the Germans to defeat. The president realized our country needed a way to get around faster. Woody was hoping he would not hit a red light or stop sign before he got to Newport.

Woody's first memory of an American president was Dwight David Eisenhower. When Woody was in the fourth grade in January 1953, his class walked to the home of the one student in his class whose family had a television set and watched the presidential inauguration of the hero. The television commentators discussed Ike and World War II, and that evening, after school, Woody asked his dad about the war. His dad told him it was bad, it lasted a long time, it was cold, and he didn't want to talk about it. Woody Senior didn't tell Woody that his World War II experience had probably shortened his life expectancy.

The Basic School had been quite the experience. Woody now knew how to fire and clean a rifle and a .45 pistol—an officer's standard-issue firearm. He knew how to call in artillery fire on a target. He knew how to read a topographical map, at least one of the woods around Quantico, Virginia, and he hoped that would be enough experience for him to read a map in the middle of a rice paddy or under a jungle canopy. Most importantly, Woody learned how to lead men. He thought every officer and enlisted Marine who instructed him at OCS and TBS had served in Vietnam. Just as every professor he had at Wake Forest had a PhD, the instructors at TBS had advanced degrees in warfare.

As he headed north to Newport, Woody realized that the next time he started a long road trip, he would be heading west to the Marine Corps Base at Camp Pendleton, California, for duty as the executive officer of a training battalion, after which he would deploy to Headquarters Company, Third Marine Division, in Quang Tri, South Vietnam, which was right below the DMZ that delineated the northern border of South Vietnam and the southern border of North Vietnam. He didn't know what he'd be doing with the Third Marine Division, but after OCS and TBS, he felt as prepared as one could be for the fog of war.

Now he was going to be instructed on how to be a military lawyer. He hoped that when he reported for duty with the Third Division, he would have the opportunity to use his soon-to-be-acquired legal skills rather than go into battle.

Woody arrived in Newport at 1300 hours on Sunday, 4 May. He had a wonderful lunch of the best fried shrimp he had ever eaten, but the coleslaw couldn't touch the coleslaw served with barbeque at Respass Brothers in Greenville. The two Bloody Marys were perfect. When he came into the restaurant, he bought a copy of *The Boston Globe*. He had been a Red Sox fan since his dad took him to see Ted Williams and the Sox play the Washington Senators. The American League had split into two divisions in the 1969 season, so Woody checked the sports page for the schedule of the Sox at Fenway Park. He wanted to see Ted and the fabled Green Monster.

He reported to the Naval Justice School the next day. There were twenty-two other officers in Woody's NJS class, sixteen Marine second lieutenants, and six US Navy lieutenants, which was the equivalent rank of a captain in the Marines. Woody didn't know any of his classmates.

When a Marine captain entered the room, each Marine stood at attention. The Navy officers did not initially stand, but after they saw the Marines stand, they stood—but not at attention.

The captain addressed the group. "I'm Captain Isaac Hite. I'm a captain in the Marine Corps. You may take your seats. I will be your *only* instructor for your six weeks at NJS. How many of you Navy guys are graduates of an Ivy League school, either undergrad or law?" Three of the six Navy lieutenants raised their hands. Captain Hite asked the other three where they went to school and was told UCLA, Northwestern and Wisconsin.

"Did any of you Marines go to an Ivy League school?" No hands were raised. "I didn't think so. This is my second year at NJS. I served in Vietnam from '67 to '68. I tried cases, *and* I led men in combat. Do any of you Marines think you will go to Vietnam?" All hands shot up. "Well, you're right. And how many of you think you will lead men in combat during your tour?" All hands were raised.

"Well, you may be wrong. I'll explain later. But first, a little exercise. Get out a sheet of paper, write your name and whether you are Marine or Navy on the top, and look up when finished." When all were looking up, Captain Hite addressed the lawyers. "In this exercise you are the trial judge. The defendant, a private first class, has just been convicted by the military panel of stealing the wallet and watch of a fellow Marine who left them on his bunk while he was in the head, which is the bathroom for you Navy lieutenants. For the purposes of this exercise, your sentencing options are one, fine and reduction in rank, or two, bad conduct discharge. That's all you know. You've got fifteen seconds to write down your sentence and pass the sheets to the front."

When Captain Hite had all the papers, he looked at each and put them in two piles on the desk he stood behind. "Well, I have the results. Every Navy lieutenant gave the defendant a fine and reduction in rank, and every Marine gave a BCD." He looked at the clipboard he brought to class. "Navy Lieutenant Peabody—what do you think about all the Marines giving the defendant a BCD, and don't hold back."

When Peabody stood up, Woody thought his name fit his appearance. He was tall, thin and had a pointed nose, one on which prez nez glasses would perfectly fit the haughty image. He talked in a high-pitched voice and sounded and looked rich, both of which he probably was. Even his voice sounded like he was talking down to the listener. "Sir, I think the bad conduct discharge was a barbaric sentence."

"Well, Marines, I guess Lt. Peabody thinks you Marines are prehistoric. Not sure if that is a compliment or an insult. Whichever, I'll call on—let's see—Marine Lieutenant Kitchen for a rebuttal. Kitchen, stand and defend the Marines from this vicious attack by the Navy."

Lieutenant Kitchen was five-foot-nine and weighed about a buck sixty. "Well, my guess is that the lieutenant—was it Peabody?—is not stupid, he is just uninformed in the ways of barracks life and military life. In the Corps, you are trained to be trusted by and to trust fellow Marines. Your life may depend on it. This defendant violated that trust. He has to go. That's the way I see it."

"Exactly." Captain Hite went to the front of his desk, sat on it, and faced his class. "Here's the point. And, by the way, I do this same exercise at the first of every class, and the sentencing results are the same every time, although, this is the first time Marines have been referred to in prehistoric terms. You Navy guys—you've been in the military, what, two weeks?" They all nodded yes. "And that consisted of what I call 'salute school,' where you learn how and who to salute, who is a higher rank than you, how to wear the uniform of our country properly, and some other military protocol. But through no fault of your own, even though you aren't experienced in military matters, you are expected to know something about the military lives of the men you will be representing, prosecuting, and advising. Therefore, you're giving advice and counsel to someone when you don't even know or understand his military environment. Every Marine in this class has earned his second lieutenant's commission through OCS or PLC, and then they all went to TBS, where they not only learned how to lead men in combat, but they also learned a lot about life in the military.

"So at this school, in this class, I am going to give you Navy guys as much of a taste of military life as I can in the time we have, so when you report to your first command you will not only be book smart, but you will also have some idea about things military. You all *will* know military law if you pass my test and become certified as a military lawyer. If you Navy guys pay attention, you will also learn a little bit—better than nothing—about how the military operates and how sailors live their everyday lives. You can't give good advice, prosecute, or defend a case if you don't have some idea about the environment in which sailors live. The law is more than what is in the books; it involves the practical experiences people have and how the law impacts their lives.

"Now, remember when I said that I had been to 'Nam, tried cases there, and led combat patrols? Remember I asked if any of you Marines thought you'd be lawyering and in combat in 'Nam and you said 'yes'? And remember when I said that you may be wrong? Well, now you're going to find out what I meant by all of that. I call on Lieutenant Woodrow White."

Woody came to attention.

"Men, when called upon, you do need to stand, but not at attention. Lieutenant White, why do you think you will be in combat in 'Nam even though you have passed the bar?"

"Sir, you come out of Marine OCS and either go air wing or grunt. I can't fly, so I'm a grunt. That is what I was trained to do. The way this war is going, they will need a lot of lieutenants in combat positions. So I'd be pleasantly surprised if all I did in Vietnam was to try cases."

"Well, Lieutenant, let's hold that thought. Have you heard the name Clarence Gideon?"

"Yes, sir, I have."

"Now, all of you pay attention to what just happened. I asked him one question, and he gave one answer. He didn't tell me *who* Gideon was; he just answered my question 'Yes,' because it called for a 'yes' or 'no' answer. We will be conducting mock trials in this class. You will be prosecutor, defense counsel, military judge, or military court panel members in these mock trials. The number one rule of preparing your own witness is to train him to answer only the question either you, opposing counsel, or the judge, asks him. Now, Lieutenant White, tell us what you know about Clarence Gideon."

"Sir, he had been convicted of several crimes before he was charged, I believe, with the felony which gave rise to the Gideon matter. He asked for a lawyer to be appointed to represent him because he was indigent and faced prison, but his request for counsel was denied. He was convicted and sentenced to prison, and then he handwrote a certiorari petition requesting the Supreme Court reverse his conviction on the grounds that the Constitution entitled him to have a lawyer appointed to represent him since he faced a prison sentence and could not afford to hire a lawyer. The Supreme Court allowed his petition for cert, heard the case, and decided that Gideon was entitled to appointment of counsel because he was indigent, faced a prison sentence, and couldn't afford an attorney. I believe the decision was handed down in 1963. Anthony Lewis wrote an excellent book about the case called *Gideon's Trumpet*."

Captain Hite responded. "That's exactly right. And what difference does it make to the military lawyer that the Supreme Court handed down *Gideon v. Wainwright*? Anybody? Well, I wouldn't expect you to know this, but to you Marines, it is the most significant legislation you could imagine. Lt. White, what were you doing on 10 October 1968?"

Woody answered, "Sir, I was at OCS at Quantico."

Captain Hite continued. "Lieutenant White, is that a southern accent?"

"Yes, sir."

"Well, do you know who Sam Ervin Jr. is?"

"Yes, sir."

"Who is he?"

"He is one of the senators from North Carolina."

Captain Hite continued. "That is right. The honorable senator has enjoyed the well-earned reputation of being a fair-minded man. He has a law degree from Harvard, I believe. He thought it was right and fair for a civilian like Gideon to have an attorney represent him if he faced a prison sentence and was indigent, but—and here's the point—Senator Irvin did *not* think it was fair for military defendants to not have a licensed attorney represent them if they faced a discharge or a prison sentence.

"The old rule was that an officer, not necessarily an attorney, would represent a defendant. The good senator felt that had to change, and there were other things Senator Ervin didn't like about the laws for men and women in the military. It took him several years, but he got Congress to pass a bill, which in effect provides that military defendants have the right to have a *real* lawyer—a lawyer who has passed the bar—represent them when they are a defendant in a court-martial that could result in their being discharged or receive a prison sentence.

"That law is called the Military Justice Act of 1968, and the House passed it on 3 October 1968, and the Senate on 10 October 1968. So when you jarheads get to 'Nam, there is a good chance you will not be in the bush, rather you'll be in a courtroom, defending or prosecuting some Marine in a special or general court-martial facing a BCD or a dishonorable discharge or a prison sentence. Maybe you can now breathe more easily."

"Now, the Uniform Code of Military Justice, the UCMJ, is the bible of military law. It came into existence in 1950 and has been changed over the years. I am *not* going to teach you the military law by having you sit down and memorize the elements of the crime, the rules of evidence, and all that stuff. You are going learn it by living it, practicing it. You are the third class I have taught this to. We will learn through mock trials. If you are the prosecutor, you'll draft the specs of the crime and try the case. If you are the defense counsel, you'll prepare the defense. If you're a court member—a juror—you will decide guilt or innocence. After each exercise, we'll critique the work of each of you and learn that way. Let's get started."

And so it was that on his first day at Naval Justice School, Woody found out he would probably be in a courtroom and not in the jungles of South Vietnam. He had six weeks to learn how to be a military lawyer, and after thirty days leave, he had to drive to California to catch that Big Bird to South Vietnam.

Operation Apache Snow

0600 Hours, Sun, 2 Jun 69
Alpha, 1/9, A Shau Valley
I Corps, South Vietnam

"Lieutenant, just how long have we been in this godforsaken valley?"

Jordan Crawford, First Lieutenant, USMC (R), had previously been with Second Battalion, Ninth Marine Regiment but had taken command of Alpha 1/9 about seven days before Apache Snow, his first operation with Alpha. He answered Second Lieutenant Overton. "Now Lieutenant Overton, you know the Corps wouldn't send us to a godforsaken place. This is a wonderful, tropical paradise. It has elephant grass eight feet high, which is so pleasant to walk through, even when it cuts your jungle utilities. It has triple canopy trees, which provide wonderful shade from the tropical sun and provide excellent hiding spaces for the PAVN and do a great job of keeping the humid weather from being reached by any wind. In fact, when—make that if—this so-called war ends, I'm thinking about building a golf course here. It has great elevation changes, which are probably easier to hump with a golf bag than with the military gear, weapons, and ammo we are carrying. This could well be a destination place. But to answer your question, the choppers dropped us off on 10 May, so—about three weeks. I'm assuming the Army and ARVN were airlifted at the same time, but who knows."

Lieutenant Overton replied, "Well, thanks for the tourist info, Lieutenant. I beg to differ with you about the triple canopy trees, 'cause some of them don't even have leaves after the folks in charge of this war sprayed that orange crap on them. You know, if that orange stuff will eat through leaves and kill them, what the hell is it doing to our lungs or eyes? No telling. Besides, who comes up with the names for these ops? Who ever heard that Apaches had snow?"

"Lieutenant, I can't believe you are so cynical about our beloved—"

Crawford heard the rifle shot at the same time Lieutenant Overton's head exploded, filling the air with the mist of Overton's blood and brain matter. He immediately knew nothing could be done for Lieutenant Overton. Instinctively, he ducked behind a tree and yelled "Sniper!" and grabbed his M16 and looked up at the trees. He saw a puff of smoke from a tree above their position about thirty feet high. He fired his entire clip and was reaching for a second clip when he looked up. The rounds from his M16 had shredded the branches and leaves between him and the puff of smoke. He could now see the sniper with blood coming from the limp body, but Crawford fired more shots at him, not so much to make sure he was dead—he knew the shooter was dead—but out of frustration for having lost a man under his command. He could see the shooter was tied to a tree limb. Crawford thought there was no way this war could be won by the United States and South Vietnam when the enemy was willing to go to such extremes as this shooter did by essentially committing suicide.

His platoon sergeant came to his side, and Crawford gave orders. "Sergeant, the lieutenant is dead. No need to call the corpsman. Have the RTO get up here and get 1/9's CO on the horn."

In a minute, the company's radio transmission operator, PFC Ronald Lassiter, whom everyone called "Sparky," came to Crawford's position. The long aerial for the PRC-25 radio was wrapped around the radio, so it would not present a target. Sparky contacted regiment's frequency.

Crawford talked to the regimental commander of 1/9. "Colonel, we're down to one platoon CO and myself. Lieutenant Overton was just KIA. Yesterday a platoon commander was WIA and airlifted to battalion aid station. I know we're here as a blocking force when the NVA push toward us heading for Laos, but we need at least one more platoon leader. Could really use two. And we can use some M16 rounds, some .50 cal rounds, and some M-60 rounds."

"Lieutenant, has a dust-off chopper come to get the KIA's body?"

"No, sir. I called you first, and no call has been put in for the dust-off."

The battalion commander responded. "Lieutenant Crawford, I'm in touch with the 101st Airborne. They are driving some NVA your way. You need to set up an ambush for the NVA. I'll give you the radio frequency for that CO, so you can contact him to make this happen. I'll personally order the chopper to you, and I'll make sure there is a lieutenant on that bird. I'll make it happen. And the chopper will resupply ammo and C-rats. We have some Cobra gunships on call. Go through me if you need them. What is your position?"

After giving the colonel the company's coordinates, Crawford called the platoon commander and platoon sergeants of Alpha 1/9 to meet with him for a situation report, and he ordered the company to get into a defensive position as they awaited the chopper.

It soon started raining hard, so it took the Huey some time to get to the position of Alpha 1/9. The platoon sergeant popped a red smoke grenade to mark their position. When the chopper landed, a Marine jumped to the ground. When Sergeant Smith saw him, he said, "This be bad news."

Crawford asked the sergeant what he meant.

"Well, Lieutenant, it means that if that Marine be the replacement for Lieutenant Overton, we's got a problem. Can't remember his name—Smith maybe—but he was with us on Dewey Canyon and screwed up so bad our platoon leader asked the brass to get him out of the bush and to some desk job, where he won't get men killed, 'cause he's stupid. Sorry, Lieutenant, shouldn't speak that way about a officer, but this ain't some place to be nice."

"No problem, Sergeant. I like to know what I'm dealing with. No need to detail his screwups. I'm going to put him with you, tell him why, and have you keep him from screwing up."

Sergeant Smith replied, "Yes, sir. I keep a sharp eye on him."

Crawford signaled Speight to come to him as members of his company were off-loading boxes of ammo and C-rats and placing Lieutenant Overton's body bag in the chopper. He gave Speight a rundown of the company's mission and position and told him he would be platoon commander of first platoon again and that Sergeant Maurice Smith would again be his platoon sergeant. "Now, Speight, you listen to what Sergeant Smith says and follow his advice. He's very experienced, as you know, and you're not. You can't go wrong listening to him, got it?"

"Yes, sir, got it."

But Speight did *not* listen to the sergeant.

Private Roosevelt Grant was shocked to see Lieutenant Speight back in the field. He remembered that Speight had triggered the ambush on Dewey Canyon too early and that the platoon commander had blown him out about it. Grant also remembered that Speight's decision to return to base camp Jasper by the same route they left on caused Scully to lose his leg to a land mine. Grant was hoping Speight would get WIA or KIA, and then he wouldn't have to worry about Speight messing up again. Grant knew that one way or another, Speight had to go.

Two hours after the chopper left with Lieutenant Overton's body, the men of Alpha 1/9 heard sporadic gunfire from the east. Lieutenant Crawford called Sparky to his side and pulled a piece of paper from the left pocket of his utility jacket. "Sparky, this is the 101st's frequency, don't know which unit. I was given this so we could coordinate with them if it turned out they were driving the NVA toward us, which it sounds like is happening. Get them on the hook for me."

Sparky unhooked the radio aerial, so it was at full length. He then adjusted his frequency button to the frequency of the 101st, pushed the transmit button, and said, "This is Alpha 1/9, USMC, calling CO of 101st, over."

Within ten seconds, a voice came over the radio. "This is Captain Witherspoon of the 101st, over."

Crawford responded, "Lieutenant Crawford, Alpha/1/9, Marines here. Sounds like you've got them on the run just as was planned, over."

Witherspoon replied, "Roger that, Lieutenant. There's about two companies of NVA, no heavy weapons that we know of. They're doing the 'fire and maneuver thing' so that about half of them fire, and the other half move toward your position and then vice versa. What are your coordinates?"

After hearing the coordinates for Alpha 1/9's position, Witherspoon keyed his transmission button and spoke. "If we keep them going the way they've been going, they'll be at your place in an hour or so. What can we do to help you get the welcome mat out?"

"Captain Witherspoon, if you can, pinch them in on their north and south ends and drive them this way, kinda like herding cattle into the pen. We can have sort of a horseshoe ambush to deal with them, over."

"Crawford, no guarantees, but we'll try. We don't want to be in your line of fire, so when you're ready to unload on them, let us know, and we'll stop our pursuit and leave them for you, over."

Crawford replied, "Sounds like a plan. Thanks. By the way, you know you airborne guys are a bit nuts, jumping out of perfectly safe airplanes, don't you?"

"No, just another way to show you that the Army has bigger studs than you pansy Marines. Good hunting, over."

After completing the transmission, Crawford ordered all platoon leaders to his position to give them a rundown of Witherspoon's report. He brushed some leaves out of the way, and using a stick, drew his ambush plan in the dirt. Moving the stick from left to right, Crawford said, "We're going to set what I'm calling a modified horseshoe ambush. Speight and Sergeant Smith, first platoon will be on the left end, the north end, then second platoon, then weapons platoon in the middle where you can support the entire company, and I'll be with weapons. Third and fourth platoons, you'll hold down the south end, the right end, of the ambush. The 101st says they think these bad guys have only small arms, no heavy weapons that we know of so be ready. The 101st is going to try to drive them to us and pinch them in on each end, so when they get to us, they're like cattle being herded into a pen.

"The woods are so thick we won't be able to see them until they are on the other side of that stream, but they'll have to slow up when they're crossing that stream, and that's when we'll unload. Whatever happens, we cannot let any of them get outside either the first or fourth platoon positions. Then they'd be behind us. Can't let that happen. Have your men at least ten feet apart—don't want one grenade taking out two men—and set up your firing lines so the first and fourth platoons don't fire at each other. First and fourth, pick a point at the end of your position, and make sure your men don't shoot back of that point 'cause if they do, they'd be shooting our men. Give that point to the other platoons. If we can pinch them into our middle, we'll be OK. This valley is too narrow for us to call in arty or napalm—don't want to get hit or roasted ourselves. We're on our own, and the NVA ain't got a chance. Questions?" There were none. "OK, set up, lock and load, and we'll open fire on my command. Got that Lieutenant Speight?"

"Yes, sir."

"Oh, I forgot one important thing. Everyone needs to have some tracer rounds in their ammo clips to make sure they can see where their rounds are going, so we aren't shooting each other. OK, let's get ready."

Crawford moved to his position with the weapons platoon, which put him in the middle of the spread-out ambush. Sparky and his radio were with Crawford, so he could contact the 101st when the time was right.

Sergeant Smith, Lieutenant Speight, and the platoon commander and platoon sergeant of fourth platoon went to the northern end—the left side—of the ambush site and discussed their respective lines of fire. The platoon commander of fourth platoon spoke first. "It looks to me that if first platoon sets up right here and doesn't fire to the right of that big tree at the right end of our position, the one with bark missing"—he pointed to the tree—"and if fourth platoon doesn't fire at anything to the left of this tree we're under and if that info is given to second, third and weapons platoons, we won't be shooting at each other. Sound OK?" They all agreed and went to their respective fighting positions and gave the order to the rest of the men of Alpha to fire only outside the restricted areas.

After the group assumed their positions, Sergeant Smith spoke to Lieutenant Speight, "Sir, we can't shoot to the right of that tree with no bark, 'cause we'd be firing at fourth platoon."

"I know that Sergeant. Let's get in position."

Roosevelt Grant had been in ambushes before and knew what he was doing. Sergeant Smith was to his immediate right, and Lieutenant Speight was to the sergeant's right. Grant was glad he had his eyes on Speight and wondered if he'd screw up again.

And then the men of Alpha 1/9 waited for the enemy.

As the small arms fire between the 101st and the NVA got closer, Lieutenant Crawford began to see NVA soldiers moving toward the stream in front of the ambush site, hiding behind trees. Crawford thought, *They ain't dummies and probably smell our ambush.* He had Sparky raise Witherspoon of the 101st on the radio. "This is Crawford of Alpha 1/9. Can you read me?"

"101st here. Affirmative. Can read you."

Crawford continued. "We're beginning to see the NVA. You need to back off. We're going to open up in a couple minutes."

"Roger that. We'll push them a little and then back off. Looks like we've got them herded like we talked. Good luck. Over and out."

The men of Alpha 1/9 had either scooped out fighting holes in the dirt of the A Shau Valley or positioned themselves behind a tree or rock. Each Marine was intensely looking across the stream, ready for the NVA to emerge from the thick woods on the east side of the stream. They took their weapons off safety and were as ready as they could be.

Lieutenant Crawford did not know the size of the enemy force, except for Witherspoon's estimate of one or two companies. It was going to be difficult to know when to spring the ambush. If sprung too soon, too many of the NVA could take cover in the thick trees on the other side of the stream and would be hard to deal with. If sprung too late, the forces of the NVA may be large enough to engage in close combat with Alpha 1/9. When Crawford estimated twenty NVA had crossed the stream, he yelled the order, "Open fire!"

The firepower from the M16s, the M-60 machine guns, and the M-79 grenade launchers manned by Alpha 1/9 brought down most of the NVA who had crossed the stream. The remaining NVA took positions behind trees, rocks, and anything else they could find on the east side of the stream and began moving from tree or rock, closing in on Alpha 1/9's position.

Grant knew from his tracer rounds that he was killing NVA. He emptied his first clip and was reaching for another when he heard Platoon Sergeant Maurice Smith cry out. "No, Lieutenant!" Grant looked up and saw that the tracer rounds from Lieutenant Speight's M16 were to the right of the tree with no bark, landing in fourth platoon's position. Speight was shooting at his fellow Marines!

Smith grabbed Speight around the neck with his left arm, grabbed the stock of the M16 with his right hand, and pointed the barrel to the sky. "Dammit, Lieutenant, you be firing into our own positions. See that tree with no bark? Don't fire to the right of that tree."

The firefight intensified as more NVA came across the stream. They knew they could not retreat—the 101st was waiting for them. They knew if they stayed in the kill zone—between the stream and Alpha's position—they would be killed. They could only move forward into the Marines of Alpha 1/9.

They never had a chance. The ambush was so well conceived and executed that the firefight was over in about fifteen minutes with only two friendly WIA, both from the fourth platoon, whose positions were near the tree with no bark.

When the NVA stopped firing, Lieutenant Crawford ordered Alpha to stop firing and gathered his platoon leaders and sergeants around him. "We're taking no prisoners. We aren't the Red Cross, and prisoners would slow us up. Each of you assign a man—a total of five men—from your platoon to make sure each of them is dead. If a man is wounded, just leave him there. And remember, those bastards will pull the pin on a grenade, so it explodes if you move their body. Be careful. Gather all their weapons, get the ammo clips and rounds, and dump them in the stream, so they are hidden. Lieutenant Speight, you and your platoon dig a pit big enough to dump all their weapons in it, and we'll burn 'em. Have the man you select to check on the dead make a count of NVA killed. Battalion will want to know."

Crawford was disgusted that the brass—the colonels, the generals, and the folks in the administration in D.C. who were supposedly running the war—often seemed to be most interested in the number of enemies killed as a way to judge the success of the American war effort. He thought it was stupid to keep score but knew to keep his mouth shut. Marines just followed orders.

For the next few minutes, the Marines of Alpha 1/9 carried out Lieutenant Crawford's orders. Sometimes a Marine fired a round into the head of a NVA soldier because that was the quickest way to make sure he was dead.

No one said anything about it. They reported to Crawford that 103 NVA had been killed. Crawford got on the horn and notified battalion that the ambush was successful and asked for enough choppers to ferry the company back to VCB.

Alpha 1/9 formed a defensive perimeter around what would become the LZ for the choppers and kept a sharp eye out for the NVA or the Viet Cong. In a few minutes they heard the "whop-whop" of the choppers heading toward them. Sergeant Smith popped a smoke grenade, which gave the chopper pilots the location of the LZ and the wind direction. There were several choppers, and since the LZ could handle only two choppers at a time, it took Alpha about thirty minutes to evacuate the area.

Grant was on the last chopper to leave the LZ. He had time to think about Lieutenant Speight. He knew he'd never know for sure if the two WIAs in fourth platoon were shot by Speight, but given the direction of Speight's firing shown by the tracer rounds from his M16, Grant was satisfied that Speight had messed up again.

He knew he had to kill him.

The questions were when and how.

Those questions were about to be answered.

Typhoon

Typhoons can form in the Northwestern Pacific Basin. On 13 Jun 69, the surface temperature was sufficiently warm in the South China Sea near the Paracel Islands for the formation of a typhoon. There were other meteorological circumstances which contributed to the formation of the typhoon: atmospheric instability, a high humidity force to develop a low-pressure center, and a low-level focus or disturbance which existed prior to the surface temperature becoming warm. At high noon on 13 Jun 1969, a typhoon formed.

It then gained strength and knot speed from the water and atmospheric circumstances as it moved west toward South Vietnam.

When the typhoon's leading edge reached the shore of South Vietnam in the Da Nang region it covered more than a hundred miles in all directions out from the eye, and its winds were reaching one hundred knots. It veered sharply in a northwesterly direction toward Quang Tri Province and Vandergrift Combat Base. The leading edge reached Quang Tri at 1700 hours on Saturday, 14 June.

At the office of the commanding general of the Third Division, the powers that be realized that the force of the typhoon would severely impact the capabilities of Marines to wage war, primarily because the air and vehicular support essential to the efforts of Marines would not be available for use in this weather. Word passed down the chain of command to stand down until the all clear was given after the typhoon had passed. The Third Division Marines were reminded to be on the lookout because the enemy could use the weather to its advantage.

When Grant heard the stand-down order, he knew three things: First, the typhoon would give him his best—maybe his last—chance to murder Speight; second, the M61 grenade he had failed to return to the armory after Apache Snow was the perfect murder weapon; and third, he couldn't use his left hand because he had paid someone to slam the stock of an M16 on his hand to break it so he could stay off the line.

Grant needed someone to open and hold the door while he pulled the grenade pin and safety clip before tossing the grenade under Speight's rack.

He needed someone weak.

He needed someone he could fool.

He needed Greenfield.

Fragging
0300 Hours, Sun, 15 Jun 69
Alpha 1/9
VCB, I Corps

"Your son is slow."

This assessment by Garland Greenfield's fourth grade teacher did not come as a complete surprise to his parents. Garland often failed to follow directions as he helped his dad on the dirt-poor farm leased from a wealthy Tulsa businessman. But when the teacher advised the Greenfields to have their son placed in a school which concentrated on the education of the mentally and physically challenged students, the argument became so heated that the principal of the small school intervened and suggested an IQ test be administered to Garland. The uneducated Greenfields had never heard of an IQ test but agreed that one could be administered to their son.

They did not understand the significance of the score of 68, but the teacher and principal did and insisted that Garland be separated from his classmates and placed in the 'special' school. The Greenfields objected and removed fourth grader Garland from school. These events were reported to the school board, which unanimously agreed to let the matter drop, since it would take time away from educating the 'smarter' kids if they had to educate poor Garland.

Garland hated working on the farm but didn't know what else he could do. But then, he went to town one Friday when it was storming so badly there was no work to be had at the farm. As he came out of the only store in town, drinking his Pepsi and eating his M and M's, Garland noticed the poster in the store-front window across the street. After crossing the street, he saw the poster was a picture of a handsome young man, with a close haircut, wearing a blue coat with an eagle, globe and anchor pinned to the collars. He was holding a rifle, and the background was framed by a big ship and an airplane.

A man came out of the store. He was wearing a brown shirt, a tie with a tie clasp, blue pants with a bright red stripe, and the shiniest shoes Garland had ever seen.

The man said, "You want to see the world?"

"Damn sure do."

Garland was invited inside. The Marine recruiter immediately knew that Garland could not read, so he read the enlistment contract to him. He also knew that because of the man-power demands of the Vietnam war, the Corps had dropped its standards for recruitment. When the recruiter finished reading the enlistment contract, Garland signed it and became a Marine recruit.

The recruiter gave him a bus ticket to San Diego, a place Garland did not know existed, and orders to report to MCRD, the Marine Corps Recruit Depot. No more farm! When he showed his mom and dad his copy of the contract and the bus ticket, his dad said, "Good riddance."

Garland barely graduated from boot camp and AIT, advanced infantry training, but upon graduation, he received orders to report to First Battalion, Ninth Marine Regiment, Third Marine Division, Quang Tri, South Vietnam, for duty as a rifleman.

It took the men of First Platoon, Alpha Company about five minutes to discover that Garland was a weak, gullible guy. When the platoon was at VCB, they pushed Garland around and ridiculed him every way imaginable. Garland began to wish he was back on the farm. He needed someone to help him out, to protect him. That someone was Roosevelt Grant.

Grant knew he could do something for Garland by protecting him from the harassment which occurred when the platoon was not in combat. Grant had noticed that even though there was racial discord and disagreement about almost everything when the Marines were not in the bush, they were all Marines hell-bent on protecting each other when engaged with the enemy.

Grant felt Garland could, and would, do something for him in return for Grant's protection, everything from cleaning Grant's M16, to running to the little PX they had at VCB to get him a drink, and other 'gofer' errands.

Grant knew that because Garland was gullible and weak, he could trick Greenfield into helping him murder the lieutenant.

But Roosevelt Grant knew he could not discuss his plan to frag the lieutenant with Garland Greenfield before it was time to kill the lieutenant. He had to surprise Greenfield, giving him no time to think about it and minimizing his chance to back out. Grant hoped the cover of the typhoon would help them get away with it.

Grant went to Greenfield's rack and placed his right hand over Greenfield's mouth to keep him quiet as he shook Greenfield awake and whispered, "Keep quiet, and come with me." Greenfield got out of his rack and followed Grant out of the hooch. It was raining like hell, and each man was instantly soaked. "I'm gonna play a joke on Lieutenant Speight. I got me a green smoke grenade from that last op and I'm gonna toss it into the lieutenant's hooch. But I've got this bad left hand and can't hold open the door and pull the pin on the smoke grenade with my good hand. I just need you to hold the door. I'll toss the smoke grenade, and then we'll run back to the hooch. All right?"

Greenfield was intimidated by Grant and felt he had no choice but to agree, so he told Grant he'd help. The lieutenant's hooch was about one hundred yards from their hooch. They crouched as they ran to the hooch. The thunder, lightning, howling wind, and sheets of rain gave them cover. Grant couldn't imagine anyone would be up and about in this weather.

Grant was wrong.

They reached the lieutenant's hooch. As Greenfield opened the hooch door with his left hand, Grant turned his back to Greenfield and bent at his waist. He then threw the grenade into the hooch. They heard it roll on the wooden floor as they ran from the hooch. They were about ten yards from the lieutenant's hooch when the M61 fragmentation grenade exploded. Every Marine has thrown an M61 grenade and knows the sound when it detonates. Even with the thunder, lightning, and rain, Greenfield heard the grenade explode, and he knew Grant had not tossed a harmless smoke grenade. He had fragged the lieutenant.

When they got to their hooch, Greenfield stopped running and turned to Grant. "You fragged the lieutenant, and he's probably dead. I can't believe this!"

Grant grabbed Greenfield by his wet T-shirt. "You're damn right I killed him. He was a shitty officer. He deserved to die. You're just as guilty as I am. Better keep your mouth shut, or you'll go to jail for as long as I do. We both keep quiet, and no one'll know who did it. No one saw us. We'll say we were up talking when we heard the grenade go off. Nobody liked the lieutenant. Keep quiet, and we're OK."

Greenfield went back to his hooch, changed out of his wet utilities, and climbed back onto his rack. He was more afraid than at any time in combat. He knew Grant would kill him just as soon as a bug and realized his only hope was to keep his mouth shut. He knew he was in a hurt locker in the worst way and could see no way out.

"Breckinridge, You're the Investigation Officer"
0600 Hours, Sun, 15 Jun 69
Office of Commanding Officer
Alpha Company, 1/9
VCB

Jordan Crawford, First Lieutenant, USMC Reserve, had replaced Jason Evans as CO of Alpha 1/9 a few days before Operation Apache Snow. At six-foot-two and with the body of an NFL defensive back, he looked like a Marine, even in jungle utilities, which hung loosely to be as cool as possible in the steamy, hot environment. Lieutenant Crawford was born ready.

His father was a lawyer in Rawlins, Wyoming, and knew John Joseph Hickey, who also practiced law in Rawlins. Mr. Hickey was appointed US Senator from Wyoming in 1961, Jordan's junior year in high school. Jordan's dad sent a letter to his friend the senator, requesting an appointment for his only son to the Naval Academy at Annapolis, Maryland. The appointment was speedily dispatched, and by the end of January 1962, his senior year in high school, Jordan knew he was headed to Annapolis.

In his fourth year at the Academy, he opted to select his commission as a second lieutenant in the Marine Corps rather than the Navy. The Corps selection committee, after reviewing Jordan's record at the Academy, gladly welcomed him as one of their own. He was proud, but in a quiet way, that he had graduated from the Academy class of 1966.

Jordan graduated first in his TBS class and was then posted to Second Battalion, Ninth Marine Regiment as platoon leader of second platoon.

On Thursday, 30 January '68, he and another platoon commander and two sergeants from 2/9 were ordered to drive from Quang Tri to Huế, the ancient imperial capital city of Vietnam, to reconnoiter the lay of the land and the streets and buildings. The battalion intelligence officers felt the NVA and the Viet Cong may attack Huế.

Their intelligence was accurate. At approximately 0230 hours on 31 January '68, the NVA and the Viet Cong launched a full-scale attack on Huế, as well as numerous other sites in South Vietnam. Since he was somewhat familiar with Huế, Lieutenant Crawford was ordered to plan and command the effort to retake Huế from the enemy.

The Marines engaged in a furious battle with the NVA in Huế, including vicious house-to-house fighting, even though the Marines had received little training in house-to-house warfare at OCS or TBS. Crawford's leadership during the battle for Huế was exceptional. As a result, he was awarded the Bronze Star with "V" device for valor and was promoted to first lieutenant.

During the presentation of his after-action report, Crawford suggested to the battalion commander that the Corps start house-to-house combat training at The Basic School, an idea that was almost immediately implemented. First Lieutenant Crawford was highly regarded by the brass—the ranking officers—of the Third Marine Division.

When he was assigned to Alpha 1/9, Lieutenant Jordan Crawford contemplated his short military career. He felt the Academy, as well as his in-country experience as platoon leader, had prepared him for anything that would come his way as he continued his tour of duty in South Vietnam.

Jordan was wrong.

He was not prepared to deal with the murder of an officer under his command.

Jordan was winging it at 0600 hours on 15 Jun '69 when he met with Lieutenant Donald Breckinridge, his new executive officer, Sergeant Maurice Smith from first platoon, and the platoon leaders of Alpha. There was no textbook that gave direction to a CO on how to handle the murder of a Marine under his command. There was also the challenge of the vestiges of the typhoon because even though the winds had abated, torrential rains continued.

Crawford started the meeting. "Here's where we are now. The body of Lieutenant Speight has been placed in a body bag, and the bag has been placed in the reefer for cold storage until a chopper can get out here to move it to the division morgue though, with this weather, there really is no idea when that will be. There is no point in endangering a chopper and its crew to get out here to take a body back to division. It may be different if we had a seriously wounded Marine who needed immediate medical attention we couldn't give him, so the chopper will get here when it gets here. Except for Sergeant Smith, each of you was in the bunker Speight was in, so I need to know what you know."

Second Lieutenant Jerry Johnson spoke up. "Lieutenant, we've discussed this and knew you'd want a summary. We agreed I'd give it to you, but we don't know much. If I misstate something, forget something, or say something that doesn't match the memory of one of the other guys, they'll pipe up. None of us heard anything before the grenade detonated. Lieutenant Speight's rack was next to the door. The plyboard deck below the lieutenant's rack is blown all to hell. I guess the explosion would have been more widespread if the deck had been concrete. The racks in that hooch are only a couple of feet off the deck, so the blast probably killed him instantly. None of us heard the door open. Not sure we could have done anything had we heard anything. The thunder and lightning and the rain on the metal roof made it tough to hear yourself think. None of us was hit. We got to the lieutenant within seconds after the blast, but he was not breathing or moving. There was blood—"

Crawford interrupted Lieutenant Johnson. "I saw the body and the damage to his rack and deck. Don't need to discuss that more. We've got to figure out who did this. None of us is trained in murder investigations, but with the uncertainly of communication with HQ or Naval Investigative Service, we're on our own until we can tell HQ what happened and they can get an investigative team out here.

"This is what we're going to do. First, Jerry, get ahold of a good camera. If none of you have one, get the platoon sergeants to check with the men in their platoon. We need a nice Nikon or Minolta. We need to take as many pictures as we can of the door, the rack, the deck, and the hooch. Then go to the reefer, and remove the body from the bag, and take pictures of it. We can give the film to NIS or the trial counsel for development.

"But second, the most important thing we can do is to start asking questions and get someone talking about who did this. I know Speight—I mean Lieutenant Speight—had some big problems in the bush because he had some KIAs and WIAs in first platoon that may have occurred because of what he did or did not do. Members of his platoon may have had it in for him. Sergeant Smith, you're his, or you were his, platoon sergeant. What are you hearing, or what have you heard, from the Marines about Speight's performance that would lead to this? We've got to find this killer ASAP, hopefully before NIS gets here."

Sergeant Smith answered, "Sir, Lieutenant Speight won't a good field commander. After Dewey Canyon, before you got here, on his first op, he was taken off the line—"

Crawford interrupted. "Well, we know he could not, or did not, hack it in the field. We can't do anything about any screwups, so no need to discuss them unless his screwups help us ID the murderer, or murderers. Sergeant Smith, who do we start with to find out who did this?"

Sergeant Smith replied, "Lieutenant, the best place to start is to round up the guys who hang out in that underground bunker. They get in there, shoot the shit, grab a few beers, probably smoke some pot. I'm not saying one of them did this, but they maybe got a feel for who is doing what in the platoon."

Lieutenant Crawford replied. "OK, so Sergeant, you'll need to find out if there were any Marines in that bunker last night or this morning, and if so, round them up. We need to set up the plan for asking those guys questions. Since the weather is keeping NIS from getting out here, we need to start the investigation, even if it won't be done the same way NIS would do it.

"XO, you're in charge of interviewing those people. One or more of them may be the guy or know who we are looking for, so question them one at a time.

"Sergeant Smith, I want you to find as many of the men in the bunker last night as you can and escort them here. Don't tell them what is going on—although they'll probably know what it's about. Stay with those waiting to be interviewed until the XO is ready for the next man, and make sure the one interviewed does *not* talk to those to be interviewed. Keep an eye on the situation.

"XO, you'll need to make notes of what each of them says, even if there is no info about who may have done this. Just get details from each of them, kinda the who, what, when, where, and how of what they were doing, what they heard, and what they saw last night—before and after the murder. Be sure to make a list of who you talk to for the SJA and NIS. If the stand-down order is lifted while you're doing your investigation, you're off the line until we hand this off to the SJA's office and to the NIS. This is your job one. Got it?"

"Yes, sir."

The XO got it loud and clear: He was off the line for the foreseeable future, and that was damn fine with him. In fact, First Lieutenant Donald Breckinridge the Fourth was ready to get out of Corps. He still had a couple months left in 'Nam, then less than a half year remained on his three-year commitment, and then he was out. His field commander skills weren't really up to snuff with what was needed from 1/9 in I Corps.

One reason Lieutenant Breckinridge was ready to get out of the Corps was that he just did not fit in. He was not "one of the guys." He didn't know why he wasn't accepted, but his fellow officers didn't like him. One of them suggested you instantly disliked him because it saved time. They also did not respect him. Donald always let it be known that he came from blue blood of the bluest kind—the Main Line in Philadelphia. Even though both his granddad and dad had graduated from Penn and Wharton, their combined pull fell short when Donnie—as his mother called him—applied to Penn. He was lazy, and his Ivy League prep school grades reflected it. He graduated from Hampden Sydney, an all-male school located in southern Virginia. During his sophomore year, he enlisted in the Marine Corps Platoon Leader's Course—the PLC, and attended those sessions at Quantico during the summers of his sophomore and junior years in college. His enlistment had less to do with a desire to serve his country than with his idea that the dress blues of the Corps would be attractive to the fairer sex. Donald didn't think he'd go to war as a Marine, since Vietnam was not a page one story in 1967.

Upon graduation from PLC, Donald received his gold second lieutenant's bars, and since he had no postgraduate work, he immediately began active-duty training at The Basic School.

Near the end of TBS training, the Corps conducts a peer-eval, the only question of which was to list, in order, the top five men in your TBS platoon you would want to lead you in combat. No one in his forty-nine-member platoon listed Donald. His TBS platoon leader tried to counsel Donald about his attitude and demeanor, but Donald, who didn't think anyone was better than he, didn't listen or learn.

Even as XO at VCB, Donald demonstrated an ability to get people pissed off at him. On one occasion, he became angry with a Marine who did not salute him. The Marine was outdoors, filling sandbags and wearing his T-shirt and his cover (Marine for "hat") but did not salute the XO when he came into the Marine's area.

When outside and wearing your cover at a state-side billet, not saluting an officer when outside would, at a minimum, earn the offending Marine a rebuke from the officer, but at a combat base like VCB, the requirement of such military protocol was over the top. Donald's fellow officers tried to talk him from writing up the Marine for such a minor offense, but Donald insisted on getting back at the Marine, who then faced what was commonly called "office hours." Donald had made a big deal about the "offense," so when the hearing officer found the Marine was not responsible for violating a rule or regulation in the combat zone, Donald was razzed unmercifully by his fellow officers, mainly for being stupid and unreasonable. If there was one thing Breckinridge couldn't handle, it was being made fun of.

The Marine was Lance Corporal Ricardo Jackson. Breckinridge vowed to never forgot his name and to get back at him.

As far as Sergeant Smith could tell, he had rounded up the seven men who had been in the bunker. They were outside the company office, waiting for the XO to begin the interviews. The first Marine called in by the XO was PFC Ratcliff. Smith and the other Marines could see, but not hear, the XO and Ratcliff.

Breckinridge decided to file his notes from each interview in a folder. On the outside of the folder, he wrote, "Speight murder investigation. Interview of Gov't Witnesses—Prepared by 1st Lt. Donald Breckinridge IV." He then wrote Ratcliff's name, rank, and service number on the inside of the folder and prepared to write notes of his questions and Ratcliff's answers on a legal pad. He asked Ratcliff to have a seat and began the questioning. He wanted the Marines he was interviewing to be as comfortable as possible.

"Ratcliff, were you in the underground bunker last night or this morning, during the storm, and before Lieutenant Speight was murdered?"

"Yes, sir."

"Who else was in the bunker from the time you got in it until you left it?"

"There was guys in and out, can't remember all of them. But when I left out about midnight, Jonesy was there, Parker was there, Walters, Evans, Singletary was there, and Douglas. And, I forgot, Jackson was there for about a minute, but he left before the rest of us left. That was it. And Singletary, he came in after Jackson left."

"Ratcliff, while you were in the bunker, did anyone discuss anything about Lieutenant Speight, good or bad?"

"Oh, sir, I don't wanna…"

"It's OK to speak freely, Ratcliff. We're just trying to figure out who did this."

"Well, sir, he was a sorry platoon leader in the bush. At Dewey Canyon after an op, he ordered us to come back up the hill to the firebase the same way we left out, and one of the guys—it was Corporal Scully—tripped a mine and lost his leg. We was always taught to not come back the same way we left out 'cause the bad guys may mine or ambush the route you left on, which they did. The lieutenant just didn't know his stuff."

"OK, Ratcliff. Did you hear anyone say anything about wanting to hurt or kill the lieutenant?"

"No, sir, but we were afraid he didn't know his head from his ass—sorry, sir. But no one really said anything about wanting to hurt him."

After a pause, Ratcliff said, " Jackson was real close to Corporal Scully, the guy who got his leg blown off with that mine on Dewey Canyon. That hit Jackson hard. We were talking about the lieutenant when Jackson left the bunker, and Jackson said that he wished the lieutenant was dead. He did say that."

"Do you know if anyone else heard him say that?"

"I guess everyone heard it. Even with the storm and rain, you could hear OK in the bunker. None of us talked about what Jackson said; he just said it. I ain't heard nothing else about this."

Lieutenant Breckinridge asked, "So do I have this clear? When you left the bunker, there were six Marines left, Jones, Parker, Walters, Evans, Singletary, and Douglas, and Jackson had come and gone, right?"

"Yes, sir."

Sergeant Smith could see the lieutenant interviewing Radcliff but could not hear what was said. He also saw that Lieutenant Breckinridge remained seated when he dismissed Ratcliff and that he tore the legal pad page on which he made interview notes and put it in the folder.

Breckinridge then ordered Sergeant Smith to send in the next man, a Lance Corporal Jones. As Jones was sitting down, Breckinridge wrote Jones's name on the inside of the folder, below Ratcliff's name. He was trying to be meticulous.

Breckinridge wondered if Ratcliff and Jones had discussed what they each would say because Jones's report of his time in the bunker was almost verbatim to Ratcliff's statement. Sergeant Smith saw that the lieutenant remained seated as he dismissed Jones and that he again placed the notes of the interview in the file folder.

Breckinridge followed the same procedures with Parker, Walters, and Evans. Their stories were so similar that it was again difficult for Breckinridge to know whether they had previously discussed what they would say or if they were all telling the same truth as they saw it. But Breckinridge didn't need to figure that out; all he had to do was to give the witness file to the NIS, whenever they got to VCB.

The sixth Marine interviewed by Breckinridge was Corporal Jason Singletary. A raw-boned farm boy from South Dakota, Singletary volunteered for the Corps two years after he graduated high school. He was tired of working as a mechanic at his father's garage, a six-day and Sunday afternoon job (church on Sunday morning) which left little time for Jason's passion, hunting anything and everything. He knew the times and dates of the opening of every hunting season near Lake Oaha in South Dakota, particularly the pheasant hunting season.

He enjoyed learning and finished in the top ten of the fifty graduates of his senior class. During the spring of that year, at a school high school assembly, an Air Force officer and an enlisted man, who were stationed at Ellsworth Air Force Base in Rapid City, South Dakota, presented a program hoping to recruit students to join the Air Force. Their presentation only partially registered with Jason, because although he felt a need to serve his country, just as his dad had in the Second World War and his granddad in the First World War, he was not interested in being an aircraft mechanic, which was the job the recruiters pitched. Jason had enough of working with tools and grease.

Then he saw the movie *Beach Red*, about US Marines in the Pacific in the Second World War. He could see himself as a Marine and enlisted as soon as possible.

Jason initially had difficulty at boot camp in San Diego, in part because he was smart and tried to figure out the 'why' of orders. The Marine Corps was not interested in telling anyone who was given an order *why* the order was given. When Jason learned the valuable, necessary lesson that a Marine did not question orders, he just followed them, he excelled and finished as one of the top recruits in his class.

One morning in Vietnam, the strength of Jason's belief in that lesson would be seriously tested.

Jason was assigned to Alpha 1/9 and because of his skills with weapons was placed in the weapons platoon. He was not certain why he and the others were being summoned to the company office the morning after Lieutenant Speight had been murdered, but he felt they would be asked what they knew about that murder. The Marines were ordered by Sergeant Smith to not talk to each other either before or after their interviews. Jason was the next-to-last to be interviewed by Lieutenant Breckinridge.

After the XO wrote Singletary's name on the inside of the folder, he asked Singletary to have a seat and began asking questions and writing Singletary's answers on the legal pad. Sergeant Smith remained outside the CO's office because there was one more Marine to be interviewed.

After a few minutes, Smith saw the XO stand, and then he saw Singletary stand and come to attention. Breckinridge said something to Singletary but Sergeant Smith couldn't hear the lieutenant. Smith then saw Singletary do an about-face and leave the office. As Singletary left the CO's office, Sergeant Smith saw the XO turn his back to the sergeant and walk to the corner of the room and, with his back to Smith, bend over. Smith could not see what the XO was doing, and he wondered what was going on.

The seventh and last Marine to be interviewed was PFC Douglas. After he was ordered to sit, the XO wrote Douglas's name on the inside of the folder, and the questions began. "Were you in the bunker last night or this morning before Lieutenant Speight was murdered?"

"Yes, sir, I was."

"And was Jackson in the bunker along with Ratcliff, Jones, Parker, Walters, Evans, and Singletary?"

"Yes, sir, he was, but Jackson left before the rest of us?"

"Did Jackson say anything about Lieutenant Speight?"

"Yes, sir, he said he wished the lieutenant was dead. Then he left. But, sir, I saw him later."

The XO looked up and paused. "Where?"

"Sir, after I got to my hooch, the thunder kept me up, and I seen Jackson was running with Grant away from the lieutenant's hooch, right after I heard the grenade explode. They was running back toward their hooch."

"How did you know it was Grant?"

"Sir, 'cause Grant is so big, the biggest man in our platoon. It was Grant."

"Are you sure it was Jackson with Grant, PFC Douglas?"

"Yes, sir. It was dark, and the storm was really bad, but I knowed Grant and Jackson was close, they spend a lot of downtime together and shoot the shit a lot of time. It had to be Jackson. I could see him when it lightninged."

"Did you see them at Lieutenant Speight's hooch right before the grenade exploded?"

"No, sir, I didn't, but when I see them, it was after the grenade exploded. They weren't more than a few yards from the lieutenant's hooch, and they was hauling ass, like they'd done something."

The XO continued. "Now, Douglas, you're sure it was Jackson with Grant, right? I mean there's no doubt about that, is there?"

"Well, sir, it was dark and raining like hell and lightning, but as best I could tell, it was Jackson. Grant is black and he had a cast on his hand, and Jackson is white. It was Jackson, as best I could tell."

After Breckinridge dismissed PFC Douglas, he knew he was ready to report to Lieutenant Crawford, and he knew what he would say. He found the CO in the mess hall, nursing a cup of coffee. Breckinridge sat down and reported. "I interviewed six men, and the killers are Grant and Jackson. PFC Douglas heard Jackson say—all of them heard Jackson say—that he wished the lieutenant was dead, and then after Douglas went to his hooch, he saw Grant and Jackson running from Speight's hooch after the grenade exploded. Grant was never in the underground bunker, but Jackson was. Looks like we've got this solved—in record time, I might add. What's the next step, arrest them, or what?"

Crawford answered. "Well, good job, but we're not arresting anyone. We're not the NIS. Even though the winds are too high for the choppers to get up, except for emergencies, the rain has stopped in Quang Tri and probably between there and here. There are some NIS agents—don't know how many—in Quang Tri, and so we will contact them and get them to round up a convoy to drive up here. Could get here soon unless there is road washout on the way. We're not going to do anything until NIS gets here, and then we'll confab with them and hand it off to them.

"The Naval Investigative Service knows what to do. We'll meet with NIS and tell them what was told to you. There will be an Article 32 preliminary hearing which legal will handle, and then legal will decide whether and who to charge with what. You and I are the only people who know what these six guys said, and I'm not telling anybody. If it gets out, it's on you, and I'll be a very unhappy lieutenant. Keep your mouth shut about his, and that's a direct order. Understand?"

The XO replied, "Yes, sir. I'll talk to NIS when they get here and shut up until then."

It is the responsibility of the Naval Investigative Service to investigate alleged criminal activity in the Navy, Marine Corps and Coast Guard. Its agents are civilian, not military, so they are not under the command of the officers and enlisted they investigate.

John Gates and Ben Harrelson had been NIS agents since they completed training in 1964, and they were very good. They worked in tandem so well that they were assigned the same duty stations. They knew how to solve crimes, and they were legendary. Throughout the Navy and Corps, wherever they were assigned, Gates was known as "Sherlock," and Ben was known as "Doctor Watson" after Sir Arthur Conan Doyle's characters.

Their convoy from Quang Tri to VCB encountered no road problems and no interaction with the NVA or the Viet Cong. Gates and Harrelson arrived at VCB around 1300 hours and immediately went to Alpha 1/9 headquarters where Crawford and Breckinridge were waiting for them.

After Crawford introduced himself and Lieutenant Breckinridge, he began his summary of the murder case. "Second Lieutenant Alvin Speight was the platoon leader for first platoon. We came off an op in Apache Snow. During the typhoon last night—I need to back up. When the typhoon hit us, we got the stand-down order, so everyone hunkered down. About 0300 hours this morning, someone fragged Lieutenant Speight—opened the hooch door and rolled or tossed a grenade under his rack. You can, of course, see the murder site. We have taken beaucoup pictures, but they are not developed. The person, or persons, who did this had to know where he slept. There were other officers bunking in that hooch, none of whom saw who did it. When the other officers in that hooch—none of whom were wounded fortunately—got to him right after the explosion, he was not breathing or moving. He probably never heard or felt a thing.

"I ordered my XO, along with Sergeant Smith—Speight's platoon sergeant—to start questioning members of Speight's platoon. Smith suggested they start with the Marines who regularly hang out in an underground bunker we have here. They didn't bunk there, but it was a kinda hangout place for the enlisted in Alpha, and I guess other companies too. That turned out to be a good idea, thanks to Sergeant Smith 'cause Breckinridge, we think, may have hit the jackpot with one of the witnesses, a PFC Douglas. He ID'd two Marines as the murderers, or at least he ID'd two Marines running from Speight's bunker right after the grenade exploded. The XO and I haven't told anyone what we know. He took notes when he interviewed the guys from the bunker." Crawford nodded to Breckinridge.

Breckinridge pulled out papers from a folder. "I've got these notes from my interviews with the six Marines. One of them—"

John Gates interrupted. "Hold on a second, Lieutenant. First, y'all did a perfect job of interviewing the Marines and we appreciate it. But Ben and I have a protocol in every case, and that is, even if someone else has interviewed witnesses, we want to start with a clean slate with each potential witness when we interview them. We don't ever look at interviews someone else has done until maybe after we've interviewed those potential witnesses. So, Lieutenant, I appreciate your good work, but what you need to do with that interview file is to give it to whoever is assigned as trial counsel, you know, the prosecutor, and we can look at it later if we need to.

"I don't know who trial counsel will be in this case, probably Captain Mike McMurry or Navy Lieutenant Kevin Ross. They're the most senior trial counsel, and they absolutely know what they are doing, so it won't surprise me if one or both of them get the case since it is a big case. Just give that interview file to them. They'll probably show it to the defense counsel, but that's up to them."

Gates continued, "Our plan is to conduct our investigation and then meet with the SJA and the assigned trial counsel who will prepare the charges if they think there is a case, and then we'll arrest the defendant or defendants."

Breckinridge interjected, "But I've got statements from…"

Ben Harrelson spoke quickly and harshly to the XO. "Lieutenant, you weren't listening when we told you our protocol. We don't ever look at what someone else has done. We do our own thing. Then we may look at your work. So please butt out."

Ben continued. "Lieutenant Crawford, is it possible for first platoon— well, first, I guess we have to know if there is a thought that someone from a platoon other than Lieutenant Speight's who may have done this. Doesn't seem likely, but should we look elsewhere?"

Crawford answered. "You should certainly be free to ask around, but we doubt anyone from any platoon other than first platoon had any issue with Speight. He was not a very good field commander. In fact, after Dewey Canyon, at the first of the year, he messed up so badly his company commander asked regiment or battalion CO—I don't know which—to give Speight an admin job, which happened. Unfortunately for Speight, we had to get him back in the bush during Apache Snow 'cause of some of our lieutenants were WIA or KIA. Then he messed up again. But I'd say his biggest detractors—the most likely suspects—are in first platoon."

"OK," Ben replied. "Is it possible for first platoon to be off the line until we make our report both to the SJA and to the trial counsel and until we make the charges and arrest anyone we think should be arrested?"

"Well, we've still got that stand-down order 'cause of the storm. I don't know when it will be lifted, but I can discuss your request with battalion to see what they say."

Gates spoke. "OK, please do that, and let's get started. Can you provide us a place to meet, and can we start with the—how many was it, seven?"

Lieutenant Breckinridge corrected him, "Six, there were six, and I can get them for you to interview if you like."

Gates answered, "That would be good. Also, we'll need somewhere to bunk 'cause I don't imagine we'll be done today. And although we know the cause of death, we'd like to see the lieutenant's hooch."

Lieutenant Crawford responded, "You can use this office. I'll take you to Lieutenant Speight's hooch. XO, you get the witnesses you interviewed back to this office. The agents will be back after we've looked at Speight's hooch."

Neither Sherlock or Watson felt they would learn anything to help their investigation by seeing where Lieutenant Speight had been murdered, but as part of their investigation, they followed Crawford to the murder scene.

They were familiar with the explosion radius of an M61 grenade, which was the type issued to Marines and which was probably used to kill the lieutenant. They didn't believe there was evidence to be gleaned from the lieutenant's hooch regarding the murderer's identity. The lieutenant's rack was only eight feet from the door, so they pictured the killer opening the door, probably with his left hand, letting his body keep the door from closing, and then pulling the pin and safety clip and tossing the grenade right under the sleeping lieutenant. That was probably the "how." They knew the "when" was around 0300 hours earlier that day. The question was: "who?"

They returned to Lieutenant Crawford's office. His "desk" consisted of a piece of plyboard placed on two sawhorses with two fans with green blades blowing toward his chair. Gates sat at the desk, and Harrelson pulled up a chair. Lieutenant Breckinridge said he had the six witnesses waiting and was told to bring one of them in. Ratcliff came to the door, knocked, and was told to enter.

Gates and Harrelson had a routine for interviewing witnesses which worked for them. One would ask questions, and each would take notes. If the other agent had any follow-up questions, he would ask them after the other agent had finished. Neither would interrupt the other during his interview. After each interview, they would compare notes to see if they had captured the same information. They would alternate being the primary interviewer.

After they had interviewed Ratcliff, Jones, Parker, Walters, and Evans, they stopped for some chow and talked before they interviewed Douglas, the last witness.

Even though there was no one else in the mess hall, they sat in a corner. Gates spoke first. "Either they all heard the same thing, or they got together and agreed what they'd say. No way probably to know which it was, but so far none of them liked Speight. All of them wanted to have a different CO, but only Jackson said anything specifically about the lieutenant."

Harrelson said, "I agree. So far we have nothing of any use to charge anyone. I don't think either Mike or Kevin, if they are appointed trial counsel, would issue articles and specifications against Jackson based on what he said when he left the bunker. But we've got to talk to the last Marine Breckinridge talked to."

When they got back to Crawford's office, PFC Douglas was waiting for them. They went inside, and after Ben asked Douglas a few preliminary questions, he began to focus on timelines.

"Was Jackson in the bunker when you left the bunker, and how long after you left the bunker did the fragging take place?"

Douglas answered. "No, sir, Jackson left the bunker before I left. Don't have no watch—really no reason to worry about time, 'cept the day I rotate back home. The fragging happened maybe an hour or two, maybe more, after I left the bunker."

Ben continued his questioning. "Did Jackson say anything about Lieutenant Speight at any time while you were in the bunker?"

"Yes, sir, I heard him say he wished the lieutenant was dead."

"Did anyone else hear him say that?"

Douglas answered, "Yes, sir, I think all of us heard him say that."

"Where did you go when you left that bunker?"

"Back to my hooch."

"Where is your hooch in relation to Lieutenant's hooch?"

"I'm on the same side as the lieutenant's, and I'm two—no, three—down from his."

"Did you see anything about the fragging while you were in your hooch?"

Douglas answered. "Well, the thunder was so loud it woke me up. I got out of my rack and looked at the storm. It was lightning, and I seen Grant and Jackson running from the direction of the lieutenant's hooch, and then I heard the grenade explode."

Ben asked, "How far were you from them?"

"I don't know, maybe about twenty yards."

"Were you looking at them from their left or right?"

"Right."

"How long did you see them, Douglas?"

"Sir, I don't know, just a few seconds."

Ben continued his questioning. "Well, could you see their faces with all the storm?"

"Yes, sir. Grant is the biggest guy in the platoon. About six and a half feet tall. He's black, and you can't miss him. His best pal in the platoon is

Jackson, who is white. I seen them together all the time. It was Jackson with Grant. I could see them when it lightninged."

"Douglas, how many times did it lightning while you saw them running?"

Douglas answered, "Sir, I don't know."

"Where is Jackson's hooch?"

Douglas answered, "It's across from mine and down about three hooches, next to the head."

Ben had another question. "Where is Grant's hooch?"

"Sir, it's past Jackson's and on the same side as Jackson's."

"Did you see either Jackson or Grant go into their hooch?"

"No, sir."

Ben asked Douglas to step out of the office for a minute.

When Douglas was out of earshot, Ben leaned close to John. "What do you think?"

John replied, "Well, it's eyewitness testimony of two men running, and his ability to see and ID isn't the strongest I've ever heard. I mean, making an ID on seeing someone running when it lightninged is kinda weak. I don't know what Mike and Kevin will think of it, assuming they are appointed as trial counsel. I think we need some more evidence. We should get Grant in here, see what he says, and then talk to Jackson. I think we should warn Grant and Jackson of their rights though."

"Agreed," Ben said. He got up, walked to the door, and told Douglas he was free to go. Then he waved to Sergeant Smith to come over. "Sergeant, we need you to bring Grant to us." Smith left the office area, and Ben went back in and sat at the desk.

Douglas was right about one thing: Grant was huge. He had to duck coming into Crawford's office. He was invited to sit but remained standing. He loomed over the NIS agents.

After introducing himself and Harrelson, John began his questioning of Grant. "We're here to investigate the fragging of Lieutenant Speight. You were in his platoon. We want to ask you some questions."

"I ain't saying nothin' to nobody."

John responded. "Well, all we're doing is interviewing you. We aren't charging you. We're just gathering facts through this investigation. We just want—"

"Don't care what you want. I ain't saying a damn thing."

John responded. "Well, you must have done something wrong if you won't talk to us, so what was it?"

Grant just crossed his arms, glowered at John and Ben, and said nothing. Both agents were certain they would get nothing from Grant. They called Sergeant Smith and asked him to have Grant report back to his unit. At least they didn't have to worry about him leaving the area—too many Cong and NVA. After Grant left, they asked Smith to bring Jackson to the office.

When Jackson came in to be interviewed, John's first thought was that he didn't look like he could kill anyone, but he also knew that meant nothing. He'd seen killers come in all sizes and shapes. Jackson was scrawny, had acne, and had the biggest nose John had ever seen. He asked Jackson to sit down, and he and Ben picked up their pads to take notes.

John began, "I'm NIS Special Agent John Gates, and this is NIS Special Agent Ben Harrelson. We're here investigating the death of Lieutenant Speight. We'd like to ask you some questions. Do you mind talking to us, or would you like to have a lawyer? You have the right to."

Jackson interrupted, "I don't need no lawyer. I'll answer what you ask. I ain't done nothin', wrong, got nothin' to hide."

John thought for a minute and decided to go straight to the jugular. "Last night, when you were in the bunker, did you say that you wished Lieutenant Speight was dead?"

"Yes, sir, I did."

"Why did you say that?"

Jackson replied, "Well, I didn't mean it, but I was just sayin' that he was a shitty platoon leader, and I wished he won't our PC. He got us, and kept us, in trouble. He ordered us to do something that caused one of my best buddies to get his leg blowed off."

"What did he do?"

"Well, he screwed up a couple of times when he got here when we were on Dewey Canyon. We was goin' back to the firebase after the patrol, and the lieutenant, he wanted to get back to our firebase using the same path we left out on. It won't as steep as the other paths, and he said he had the red ass and needed to get back to our position ASAP. My friend Scully told him he shouldn't go back the same way he left, 'cause the NVA or Cong may set up an ambush or plant a mine. The lieutenant said go anyway. The NVA, they planted a mine on the path, and Scully stepped on it, lost his leg. Lieutenant Speight also screwed up on Apache Snow."

Gates interrupted Jackson. "Let's focus on what happened last night. Where did you go when you left that underground bunker, and what time was it?"

"I don't know the time, ain't got no watch. But I went back to my hooch and tried to sleep, which was hard with the storm goin'."

"Who else was in your hooch, either when you got there or after you got there?"

"No one, sir. They only there other guys in my hooch, and none of them was there when I got there."

John continued. "Did you later leave your hooch?"

Jackson answered, "Yes, sir, I did, don't know what time, but I left to take a leak."

"Where's the head in relation to your hooch?"

"Right next to it."

Gates continued, "Well, we have a statement from someone that he saw you and Grant running from the lieutenant's hooch right after the grenade exploded."

Jackson stood up—all five feet, six inches of him. "That's a damn lie. I ain't done nothin'. I didn't kill the lieutenant, and I don't know who did. Who said that?"

John didn't answer Jackson and resumed the questioning. "Sit down, Lance Corporal. Can you prove where you were when the lieutenant was murdered? Did anyone see you in your hooch, or did anyone see you go into your hooch when you left the bunker?"

"I done said, no one else was in my bunker, and I didn't see no one."

"Do you know Grant?"

"Yeah, I know him. I know all the guys in the platoon, 'cept some of the new ones. Grant is a buddy of mine."

John took off the gloves. "He's such a good buddy, you and he agreed to kill the lieutenant, didn't you?"

"I done tell you. I didn't kill the lieutenant. Besides, we got to turn in all unused ordinance to the armory here. I had two grenades on me when we came back from Apache Snow, and I turned in both of them in. I didn't have no grenade to toss at the lieutenant."

John pulled his chair back and stood up, dismissing Jackson. "Well, Lance Corporal, thanks for your help. You can go back to your unit."

Jackson stood up. "What's gonna happen?"

John answered, "Well, we haven't completed our investigation, so we'll keep you posted. You can go now."

After Jackson left, Ben asked, "What is our plan of attack now? Think we should take this info to the SJA's office, meet with Mike and Kevin, and see what they think? We've done all we need for this preliminary investigation. No need to interview every man in each platoon at this point."

John responded. "Agreed, but first I think we should take a casual stroll in the company area and ask Sergeant Smith the locations of everybody's hooch. I don't think we should really inspect the area carefully—don't want to show what we're interested in it. How does that sound?"

"That's a good plan. Maybe Sergeant Smith can help us get a hop back to Quang Tri. This didn't take as long as I thought it would. Sergeant, can you come in here?"

After getting an idea of each Marine's hooch, Gates and Harrelson walked around the company area while Sergeant Smith arranged for them to get on a chopper back to Quang Tri. When they got to Quang Tri, they hitched a ride to the office of the SJA of the Third Marine Division and were told to meet with the SJA and chief trial counsel McMurry and Ross at 0900 hours the next day. They were assigned bunks for the night, and they finished their day at the O Club, where the beers were cold.

Trial Counsel
0900 Hours, Mon, 16 Jun 69
Office of the Staff Judge Advocate
Headquarters Company, Third Marine Division
Quang Tri

"Well, lookie here, it's Sherlock and Watson. Put your hands on your wallets, they aren't safe with these guys around!" Mike McMurry and Kevin Ross, the best trial counsel/prosecutors in the Third Marine Division, were happy to see NIS agents John Gates and Ben Harrelson. The four of them had been involved in four major cases for the Third Marine Division in Quang Tri, all of which were successful, at least from their perspective. The defendants who were convicted, and in two cases dishonorably discharged, probably didn't care a bit for NIS or the two most senior trial counsel in I Corps. They met in the outer office of the SJA's office.

John and Ben were just as happy to see Mike and Kevin again. They knew how zealous and fair these experienced military prosecutors were. They also felt Mike and Kevin would be tested in what was shaping up as a "he said, he said" murder case, the type of case that was always problematic and unpredictable.

Mike McMurry grew up in a Catholic family in Indiana about one hundred miles from Notre Dame. He was an altar boy at their church and became a devout Catholic. Even though no one in has family had attended Notre Dame, or any other college, everyone in the family was a rabid Irish fan. His dad was a county clerk and a small claims judge, a position for which a law degree was not necessary. Mike spent a lot of time in his father's "courtroom" and was quite impressed with the lawyers who appeared before his dad. Even though his dad was not a lawyer, he was highly respected by all the lawyers in the county.

One year, Mike's Christmas gift came in November when his dad took him to see the Fighting Irish play Michigan in South Bend. It was Mike's first trip to Notre Dame. They had seats in the first row at the fifty-yard line, right behind the Irish bench. And at that game, Mike decided he wanted to be a US Marine after he saw the Marine in the color guard wearing his dress blues. He knew he wanted to wear that uniform one day.

He was accepted to Notre Dame, joined a fraternity, and was given the nickname "Lep," short for leprechaun, because he was short, had a perpetual grin, and his eyes seemed to literally twinkle. He also had a great sense of humor, which endeared him to those who got to know him. During his freshman year, he took the first step to wear the dress blues of a Marine by enlisting in the Corps. He attended the Platoon Leaders Course during the summers of his sophomore and junior years. His major was political science, and during his senior year his favorite professor advised him that there were more than enough political science professors and that law school was a better plan for him. When Mike graduated from Notre Dame, he had a degree in political science, a seat in the Notre Dame law school, and the gold bars of a US Marine second lieutenant, which were pinned on him by his proud mother. Mike's active-duty report date was deferred, so he could attend law school.

Kevin Ross was born and reared in Charlestown, near Boston. His mom worked at a dry cleaners and his dad worked for the Charlestown sanitation department. They were the prototypical "paycheck-to-paycheck" family. When he was twelve, Kevin got his first paying job as a bagger at the grocery store owned by the family's next-door neighbor. He contributed his small wages and all tips to the family to help pay expenses.

Kevin's older brother Paul was a troublemaker who ran with the wrong crowd. Late one Saturday night, Paul and some of his friends were drinking at one of the many Irish pubs in "The Town," as Charlestown was called, and got in a fight with some punks from a different part of Boston . One of the punks had a concealed pistol and shot Paul, who was taken to the hospital. When Kevin and his mom and dad arrived at the hospital, Paul was in extremis and only opened his eyes briefly as he signaled Kevin to come close. Before he closed his eyes for the last time, Paul's his last words, before his eyes closed the last time, were, "Do good."

Kevin attended the trial of the accused murderer. The assistant district attorney made a procedural mistake that resulted in the judge granting the defense counsel's motion to dismiss the case against Paul's murderer. So it was at age thirteen that Kevin, who understood why the judge dismissed the charge against Paul's killer, decided he wanted to be a lawyer who prosecuted criminals.

Neither of Kevin's parents were college graduates. His dad had dropped out of high school in his sophomore year to work, and his mom dropped out of school at age thirteen to take care of her five siblings. But both of Kevin's parents valued education, and they made every effort to instill in Kevin an appreciation for the benefits of education. It turned out that Kevin was an exceptional student, garnering top grades in his public high school graduating class. He was also an aggressive, quick, and intelligent hockey player who received and accepted an offer to attend Boston College on an athletic scholarship. Later he received an academic scholarship from the Boston College School of Law. During his first year in law school, he enlisted in the Marines, and after graduating with his juris doctorate, he completed Marine Corps OCS at Quantico.

Kevin and Mike were in the same Naval Justice School class. Neither was married, so they spent a lot of time together, going to Boston to see the Red Sox play and shooting the bull. The subject of religion often came up since Mike had attended a Catholic school and Kevin a Jesuit-Catholic school.

They both received orders to report to Headquarters Company, Third Marine Division, Quang Tri, South Vietnam for assignment as legal officers. Each was assigned to the trial counsel shop, so Kevin got his wish to prosecute. They tried a number of cases together, particularly the more complicated ones.

After the greetings and good-natured ribbing, Mike McMurry asked John Gates to give the NIS version of the crime and investigation. When John finished, he told the two attorneys, "That's the *Reader's Digest* version. What's next?"

Kevin answered, "Well, let's see what the colonel has to say about this. He'll probably hand this off to the ASJA, but John, why don't you give the colonel the summary you gave us?"

Kevin knocked on the SJA's door and was ordered to enter. The SJA, Lieutenant Colonel Raoul Suarez, did not move from behind his desk or look up when the four men entered. He asked Kevin, "What's up?"

Lieutenant Colonel Suarez was scheduled to rotate back home to New Mexico near the end of August and was spending as little time running the SJA's office as he could and as much time as possible planning his campaign to run for county judge back home. He often deferred his command decisions to the assistant staff judge advocate, Major Bert Forrest, who was a career Marine.

Mike introduced the NIS agents to the colonel and said they had investigated the fragging and had a synopsis for the colonel. He was interrupted by Lieutenant Colonel Suarez. "Captain, I'm involved in some important work now, and I think the best thing for you to do is run your thoughts by Major Forrest and follow his lead. Thank you."

After they left the SJA's office, Ben spoke up. "Not exactly an 'in the weeds' kind of guy, is he?"

"No, and it's a good thing, frankly," Kevin replied. "I guess it's like being in a firm with a senior partner who is senior in name only, who will let you do your own thing. Major Forrest is very much an 'in the weeds' guy who wants to know the process we recommend. He will want details, so let's go to the courtroom and discuss what we will say and recommend to him."

The Third Marine Division courtroom was in a Quonset hut, a structure that looked like a huge piece of metal underground pipe that had been cut in half and placed on top of a concrete slab. There were doors at each end, one small window on each side, a spectator seating area for no more than thirty people, a judge's bench which was flanked by the American and Marine Corps flags, a witness chair to the left of the bench, and on the front left wall seating for the military panel, or jury, which presently had three chairs, the normal complement for a special court-martial. More chairs would be required for a general court-martial. A table and chair in front of the judge's bench accommodated the court reporter.

Kevin spoke first. "Major Forrest will want to know how we're gonna attack the problem. So, what's our plan of action now that we have a general idea of what happened?"

Mike responded, "Well, there are several things to do, maybe not in this order. First, Kevin, don't we need to check out the murder site and the Alpha 1/9 area and get this guy Douglas to show us where he was and where Grant and Jackson—or whoever it was—were when he saw them running? Eyewitness cases are hard as hell when there is no other evidence. We may want to draw a schematic map of the area as an exhibit for the military panel. You know, with the storm and all, this ain't a cakewalk."

Kevin answered, "Good ideas. Then with John and Ben present, we need to interview all the witnesses they interviewed to see if their stories have changed. We need to think about interviewing other members of the platoon—and maybe even the company—to see what they may know. That may slow down the process, so we need to have someone with more rank—the ASJA—tell us whether to interview more than the six guys already interviewed, so we have a little CYA if the big brass starts hollering about why this is taking a lot of time."

Kevin continued, "We need to discuss the charges with the major. John, what does the NIS say about who and what we should charge? And one other thing—I know the XO of Alpha acted as an informal investigator when NIS couldn't get there because of the storm. Do we want to look at his interviews? And we need to have the Article 32 hearing."

John Gates answered, "I leave the charges to you guys, but regarding the XO's investigation—his name was Breckinridge—he tried to push his interview notes on us. I told him that we don't ever look at interviews done by anyone else until after we've completed our own interviews, and then we may or may not review his notes, but he should offer his notes to you guys. Ben and I started from scratch, so I don't know if those six guys told Breckinridge the same thing they told us. I suggest you get his interview file, and then if you want to, you can compare his notes with our notes and with your own interviews."

Mike said, "OK, we'll get Breckinridge's interview file and may give it a quick review, but we probably won't mess with it assuming it jives with what those six guys told us and tell you."

Mike continued, "On the Article 32, the hearing officer will have to be equal to or above the rank of the defendant's counsel, whoever that is. And there's the question of whether we charge a defendant or the defendants before or after the 32. Probably before is my thought. Based on what we now know, it sounds like the charges should be murder, accessory after the fact, and conspiracy. If my memory is right, the elements of accessory are that the accused knew, comforted, assisted, and so forth, the offender—in this case the murderer—to keep him from being caught, and that the man accused with accessory knew that the crime—murder here—had been committed. So going to the lieutenant's hooch with the man who tossed the grenade and maybe helping him toss the grenade, and then not pointing him out, should qualify for both as accessory after the fact and conspiracy."

Mike then said, "Unless the investigation takes us elsewhere, maybe both men—Grant and Jackson or whoever it was—should be charged with all three crimes since we don't know who the 'trigger man' was, and maybe we can squeeze the 'nontrigger man' to testify against the trigger man. I'm more interested in a murder conviction than an accessory or conspiracy conviction. By the way, what do Grant's and Jackson's SRBs show?"

Every Marine, from the Commandant to the lowest private, has a service record book, which contains everything of importance about the subject Marine, such as his duty stations, the schools he attended, his promotions or demotions, his marksmanship records, his fitness reports, information about their intelligence if the Marine engages in sensitive matters, and so forth.

John Gates replied, "NIS looked at both files. Grant is still a private, same rank as when he finished boot camp two years ago. Every time he gets a promotion, he gets busted for insubordination, fighting, drunk and disorderly, and other stuff. He's a troublemaker. On the other hand, Jackson is pretty squared away. At Parris Island, he did so well he was offered to try OCS, but he turned it down, probably 'cause it would have added a year or so to his enlistment. He's got high marks all around. Got a Purple Heart and Bronze Star with "V" for valor in Dewey Canyon. So if we go on SRBs, Grant was the more likely trigger man."

Kevin stood up. "Well, let's see if Major Forrest is available to meet with us, so we can lay this out for him, particularly the part about whether he wants to us to interview everyone in the company. We'll need to discuss the Article 32 also. Is everyone OK with this?" Everyone nodded. Kevin continued, asking the NIS agents if either of them had met Major Forrest. They both shook their heads no. "Well, I doubt he's ever laughed at anything. Knows the law and he is the judge in special courts martial for the division. No close buddies, but a straight shooter."

They left the courtroom and walked to the office of the assistant staff judge advocate, which was located in the same building as the SJA's office. Major Forrest was in the admin area, and Mike asked if they could meet with him. They went into the major's office, and Mike began the conversation by introducing the NIS agents to Major Forrest. The major didn't extend his hand to either Jack or Ben, so Mike proceeded to outline the case status, the plan, and the concerns for moving ahead, after which the major finally spoke. "Well, sounds like a good plan to me. What questions do you have?"

Mike said, "Sir, of course you will have to appoint a 32 investigation officer, and since the highest-ranking defense counsel will probably be a captain, the IO will have to be a captain or higher. Also, Major, we don't know whether we should take the time to interview anyone other than the members of first platoon. We don't think it is likely—though possible—that someone in another platoon did this because the murdered lieutenant apparently was not a good field commander, and that would impact the first platoon most."

The major replied, "I think the more thorough approach is for everyone in the company to be interviewed. These 'he said, he said' cases are the toughest if there is no other evidence, as in this case, so you need to be particularly thorough. If that's all, you are dismissed.

"Wait a minute," the major said. "I just thought of something. When you interview each man in the entire company, don't use the company roster to start that process. Instead make a list of everyone you interview, and then compare it to the company roster. With guys rotating in and out or going to sick call, that's the best way to get make sure all Marines are accounted for. I don't imagine anyone rotated between the murder and now, but check that out too. And I'd have each platoon leader bring his platoon to the interview site and confirm those are all his men—that no one is missing.

"I can handle any pushback you get if this takes longer 'cause it is the thorough way to do it. But just ask each Marine his name, unit, and if he heard or saw anything related to the fragging. There is no need to cross-examine each of them. This is probably not going to be a deep dive unless you stumble on something. When you get back from VCB, report to me on how it went. Now you are dismissed."

The four men went to the airstrip at Quang Tri. They were the only passengers on a CH-46 chopper, which was carrying supplies, including C-rats, so Marines would have chow, such as it was, when they were in the bush.

When the lawyers and NIS agents landed at VCB, the agents led the way to the Alpha Company area because although both trial counsel had been to VCB when preparing other cases, they did not know Alpha's location.

They were met by Lieutenant Crawford, who was asked to order each platoon leader to bring the Marines in their platoon to the area of the company office and to also bring the latest platoon roster for comparison with the men who were then interviewed. Crawford then showed Mike and Kevin the locations of Speight's and Douglas's hooches, as well as the underground bunker.

After the inspection of the area, the NIS agents and the trial counsel were seated in the CO's office. Lieutenant Breckinridge came in and addressed them. "I'm the XO, and I interviewed six Marines and have their interview sheets. Do you want them? Do you want me to help you interview the Marines?"

Ben answered him. "Lieutenant, for the second time, no; for the third time, you've tried to push your interviews on us, and as I told you before, NIS doesn't need your help. You can leave your interview file with Captain Ross." Breckinridge gave Kevin his folder with the six interview sheets and left. Kevin put the file in his briefcase to be reviewed later.

The men of Alpha 1/9 were in formation. As a Marine came into the office, Kevin asked his name, rank, service number, and unit as John wrote that information and checked that name off the company roster provided by Lieutenant Crawford. Two of the men interviewed were not on the roster since they had just joined the company.

Kevin began asking each Marine these questions: Were you at VCB the night Lieutenant Speight was murdered? Did you see anyone at or near the lieutenant's hooch at any time during the night of the murder? Did you see anyone up and about the company area after midnight and before daylight on the night the lieutenant was murdered? What have you heard anyone say about who may have committed the murder, and who said it?

There were 123 Marines in Alpha, including Grant, all of whom were asked these questions. Except for Grant, who said nothing, and Douglas, who repeated his statement about seeing Grant and Jackson running, each of the remaining 121 Marines gave the same answers: I was at VCB; I saw no one at or near the lieutenant's hooch; I saw no one up and about the company area after midnight and before daylight on the night of the murder; and I heard no one say who may have committed the murder.

Two of those Marines were lying.

After completing interviews, the lawyers and the NIS agents caught a chopper back to Quang Tri and went to the empty O Club to discuss the case. Mike began, "I don't know what else we can do to vet Douglas's story. His ability to ID whoever it was running from the lieutenant's hooch is suspect because of the distance between them and because of the weather."

Kevin responded, "From the trial counsel view, I agree that his testimony will be weak, but we've got no other cards to play. It isn't enough if all we have is that Jackson said he wished the lieutenant was dead. I don't think an Article 32 hearing officer would recommend charges based just on that evidence. I wouldn't. But we should have all the guys who heard what Jackson said, which includes Douglas, testify at the 32 hearing."

"Agreed," said Mike. "As to the possible charges, since we don't know who tossed the grenade and since Grant and Jackson were both seen running from Speight's hooch after the grenade detonated—or from Douglas's testimony they were both running—let's recommend charging each of them with murder, accessory after the fact, and conspiracy. I'm not sure who we should try first or if we should try them at the same time. I know this isn't in your NIS wheelhouse, John, but what's your gut reaction regarding the charges?"

John thought a minute before answering. "Well, from the NIS perspective, Grant was more likely the trigger man, and it is more important to convict the defendant who threw the grenade on the murder charge than the person who was with him , 'cause whoever threw it probably came up with the idea. Maybe by charging both with all three crimes, and trying Jackson first, you can get him to flip on Grant. Facing a murder charge and the death penalty could give him incentive to testify against Grant if he was the one with Grant."

Mike McMurry replied, "Damn, John, that's downright scary 'cause you're thinking like us lawyers. So let's report to Major Forrest—no point in taking the time to go to the SJA—and see if he agrees and ask him to get an Article 32 hearing officer designated. Agreed?" All nodded, so they headed to the ASJA's office.

Major Forrest had a habit of walking back and forth in his small office when discussing serious matters, and the murder of Lieutenant Speight was such a matter. Kevin and Mike had presented the plan they and the NIS agents had formulated.

The major stopped pacing. "Well, I have already appointed Major Womack as the Article 32 hearing officer. We will have to designate an attorney for both Grant and Jackson. Captain Peterson can handle Jackson's case, and Lieutenant Allen will be Grant's counsel. Are you going to serve charges on them before the Article 32?"

Kevin Ross responded, "Yes, sir. We'll prepare the charges, go the VCB, serve them with the charges, arrest them, get them in the brig here, keep them separate, and have the hearing. That way, we're moving as fast as we can."

Major Forest said, "I approve. Let me see the charges before you serve them and arrest Grant and Jackson."

Jackson is Charged
1330 Hours, Tues, 17 Jun 69
Third Marine Division
Quang Tri Province

In that Lance Corporal Ricardo Jackson, US Marine Corps (Reserve), Ser. No. 6251025. did, on or about 15 June 1969, at Vandergrift Combat Base, I Corps, Republic of South Vietnam, with premeditation, murder Second Lieutenant Alvin Speight, US Marine Corps (Reserve), by causing a live grenade to be thrown under the bed of Lieutenant Speight, causing the death of Lieutenant Speight, a violation Article 118 of the Uniform Code of Military Justice.

In that Lance Corporal Ricardo Jackson, US Marine Corps (Reserve), Ser. No. 6251025, did, on or about 15 June 1969, at Vandergrift Combat Base, I Corps, Republic of South Vietnam, knowing that the offense of the murder of Second Lieutenant Alvin Speight had been committed, assist the offender who murdered Lieutenant Speight, by hindering or preventing the apprehension, trial, or punishment of the murderer, a violation of Article 78 of the Uniform Code of Military Justice.

In that Lance Corporal Ricardo Jackson, US Marine Corps (Reserve), Ser. No. 6251025, did, on or about 15 June 1969, at Vandergrift Combat Base, I Corps, Republic of South Vietnam, conspire with another person to commit the crime of murder, a violation of Article 18 of the Uniform Code of Military Justice when one or more of the conspirators did an act to effect the object of the conspiracy, to wit, the murder of Second Lieutenant Alvin Speight, US Marine Corps (Reserve).

Jackson read the charges against him at least ten times on the ride from VCB to the brig at Quang Tri and still didn't believe this was happening to him. All he could remember was that he was in his hooch when two NIS agents—the same two he talked to when he denied killing the lieutenant—came into the hooch with two sergeants and told him he was being charged with murder, conspiracy to commit murder, and accessory after the fact to murder. Jackson had no idea what conspiracy and accessory after the fact even meant, but he sure knew what "murder" meant.

After he was handcuffed, the NIS agents and one of the sergeants left Jackson while the other sergeant guarded Jackson. The next person Jackson saw was Grant, who was also handcuffed, walking in front of the NIS agents and the other sergeant. Jackson and Grant were placed in different jeeps, and each was accompanied by a guard and an NIS agent when they left VCB. His guard told Jackson he would be placed in the division brig at Quang Tri. The road ran thorough unsecured territory, so Jackson was relieved to see two Huey gunships overhead, providing security.

Jackson and Grant were each placed in solitary confinement in separate parts of the brig, so they were unable to communicate with each other. Jackson had never felt so alone, so hopeless, in his life. He was half a world away from his family in the brig, facing three charges—one of which carried the death penalty. He knew he was innocent and did not know why he was picked out and charged out of all the other Marines in first platoon.

Jackson did have one thing going for him, even though he didn't know it. His lawyer was the best lawyer—defense or prosecution—in the Third Marine Division.

First Lieutenant David Peterson received his undergraduate degree, with honors, in philosophy from Williams College, a small, elite liberal arts college located in bucolic Williamstown, Massachusetts. He was accepted to Harvard Law School and finished in the top tier of his class. During law school, he enlisted in the Corps, obligating himself after graduation to attend the ten-week OCS class at Quantico, which began in January 1968.

David was at OCS when the Tet Offensive began on 31 January 1968. After completing OCS and TBS, David was sent to the Naval Justice School in Newport, Rhode Island, to take classes for certification as military trial counsel. In August 1968, he was assigned to a platoon leader's billet in Charlie Company, 1/9 of the Third Marine Division in I Corps.

Peterson distinguished himself in the field, earning the Bronze Star with the combat "V" device. Due to the passage of the Military Justice Act in October 1968, he was made a defense counsel with Headquarters Company, Third Marine Division in November 1968.

Most defendants represented by Peterson were not only guilty, but the government could prove it and David knew they could prove it. But he made the government work hard to win convictions by filing novel and legally appropriate motions. He was also a highly skilled trial counsel, frequently engaging in legal battles with either Mike McMurry or Kevin Ross, or both. Sometimes these legal battles were followed by the sharing of beers at the O Club. These three professionals felt it was possible to be civil with lawyers "on the other side." They were friendly, worthy adversaries who shared a love for the law and for the professional practice of law.

Major Forrest called Peterson to his office, told him of his new assignment, gave him a copy of the charges, and suggested he meet with Kevin and Mike about the case.

Kevin and Mike were upfront with David, giving him copies of the NIS interviews of the six men in the underground bunker as well as the interview folder from the XO, Lieutenant Breckinridge. David glanced at the NIS interviews as Kevin and Mike filled him in on the case. He put the Breckinridge interview folder in his file. He could sense that Jackson was in for a tough legal ride.

Jackson was at the brig in Quang Tri for no more than four hours before Peterson came for his first attorney-client conference. He saw that Jackson was a very frightened Marine with the largest nose Peterson had ever seen. Jackson told Peterson his mind was still "messed up," as he described it.

David began the interview. "Lance Corporal, anything you tell me is confidential, and that means I can't tell anyone what you and I talk about. But if you tell me something, you can't say something different in the courtroom. Understand?" Jackson nodded that he understood.

"So, Jackson, did you say you wished the lieutenant was dead?"

"Yes, sir, but I didn't mean it. I just meant he won't a good platoon leader, and we could do better if he won't our platoon leader. He messed up in Dewey Canyon. They took him off the line, but he came back to the platoon in Apache Snow, and he messed up in there. My best buddy lost his leg because of the lieutenant on Dewey Canyon."

David replied, "So you had a motive, a reason, to kill the lieutenant. That's what the prosecutor is going to say."

"But I didn't. I was in my hooch when the grenade exploded!"

"OK, tell me about that night after you left the bunker."

Jackson continued. "Well, I left the bunker and went to my hooch. There was no one there, and no one came to the hooch before the grenade exploded. I don't think no one came until daybreak. I guess they was holed up somewhere else, and it didn't matter 'cause we were on stand-down. I was in my rack when I heard the grenade, but with all the thunder and lightning and rain, I didn't go see what was going on. Oh yeah, I remember getting up and going to the head to take a whiz before the grenade exploded, but I didn't see nobody."

Peterson asked, "How did you and PFC Douglas get along, any problems?"

"No, sir, never got cross-legged with him. No problems. Why."

Peterson answered, "Douglas told NIS that he saw you and Grant running from the direction of Lieutenant Speight's hooch right after the grenade exploded. Is that true?"

"I won't with Grant at all that night. Didn't even see him. He was not in the bunker. It won't me running nowhere."

"Well," Peterson asked, "would Douglas make up something to get you in trouble?"

Jackson answered, "I never had no problem with him. No reason I know for him to make up something."

After a three-hour conference, Peterson realized two things: First, he could get no more from Jackson because Jackson had no more to give him other than the denial with no corroboration; and second, he had his work cut out for him in the toughest kind of case—a "he said, he said" murder case with no real evidence other than one eyewitness.

Peterson also realized this case was more difficult because the victim was a Marine officer murdered while sleeping. The Corps looks after its own, and the military panel for the general court-martial would consist chiefly of Marine officers. Furthermore, fragging officers happened from time-to-time in South Vietnam with both the Corps and the US Army. Fragging was a problem, and the Corps had a history of dealing successfully with problems. Things did not look good for Lance Corporal Ricardo Jackson.

David went back to his office and started a to-do list of steps to represent Jackson:

- Prepare for Article 32 hearing, esp. cross-examination of witnesses.

- Go to VCB, check out Douglas's hooch, and scope out Douglas's ability to see anyone running from Speight's hooch. Where was he standing; where were the men when he saw them running, etc.

- Re: GCM military panel makeup for murder case—requires twelve when death penalty is at play unless the convening authority specifies lesser number due to physical circumstances or military exigencies. Make objection to any number less than twelve. And request in writing the inclusion of enlisted members (at least one-third of total on panel.)

- Attempt to get meteorological evidence concerning the storm conditions between midnight and 0500 on murder date—may undercut Douglas's eyewitness testimony.

- Are there any witnesses other than the guys in the bunker and all of Alpha? Probably not likely but check it out.

When David completed this list, he knew he would be adding to it as trial prep continued. He also knew that he had to create as many issues at trial as legally permissible to be argued on appeal if Jackson were convicted. He also knew that it was entirely possible, maybe even likely, that Jackson would receive the death penalty if he were convicted of the murder of the lieutenant. David never had a case that needed his considerable skills more.

Major Womack conducted the Article 32 preliminary hearing, which did not take long. A court reporter recorded the proceedings, so Peterson would be able to review the transcribed testimony of each witness, Ratcliff, Jones, Parker, Walters, Evans, and Douglas—each of whom testified consistently with the statements they gave to the NIS agents. David had no cross-examination of the witnesses.

After the Article 32, David was informed that there was no evidence in I Corps or at VCB of the meteorological conditions when Lieutenant Speight was murdered. All anyone in I Corps knew about the typhoon was that it rained like hell, the thunderstorm was unforgettable, and the wind was blowing so hard rain fell sideways. David hoped each member of the military panel had experienced the typhoon and would know the difficulty of Douglas identifying, from twenty or so yards, someone running only when lightning flashed.

David was exceptional at judging strengths and weaknesses of cases, and he usually could accurately predict the most likely trial result. Any general court-martial verdict had to be unanimous, and David had no illusions that he could convince the entire panel that Jackson was innocent of all charges. David knew if just one panel member was not morally certain of Jackson's guilt on any of the charges—that is, if just one panel member had "reasonable doubt" of Jackson's guilt—and if that person had the guts to hold out against the pressure of all the other panel members who had no reasonable doubt, there could be a mistrial as to that charge, which would at least lead to another trial on that charge.

However, all of David's considerable instincts told him that there was just no way all members of the panel would acquit Jackson or have reasonable doubt on all charges. That meant Jackson's best-case scenario would be for the panel to find that there was not sufficient evidence that Jackson threw the grenade, in other words that he was not the murderer. David knew as defense counsel that he could argue that point effectively because there was no evidence who tossed the grenade. But the remaining charges—accessory after the fact and conspiracy—well, David believed it was highly unlikely that Jackson would be acquitted of both those charges. He never told Jackson, but David knew in his gut that Jackson was going to prison. He just hoped they dodged a guilty verdict to the murder charge, and the death penalty.

David's motion to have enlisted Marines on the military panel was granted, so one-third of the panel would be enlisted above Jackson's rank of lance corporal.

Captain David Peterson, the best trial lawyer in the Third Marine Division, then began his final trial preparation.

The Trial of Lance Corporal Jackson
0800 Hours, Mon, 7 Jul 69
Third Marine Division Courtroom
Quang Tri

The prosecution of Lance Corporal Ricardo Jackson began with the reading of each charge and the entry of the plea of "not guilty" to each charge. David's motion objecting to the reduction of the number of Marines on the panel was denied on the predictable grounds of military exigencies. After all there was a war going on.

The officers on the panel were a bird colonel, a lieutenant colonel, a major, two captains, and a first lieutenant, and the enlisted were two gunnery sergeants and one first sergeant. Except for the bird colonel, each enlisted man had more time in the Corps than each of the officers. David knew those enlisted men were what the Corps referred to as hard "Corps." They had been through it all. He and Jackson had their work cut out for them.

A corpsman testified that from his examination of the murder scene photos, it appeared from the position of the rack and the hole in the plyboard deck of the hooch that the grenade had detonated directly under the middle of Lieutenant Speight's back, stomach, or side, depending on how he had been sleeping.

The corpsman also testified that the explosion probably caused the lieutenant's body to initially move upward before it fell into the hole made in the plyboard . The corpsman's testimony ended with his stating that he was told that the on-the-scene personnel had to crawl under the hooch to reach the lieutenant to search for a pulse, which they did not find.

David did not object to the corpsman's inadmissible hearsay testimony about what the on-the-scene personnel did or said because David wanted the government to move on from this subject matter and the pictures of the scene and deceased as soon as possible.

David correctly predicted that Mike McMurry and Kevin Ross would call PFC Douglas as the government's last witness. The testimony of the other five Marines in the bunker who heard Jackson's comment about wanting the lieutenant dead didn't take any time at all. In fact, David had planned to ask them no questions if they testified consistently with their statements to the NIS agents, which they did. They were on and off the witness stand in no time at all.

Kevin handled the direct examination of Douglas, asking about all the points Douglas made in his interviews.

It was Peterson's time to cross-examine the most important witness against Lance Corporal Jackson. He started with an easy question.

Defense counsel: PFC Douglas, what time was it when you say you saw men running from the direction of Lieutenant Speight's hooch?

Witness: Sir, about 0300 hours.

DC: Did you hear the grenade detonate?

Witness: Yes, sir.

DC: How much time was there between the grenade detonating and the time you allegedly saw the men running?

Witness: Just seconds, sir.

DC: Now, describe the weather conditions at the time you say you saw the men running.

Witness: Sir, I ain't never saw a storm like that before. The wind was howling, and rain was coming down sideways in sheets.

DC: As you are looking out from your hooch, the lieutenant's hooch is about thirty yards to the left of your hooch, correct?

Witness: Yes, sir.

DC: So the men you say you saw running had their right sides to you, right?

Witness: Yes, sir.

DC: Which of the two men was closer to you?

Witness: Grant was closer.

DC: Describe Private Grant's build.

Witness: Sir, he's about six and a half feet tall, real big. He's the biggest man in in the platoon.

DC: How far apart were the two men you say you saw running?

Witness: I, um, I don't know, sir. I couldn't tell.

DC: When the men were even with your hooch, who was in front?

Trial counsel: Objection, that question assumes a fact not in evidence, namely that one of them was in front of the other.

The Court: Objection sustained. Ask another question, Lieutenant Peterson.

DC: Were the men side by side when they ran by your hooch?

Witness: I don't remember.

DC: How far from you were the two men you say were running?

Witness: About thirty yards.

DC: There was no artificial light in the area, was there?

Witness: Uh, sir, I don't know what you mean.

DC: There were no streetlights or other lights shining on the area where you say you saw men running, were there?

Witness: Oh, no sir.

DC: Well, if there were no lights, then it was dark when you allegedly saw the men running, right?

Witness: Well, sir, it was lightning all the time. I seen them when there was lightning.

DC: So the opportunity—the chance—you had to actually see and identify the men you saw running happened when lightning flashed, right?

Witness: Yes, sir.

DC: How many times did lightning flash when you say you saw the men running?

Witness: I don't know, sir.

DC: Just how long was there light when the lightning occurred?

Witness: I just don't know, sir.

David knew he could ask Douglas to explain why he didn't remember who was in front if either man was ahead of the other. He also knew that more questions would give Douglas a chance to explain the weak parts of his testimony. He knew that Kevin would ask Douglas questions on redirect to shore up his testimony, so he decided to ask no more questions. He could argue those inconsistencies in his final argument. He hoped it was enough, so he told the court he had no further questions. After some redirect of Douglas by Kevin, and no further examination by David, the government rested.

David called Lance Corporal Jackson to testify. David decided it was best to cut to the chase in his direct examination of the defendant.

Defense counsel: State your name, rank, serial number, and date of birth.

Witness: Ricardo Jackson, lance corporal, 6251025, 16 July 1949, first platoon, Alpha 1/9.

DC: When you were in the underground bunker during the typhoon on the night Lieutenant Speight was murdered, did you make the statement in the presence of the other Marines in the bunker who have testified in this case that you wished Lieutenant Speight was dead?

Witness: Yes, sir.

DC: Why did you make that statement?

Witness: Sir, Lieutenant Speight was not a good platoon leader. He made mistakes in the field. I didn't want to be in his platoon and just said I wished he was dead so he won't be our platoon leader, sir.

DC: Did you mean you wanted him dead?

Witness: No, sir, no way. I just don't want to be in his unit.

DC: Why do you say he was not a good platoon leader?

Witness: Sir, on our first op in Dewey Canyon, on the way back to the firebase, the lieutenant, he went up the same path we'd left on, even though he was told not to go there 'cause the VC may have put a mine on that path. He ordered us up the path anyway 'cause it was quicker, and he said he had the red ass and needed to get to the firebase fast, and my friend Scully stepped on a mine and lost his leg. And at an ambush on Apache Snow, he opened fire on the Marines at the other end of the ambush, even though the firing lines had been set out. But I didn't frag him and don't know who did.

DC: What did you do when you left the underground bunker after saying you wished the lieutenant was dead, even though you didn't want him dead?

Witness: Went back to my hooch, sir.

DC: Was anyone in your hooch when you got there?

Witness: No, sir.

DC: Did anyone come into the hooch before the fragging?

Witness: No, sir.

DC: Did you leave the hooch before the fragging?

Witness: Only to go to the head to take a whiz—I mean to pee. The head is next to my hooch.

DC: Did you see anyone before or after the fragging?

Witness: No, sir.

DC: Did you throw, help throw, or know who threw the grenade under Lieutenant Speight's rack?

Witness: No, sir. No way. I'm innocent.

David then asked questions about the arrangement of hooches at VCB and had him identify the map of the layout Jackson drew, particularly the estimated distance of Douglas's hooch to the pathway on which Douglas said he saw the Marines running. David completed his examination by asking Jackson about his outstanding record at Parris Island, his Bronze Star, and his receiving promotions quickly. David then told the court that he had no further questions for Jackson and awaited cross-examination of his client.

Peterson thought Jackson had done as good a job as anyone could in answering Kevin's cross-examination. He did not waiver, declaring his innocence in the face of Kevin's cross-exam. Both the government and the defendant then rested.

After final arguments from the lawyers, the military judge gave the nine-member panel instructions for deliberation by explaining the elements of each alleged crime, the definition of burden of proof, the definition of reasonable doubt, and the other standard instructions.

The jury recessed for deliberation at 1500 hours. As a defense counsel, David knew that the waiting time during jury deliberation could feel like an eternity, regardless of the actual length of the wait.

At 1610 hours, only one hour and ten minutes after being excused to deliberate, the panel informed the military judge they had reached a verdict. David thought the short deliberation time was a bad sign.

As the panel filed in, each of them looked at the defense table, and David saw no compassion in their faces. He thought the colonel, the highest-ranking officer, would be the panel foreman, and he was.

When the military judge asked the colonel if the panel had reached verdicts in each case, the colonel stood and said, "Affirmative, your honor," and handed the verdict paper to the judge.

The military judge ordered Jackson to stand. David stood also. From the look on the faces of the panel members—each of whom stared harshly at Jackson—David knew he and Jackson were not going to hear good news.

The judge read the verdict sheet.

"How do you find the defendant, Lance Corporal Ricardo Jackson, on the charge of conspiracy to commit murder?"

The colonel answered loudly, "Guilty."

"How do you find the defendant, Lance Corporal Ricardo Jackson, on the charge of accessory after the fact to the crime of murder?"

The colonel again answered, "Guilty."

"How do you find the defendant, Lance Corporal Ricardo Jackson, on the charge of murder?"

The colonel answered, "Not guilty."

No death penalty! For that, David was relieved. Now the military judge would begin the sentencing phase. David had arranged for Jackson's squad leader to testify about his bravery during Dewey Canyon, why he was awarded the Bronze Star for valor, and how Jackson was wounded for which he received the Purple Heart. His excellent SRB was also put into evidence and reviewed by the military judge as he deliberated on the sentence.

After the mitigating evidence was presented, Kevin and Mike were offered the opportunity to put on aggravating evidence—evidence for a long sentence—but they chose to argue to the court that the findings of guilty by the jury was sufficient basis for a lengthy sentence.

Having heard from both sides on sentencing, the military judge ordered Jackson to stand. David also stood as the judge announced the sentence. "It is the sentence of this court that for the crime of accessory after the fact to murder, you shall be imprisoned in the federal prison at Fort Leavenworth, Kansas, for a period of ten years, you shall be dishonorably discharged from the Marine Corps, and you shall forfeit all rank and pay. For the crime of conspiracy to commit murder, you shall be imprisoned in the federal prison at Fort Leavenworth, Kansas, for a period of ten years to begin to run at the completion of the ten-year sentence imposed for committing the crime of accessory after the fact, you shall be dishonorably discharged from the Marine Corps, and you shall forfeit all rank and pay. Guards take the convict away."

Not guilty of murder but twenty years! The trial judge granted David's request to talk to Jackson for ten minutes before he was taken to the brig. David hoped to give the stunned Marine the rundown of the automatic appeal process, but Jackson was like a man in a coma. Nothing David said registered, so he decided that he would talk to Jackson at the brig in a couple of days. But he knew he had little comfort to give his client.

Staging Battalion
0730 Hours, Thurs, 24 Jul 69
Marine Corps Base, Camp Pendleton, CA

"Lieutenant White, do you know what your duties are as the executive officer of this staging battalion?"

The question was asked by the darkest black man Woody had ever seen. He wore the silver railroad tracks, two bars, of a Marine Captain and the nametag "Barkley."

"Sir, I guess my job as your XO is to do what you, the commanding officer of this battalion, order me to do before we leave for 'Nam."

"Lieutenant, you and I are going to get along just fine. Have a seat, and we'll set out the two-week training schedule for these 160 hard-asses we've got to keep in line before all of us go to war."

Captain Barkley was a former enlisted man with a high school education who had been in the right place at the right time. He was the driver for what he called "the grief detail"—the Marine officers and chaplains who went to the homes of Marine families to tell wives they were now widows and to tell children their dads would not be coming home.

Barkley was stationed in Washington, D.C., where the procedure was that if the deceased was a field grade officer—a major, lieutenant colonel, colonel, or a general officer—the detail consisted of at least one field grade officer to accompany the chaplain. Each detail had a driver, and Barkley was often the driver, but he became more than a driver. He was frequently asked to accompany the officer and chaplain into the homes to which they were delivering the terrible news. He was a comforting force, often helping with the children of the deceased officer. He had a way about him that made people open up to him and like him. Even he was hard pressed to define what he came to think of as his "gift."

The Corps had a process to promote an enlisted man to the rank of an officer, usually a second lieutenant, and the officers Barkley drove around had the clout to make that sort of thing happen. Captain Barkley had orders to report to MAC-V in Da Nang for an assignment that Woody thought must be an intelligence position.

Woody watched everything Barkley did and how he did it. This was Woody's first real command. He didn't count the training exercises at TBS where the new second lieutenants took turns leading squads, platoons, and the company in combat field exercises. But at Camp Pendleton, Woody was ordering enlisted men, whom he didn't know, to do physical training, march, and all types of things to keep them tired and busy before their deployment to Vietnam.

On three different occasions, the company had "saddled up" and been bused to Norton Air Force Base for the flight to Vietnam, and each time deployment had been called off. Woody no longer became frustrated when one order was countermanded with another. At OCS, the platoon would be ordered to "fall in" outside, in formation wearing canteen and web belt, and then the order came for no canteen or web belt. And back and forth. Woody of course never knew, but he suspected it was just part of the practice of keeping the candidates off-balance. It worked.

But at 2300 hours on Saturday, 26 July 1969, the word came to get gear and meet the buses on the parade deck. One hundred sixty-two Marines got on the buses and started for Norton AFB. And this time, they were headed for South Vietnam.

When the bus Woody and Captain Barkley was on stopped at the terminal, Barkley pulled Woody aside. "Lieutenant, do you know what the Marine Corps protocol is for boarding modes of transportation?"

"No, sir, I didn't even know there was a protocol."

"Now, Lieutenant, the Marine Corps has a protocol for taking a crap, so you know they have one when it comes to boarding modes of transportation.

Let's see if you can figure it out. Who gets on the plane first, the officers or enlisted?"

"Sir, I don't know."

Barkly continued, "Well, the protocol is that enlisted get on first, and the officers get on last, so the officers will be the first off, which would happen if they were in a car. But tonight, we're getting on first. We're not following that protocol. Do you know why?"

Woody answered, "No, sir. Why is that?"

"Because we're getting ready to sit our asses in airplane seats for five hours to Hawaii for refueling and then maybe fifteen to eighteen hours to Okinawa, depending on the headwinds. You and I are getting on first because there are two—only two—seats with extra leg room on that civilian passenger aircraft that is going to take us on this wonderful journey, and those seats are on the starboard side of the plane, at the front of the plane, right behind the galley. And I want the extra leg room for this flight. So—follow me."

Woody had no idea they would be flying a civilian plane to 'Nam, but it made sense. The military didn't have a lot of aircraft that could carry 200 or so men across the Pacific. Woody guessed some politicians back in DC probably had a bunch of airline stock and that Ike's "military-industrial complex" was alive and well.

And there were stewardesses. Good-looking ones. Flirty ones, particularly with the enlisted. One last time of innocent flirtations before war.

Captain Barkley directed Woody to the window seat and then took the aisle seat, which had a bit more leg room. Woody settled in as the plane backed away from the terminal building. Woody diligently followed the instructions about keeping his seat in the "up" position and fastening his seat belt, but he didn't pay much attention to where he the flotation devices were because he didn't think they could be of much help if the plane ditched in the Pacific.

Woody was the antithesis of a nervous flyer. He knew he had no control, so why worry? He always fell asleep when flying, usually before the wheels were up. On the one helicopter insertion training exercise at TBS, his platoon had boarded a CH-46 chopper and flown fifteen minutes to the landing zone in the Virginia countryside. Woody had to be awakened when the chopper made its descent, even though it was a rough flight.

As Woody settled in, he thought it was a perfect "SA time," which he learned about during summer school after his freshman year at Wake. He had made a "D" in math and a "C" in biology and needed to pull up his grades, so he registered for Sociology 101 taught by Professor Accorsi. The class was held in the basement of the Z. Smith Reynolds Library in the middle of the Wake campus. Professor Accorsi was a real hoot who made learning fun.

Woody remembered two points the professor made. First, if you really screw something up, and someone is mad at you because of your screwup, go straight to that person and just tell him, "I'm a sorry SOB for messing you up." Once you've done that, the professor pointed out, it makes it harder for the person to come after you.

The second thing Woody remembered was the importance of SA time at certain junctures in your life. As Professor Accorsi explained it, "There are times in your life, or there will be, when you've been on a path for a long time, and you find yourself at a place where you are getting ready to take an entirely different path. You should use that opportunity for SA time—self-assessment time. Think about where you've been, how you got where you are, where you are, and where you're going."

Woody began the SA process. He was a high school, college, and law school graduate licensed to practice law in the courts of North Carolina. He was a second lieutenant in the United States Marine Corps—one of history's most elite fighting forces. He was a certified military lawyer, and he was heading to a war zone.

As the plane began its takeoff roll, he leaned back and closed his eyes, wondering if his dad would have been proud of him. He'd never know because of a phone call at three o'clock in the morning on Wednesday, 8 October 1958.

Jerking Sodas and the Mill Run Valley Case

Woody's sophomore year at Rose High School in Greenville, North Carolina, officially began September 2, 1959, but as far as he was concerned, school started on August 15 when varsity football practice began. The squad had "two-a-days," a practice in the early morning, usually without pads, and one in the late afternoon with pads.

By October 3, the Rose High Phantoms were 4–0 overall, and 2–0 in their conference. Homecoming versus the archrival Washington High School Pam Pack was scheduled for Friday, October 9. On October 6, the coach called Woody into his office before practice and said, "White, you're not very experienced, but you need to pick up your game because you're starting in place of Wade."

"Coach, I think that's great. What's wrong with Wade?"

"Well, Wade has mono, probably from kissing a girl who had mono. He's weak as a newborn puppy, and Doctor Aycock won't let him play. He may be out for the season. You're my new right guard—offense and defense. I'm counting on you."

"Coach, I won't let you down." Woody finished dressing out for practice and ran onto the practice field. He felt sorry for Wade, a little bit. Woody knew he could not get mono from kissing some girl because he hadn't kissed any girls. He was not someone girls found particularly attractive, and he knew he was not, and never would be, cool like some of the guys. But he was excited about starting. He was sorry his dad would be in the VA hospital in Durham and couldn't see the game.

The next day was picture day. A photograph company would take the pictures of every student at Rose High, and those pictures would be published in The Tau, *the Rose High annual. Before he went to bed, Woody picked out a tie to go with the one sport coat he owned.*

There was only one phone in the White household, and it was in the pine-panel den, which was at the front of the house. It was a very small den in a very small house. Woody's bedroom had twin beds, and you had to turn sideways to walk between them. His bedroom was only about five steps from the den. He slept with his door open, and at three o'clock in the morning, the phone rang. As he walked to the den, he wondered who would be calling at this hour.

He answered the phone.

"Is this the Woodrow White residence?" It was a man's voice.

"Yes, it is."

"May I speak to Mrs. Frances White please?"

Woody told the man to wait a minute and walked toward his mother's bedroom. His mom was out of the bed when Woody told her the call was for her. She brushed past Woody and reached the phone and said, "This is Frances White." Woody could not hear the other end of the conversation, but since he had cut on a lamp in the den, he could see his mother's expression as she listened. Woody saw her hand go to her mouth and her eyes close. She said, "I understand. I'll be up there."

She hung up the phone. "Son, do you know Uncle James's number?" Woody did not, so he looked up and dialed the number. After a while, his dad's oldest brother answered, and Woody handed the phone to his mom. She said, "James, I just got a call from the VA hospital in Durham. The man told me that Woodrow has taken a turn for the worse, and he asked me to come to Durham. I need your help." His mother listened and then said, "I'll be ready."

She looked at Woody. "Son, James is going to take me to the VA hospital. There is no reason to wake up Hailey now. You and she just need to go to school, like always." In fifteen minutes, Woody's mother left with James.

Every instinct in Woody's fifteen-year-old mind and body told him his daddy had died. There was no other reason for the VA hospital to call in the middle of the night to say his dad had taken a turn for the worse. After his mother left with James, Woody went to his bedroom and tossed and turned until early morning. He told his sister, Hailey, that their mom had gone to see their dad, and that was all he said. She didn't ask for any particulars.

Woody was in Ms. Greene's 9:50 a.m. algebra class when the school secretary came to the door and spoke to Ms. Greene, who in turn told Woody he was needed in the principal's office. His classmates made the usual "What's he done now?" comments, but Woody knew.

They had come to tell him his daddy had died.

Margaret, James's wife, was waiting in the principal's office and told Woody what he already knew. She took Woody and Hailey home while they waited for James and their mom to return from Durham. Woody noticed that within an hour of his return home, neighbors were bringing food. This was his first experience with someone dying, and he didn't know that when there is a death in the South, it was the custom for friends and neighbors to bring food. Woody thought it was a strange custom, maybe because he wasn't hungry.

James and Frances arrived about eleven thirty, and Woody's mother hugged him differently than she ever had. He knew his mother was a strong woman, but he also knew he was now the man of the house—although he wasn't sure what that meant.

After Frances and James had been there a few minutes, Frances told Woody to go with James to his dad's closet to pick out a suit for his daddy to be buried in. James was a man of very few words and said nothing as they walked to the bedroom closet. Woody picked out the one dark blue suit his daddy owned, a matching tie, and a white shirt to take to the funeral director, who had just arrived. James told Woody the funeral home did not need shoes. James looked at Woody as he turned to go to the den to see the funeral director and said, "Son, I'm going to look after you."

Woody asked him, "What does that mean?"

James didn't answer.

Woody got his answer on Thursday, May 21, 1959. The Rose High golf team, of which Woody was a member, had a match at the Greenville Golf and Country Club against New Bern High School. Woody was one down in his match when he reached the seventeenth hole, a dogleg right par 4. His second shot ended up about two feet from the hole, so he felt good about squaring the match and playing the eighteenth hole for the win. He didn't feel so good after his opponent hit a career shot through the trees at the corner of the dogleg and into the hole. An eagle two! Woody lost two and one.

James's car was at the house when a teammate brought Woody home. James and Woody's mom were seated at the kitchen table, with a bottle of Jack Danials, some ginger ale, and half-full glasses. James asked, "Aren't you sixteen on June 6?" Woody told him he was. "What day of the week is that, a Saturday?" Woody nodded yes and James continued, "Well, be at Dogs Head, the Carolina Grill, at five thirty in the morning on June 8. You're working for me Monday through Thursday of each week. Bring your lunch."

Woody asked, "How do I get to Dogs Head?"

"Walk, it's only about 2-3 miles."

Woody asked, "What about Fridays?"

"I'm getting to that. Tomorrow after school, go to Corner Drug. You know where it is—across from the courthouse. You'll be working for the pharmacists, Mr. Small and Mr. Allred, doing whatever they say to do, delivering prescriptions, selling coffee, being a soda jerk, whatever. You'll work their schedule every Friday, and they'll want you to work weekends too."

Woody wanted to ask James when he could play golf or go to the beach or have a good time, but he kept his mouth shut because he had figured out what James had in mind when he said he would take care of him.

The White family owned a small construction company, doing some odd jobs such as pouring a concrete patio and some sidewalks or putting in curbs and gutters when they won a state or city bid. On Woody's first day at work, the crew, mostly Blacks Woody had known for some time, was pouring concrete curbs and gutters on Memorial Drive in Greenville. After just one day, Woody hurt everywhere, even his fingers. He was looking forward to Friday and working at Corner Drug.

The other soda jerks at Corner Drugs were older than Woody. One of them had been a basketball star at East Carolina College in Greenville. No one gave Woody a hard time, and learning how to be a soda jerk, stock guy, and delivery man was not challenging. It beat putting in curb and gutters.

On his second Friday at Corner Drug, Woody was serving a cup of coffee to Billy Wilkins, who was three years older than Woody. Billy had barely graduated Rose High School and was wearing the uniform and badge of a Pitt County deputy sheriff. He said he was a bailiff, but Woody had no idea what a bailiff did. There weren't many customers at eight forty-five that morning when Woody looked out the side door of Corner Drug toward the south side of the courthouse. People were forming into two lines that snaked into the southern entrance of the courthouse annex.

"What's going on at the courthouse?" Woody asked Billy.

"Haven't you heard? It's the trial."

"No, I've been working so hard I haven't listened to the news or read the paper. What's going on?"

"Well, they're trying a colored guy for threatening and showing his pecker to a white woman at her house out at that new golf development, Mill Run Valley. I'm one of the courtroom bailiffs. I've heard it all."

Woody asked, "What have you heard so far?"

"Well, warm up this coffee—at no cost—and I'll give you the short version." Woody filled up Billy's cup and made a mental note to put a dime in the cash register to pay for the coffee. "The woman testified she was alone at her new house. Her husband had come to town for something. The colored guy came to the back door, which opens to a garage, said he was working construction on the new house next door, and asked for a glass of cold water. She testified she told him to wait at the door and turned her back to him to get the water, but he followed her in, told her he'd kill her if she fought him, and then he unzipped his pants and showed her his pecker and tried to push her to the floor. She got away and ran to the front of the house, and he ran out the back door.

"The husband testified that when he came home, he saw the guy walking from the back of his house to the house under construction next door. He asked his wife what the guy was doing at their house, and she told him he had threatened to rape her and that he showed her his pecker. The husband testified that he got his shotgun, locked the back door, and called the sheriff's office. When the deputy sheriff got to his house, the woman told him what had happened, and the deputy sheriff went next door and arrested the guy and took him to the jail."

Woody said, "Damn, that is something. What is happening next? Has he testified? Who are his lawyers? Is he guilty?"

"Hold on, White. Not so fast. The woman has been testifying. When we broke for lunch, the solicitor—you know, he's the guy that tries the case for the State—told the judge he had a few more questions for the lady, so when he's through with her, one of the defense lawyers will cross-examine her. Her husband already testified and was cross-examined by the defense lawyers."

"Will the guy testify?"

"Nobody knows. His lawyers are Mr. Garrison and Mr. Cavanaugh." Woody knew both from the drug store. When they came in for coffee, neither sat and talked with the other lawyers and businessmen who congregated daily at Corner Drug. Mr. Garrison and Mr. Cavanaugh always seemed busy, and with this case, Woody could see why.

"So the defense lawyers, or one of them, starts asking her questions this afternoon, right?" Woody asked.

"Yep, at 2:00 p.m. sharp, or as soon as the solicitor has finished his questions. Let me tell you, that judge is all business. Those two lines you see, what the judge has done is have the clerk of court fix up 126 tickets because he figured there were 126 seats in the courtroom, so the first 126 people in line get in, and sixty-three go up the left staircase and sit on the left side of the courtroom, and sixty-three go up the right staircase and sit on the Evans Street side. If a spectator leaves the courtroom, he don't get back in, period. That judge is from Lexington, and he is all business, let me tell you."

Woody looked at the courthouse. "I'd like to go this afternoon if I can get off work. Can you get me in, Billy?"

"Can I get you in? Damn, Woody, I'm one of the bailiffs. Of course, I can get you in—at a front-row seat next to me, but as a trade-off, I would like to come over here about twelve thirty when the judge recesses for lunch and have you toast me one—no, make that two—of those chicken salad sandwiches and fix me a Pepsi—make that a chocolate shake, courtesy of Woody—and I can make it happen."

"So I fix and buy your lunch, and if I can get off, you'll get me in, right?" Billy nodded. "How do you sleep at night, taking advantage of a young sixteen-year-old guy?" Woody turned to Chapy, his coworker on the morning shift. "Do you work this afternoon?"

"Not scheduled, but if you want me to work for you, I'll do it. And you pay me my wage rate, not yours, time and a half."

Woody said, "So let me see if I've got this right. To get into the courtroom this afternoon, I fix and buy Billy his lunch, and I pay you your wages time and a half, right?" Billy and Chapy nodded. "You guys are criminals. I'm going to call the sheriff to arrest one of his own men, but I'll take this deal. And I'll remember it too."

"OK, Woody," Billy said. "But be sure to pee and take a crap if you need to before we go to court this afternoon because that judge will not let you back in if you leave. I'll see you for my free lunch about quarter to one."

At one forty-five, Woody and Billy entered the courthouse through the new annex entrance and went up the stairs on the west side of the courthouse, past the jury room, and into the courtroom.

Woody had never been in a courtroom before. The Superior Courtroom for Pitt County was on the second floor of the courthouse, which had been built in the 1920s. Billy told Woody to sit in the chair next to a rail, which he said was called the "bar," and that only court officials or witnesses could come inside the bar. Woody estimated the courtroom was over one hundred feet long and about sixty feet wide. There were floor-to-ceiling windows at each end. The judge's bench was at the north end of the courtroom. To the left of the bench was what Woody guessed was the witness box. In the middle of the room was a section with fourteen seats in it. "Is that where the jury sits?" Woody asked Billy.

"Yeah."

"I thought there were twelve jurors, but there are fourteen seats. What's the deal?"

Billy answered, "The judge has fourteen jurors for the case, and two are alternates so if a juror gets sick or whatever and has to drop out, he will still have enough. Jurors numbered 13 and 14 will be excused for the jury deliberations. Now you need to shut the hell up. Court is about to open."

He looked at the watch Woody's mom had given to his dad as a wedding gift. She gave it to Woody on his sixteenth birthday a few days ago. It was two minutes to two o'clock.

The defendant, a large black man, sat across the courtroom behind and between Mr. Garrison and Mr. Cavanaugh. They were seated at a long table, which had several files and books on it. There were two deputies sitting behind the defendant.

The solicitor's table was directly across the room from the defendant's and also had files and books on it. Two men sat at the table. Woody knew one of them was an attorney who came into the drugstore, but he could not remember his name. The other was a Mr. Beamon, who was from New Bern, the county seat of Craven County. Mr. Beamon was a very imposing six feet, three inches tall and was wearing a light tan-colored suit with vest, a light blue shirt, and a dark brown tie.

It was getting warm in the courtroom as the spectators filed in, but Mr. Beamon looked as cool as the other side of a pillow. He was the solicitor, or prosecutor, for the Third Judicial District, which contained not only Pitt and Craven Counties but also Carteret and Pamlico Counties.

There was another man sitting behind the solicitor's table. Woody recognized him as a law enforcement officer because he had been into the drug store, wore a pistol in a holster on his right hip, and everyone called him "Detective."

Woody also recognized the lady sitting behind the solicitor, next to the wall. Her last name was Leggett. Woody assumed she was the woman who said she'd been assaulted. He had seen her at the country club pool last summer. She wore a wedding ring, but there was never a man with her at the pool. Woody had seen her tease and flirt with some of the older boys at the pool. She had a beautiful body and when she asked some of the older boys rub suntan lotion on her back, Woody could tell that the mothers at the pool with their kids didn't think much of her. Ms. Leggett was holding the hand of the man to her right, whom Woody assumed was her husband. Her chair was canted so that she was looking straight at the jury.

When the courthouse bell-clock rang twice, the door across the courtroom, behind the defendant's table, opened. The elected high sheriff went to the middle of the courtroom, and commanded, "All rise," and everyone stood. The judge walked from the door to the bench, and when he was standing behind the bench, the sheriff announced, "Court is now in session." The judge directed the sheriff to escort the jurors from their jury room to the courtroom, and the sheriff went to the door behind the solicitor's table and disappeared. He returned in a minute and held the door open for the fourteen jurors. Woody didn't know any of them. He also noticed that none of them was Black.

The judge directed Ms. Leggett to sit in the witness chair and addressed Mr. Beamon. "Mr. Solicitor, does the State have any further questions of Ms. Leggett?"

"No, sir, not at this time."

The judge looked down at a lady sitting in front of and left of the bench. She was facing the judge and the witness stand, and her back was toward the defendant's table, and she was typing on a small machine. "Madam court reporter, let the record reflect that at 2:02 p.m., the State announced it had no further questions of Ms. Leggett at this time. Does the defense have any questions of Ms. Leggett?"

Mr. Cavanaugh stood, told the court he had questions for Ms. Leggett, and then sat down to begin his cross-examination.

"Does the front of your house face north, south, east, or west?" Mr. Cavanaugh had a loud, growling voice that intimidated Woody. He wondered how Ms. Leggett felt.

Ms. Legget answered, "I don't know, and what difference does it make anyways?"

Mr. Cavanaugh stood and addressed the judge. "Your honor, please direct this witness to just answer the question and not ask me questions."

The judge turned toward Ms. Leggett. "Ms. Leggett, you can't ask the defendant's lawyer any questions. Just answer the questions. Do you understand?"

"Yes, sir I do. I don't know which way it faces."

Mr. Cavanaugh's next question sounded like a rifle shot. "Well, do know what the sun is?"

"Objection," Mr. Beamon yelled as he stood to address the court. "Counsel is trying to belittle the witness."

"Overruled, but Mr. Cavanaugh, get to the point. This isn't a geography or astronomy class."

"Yes, your honor. Ms. Leggett, when the sun comes up in the morning, it shines on the back, the rear, of your house, correct?"

"Yes."

Mr. Cavanaugh said, "Then you'd agree the back or rear of your house faces east, correct?"

"Yes."

Mr. Cavanaugh continued, "As you face the front of your house, is there a house to the left of your house?"

Ms. Leggett answered, "Yes, there is. The Davenports live there."

Mr. Cavanaugh continued, "The house to the right of your house was being built when you say may client came to your back door, wasn't it?"

"Yes, sir. The defendant who assaulted me was working at it."

"How big is your backyard?"

Ms. Leggett answered, "I really have no idea."

Mr. Cavanaugh continued, "Have you met the neighbors who live behind you?"

"No, I have not."

Mr. Cavanaugh asked, "But you have seen the people who live in the house behind you working in their garden, which is next to the rear fence in your yard, correct?"

"Yes, sir, I have seen a woman working in that garden, and I guess she lives in that house, but I've never met her."

"And you have a flower garden at the back of your yard, next to the fence between your yard and the yard of the back door neighbor's house , don't you?"

"Yes, but how do you know that?" Ms. Leggett asked. The judge reminded her to not ask questions.

"Ma'am, from where you're sitting to the back wall of this courtroom is a little bit further than the distance from your garage to the fence at the back of your yard, next to the neighbor's garden, where your flower garden is, isn't it?"

"Yes, sir, I guess so."

"And your garage opens to the backyard, doesn't it, so when you drive into the garage the front of the car is facing the street, correct?"

"Yes."

"There is no garage door, is there?"

"There is no garage door."

"So if I'm standing at your flower garden, I can see into the garage and see the back door to your house because there is nothing obstructing that view, no garage door, no trees, no bushes, or anything like that, right?"

"Yes, sir."

Mr. Cavanaugh approached the witness box. "You can read the clock hanging on the back room of this courtroom, can't you?"

"Yes, sir, it is 2:20 p.m." Every spectator and each member of the jury turned to look at the clock.

"Do you see the backdoor neighbor in this courtroom? You may stand up to look at the audience."

Ms. Leggett stood up and scanned the courtroom audience for about a minute and then answered. "No, sir, I do not."

Mr. Cavanaugh walked back toward his counsel table, pointed in the direction of the first row on the right side of the court room, and made a motion with his hand for someone in the audience to stand up.

Everyone in the courtroom, including the judge and court reporter, looked at the woman who rose from her seat on the first row. To Woody, she appeared to be about five and a half feet tall. She had gray hair and what Woody thought was a kind-looking face. She was wearing a necklace with a gold cross.

Mr. Cavanaugh stood by his counsel table and addressed Ms. Leggett. "Ma'am, this lady who is standing is your backdoor neighbor, isn't she?"

"Yes, sir, I believe she is."

"Ma'am, you know that your backdoor neighbor is Mr. Clement, the minister at First Baptist Church located on Ninth Street, and that lady who stood up is his wife, don't you?"

Ms. Leggett answered, "I think I heard that somewhere. Yes."

Mr. Cavanagh addressed the court. "Your Honor, we would like to have these three photographs marked as defendant's exhibits one, two, and three for identification."

After the photographs were marked by the courtroom clerk, the judge directed Mr. Cavanagh to show the photos to the solicitor, who examined them and said he had no objection. Mr. Cavanagh then showed the three photos to the witness and asked his next question. "If Mrs. Clement were standing in her garden at the backyard fence and was looking toward your house, she would see what these pictures show, wouldn't she?"

"Yes, sir."

"Then if Ms. Clement were standing in her garden when the defendant came over to your house to ask for water, she could see him, and she could see him standing in the garage and whether he went into your house, couldn't she?"

"Objection!" Mr. Beamon was on his feet and practically yelled. "That calls for speculation by the witness."

"Overruled," the judge said. "From the questions and answers, it is clear the witness is familiar with her own backyard and garage areas and the location of the neighbor's garden. Answer the question, Ms. Leggett."

Woody knew something important was about to happen, but he didn't know what. The only sound in the courtroom was the ticking of the second hand on the clock that hung between the two floor-to-ceiling windows at the south end of the courtroom.

Ms. Leggett squirmed in the witness chair as if she were very uncomfortable. She had a tissue in her hands and was squeezing it. She looked to her husband and the solicitor. After about a minute, she answered the question. "Yes."

Mr. Cavanaugh stood at the bar with his back to the standing Mrs. Clement, faced Ms. Leggett, and asked his next question. "If my client had come into your garage, rung your back doorbell, and stood in the garage, given the distance from the fence to your back door, given that there was no garage door or car in the garage, given the fact that there were no obstructions in the backyard blocking the view of the garage and back door, then if Mrs. Clement were standing at the fence, working in her garden when the defendant came over to your garage and back door, she could have seen the defendant come to your back door, ring the doorbell, stand in the garage, take the glass of water from you, never enter the house, and then return to the house he was working on, couldn't she, Ms. Leggett?"

Everyone in the courtroom looked at Ms. Leggett, who was increasingly uncomfortable. After about a minute, Mr. Cavanaugh addressed Ms. Leggett: "Do you want me to ask the question again?"

Ms. Leggett shook her head back and forth no.

Mr. Cavanaugh moved to the defense counsel table. "Ms. Leggett, my client came into the garage, rang the doorbell, asked for water—which you gave him—but he never came into your house, never exposed himself to you, never threatened or touched you, and after he finished the water, he left the glass on *the step, left the garage, and went back to work. You made up this story about his actions because your husband would have been mad that you gave him water. Now, isn't that the way it happened?"*

Woody again noticed there was not a sound in the courtroom, save the ticking of the clock. Ms. Leggett looked at Mr. Cavanaugh, said nothing, and then began nodding her head yes. She also began to sob, and her shoulders shook. Mr. Cavanaugh said, "Ms. Leggett, the court reporter needs to record your answer, not the movement of your head. My question is, my client is innocent of all the charges brought against him, isn't that correct?"

Ms. Leggett spoke in a whisper. "Yes."

Mr. Cavanaugh moved to the center of the courtroom and faced the judge. "Your Honor, I move for a dismissal, with prejudice, of the indictments against the defendant."

For a few seconds, the judge said and did nothing, then addressed Mr. Beamon. "What do you say to Mr. Cavanaugh's motion to dismiss, Mr. Solicitor?"

Mr. Beamon's head was bowed and in his hands. "The State dismisses the charges against the defendant, with prejudice."

The judge stood up. "In light of the testimony of the prosecuting witness that the defendant did not commit the crimes with which he is charged, and in light of Mr. Cavanaugh's motion to dismiss with prejudice, and in light of the statement by the solicitor dismissing the charges with prejudice, it is adjudicated that the charges against the defendant are dismissed with prejudice. He is free to go. Mr. Solicitor, this court will be awaiting a report from your office regarding any action you may take against Ms. Leggett as a result of her testimony in this case. Sheriff, adjourn court, please."

The high sheriff went to the center of the courtroom and announced that court was adjourned. Billy stood up and directed Woody to follow him out. When they reached Third Street, Woody thanked Billy and ran across the street to the side door of the drugstore. His head was spinning.

As he entered the store, Mr. Small, one of the pharmacists, said, "Woody, Dr. Haigwood called in another prescription for Ms. Bigelow, over on Second Street. You took one to her last week, remember, and you got lost. Think you can find it today?"

Woody laughed. "Yes, sir, I can handle it."

As Mr. Small gave Woody the prescription, he asked, "Well, did you learn anything at the trial?"

"Yes, sir. I learned that I want to be a trial lawyer, just like Mr. Cavanaugh.

In Transit

0730 Hours, Sun, 27 Jul 69
Above the Pacific Ocean
East of Okinawa

"Lieutenant. Lieutenant White." Woody heard someone calling his name, and he felt his left shoulder being shaken. At first, he had no idea where he was, but then he heard the plane's engines and opened his eyes. He was staring at the partially unbuttoned blouse of Susannah, one of the stewardesses. There was enough showing for Woody to know that she had beautiful breasts.

For reasons totally unknown to Woody, Susannah had been flirting with him during the trip. On several occasions when he went to the plane's galley to get a cup of coffee, Susannah made it her business to come up beside him and press her breasts against his arm and make comments full of sexual innuendo. All Woody could think was that it was just his luck—this good-looking woman was making a pass at him, which was the first time a women made a pass at him in his life, and she was doing it in a damn airplane that was probably 35,000 feet high, in the presence of 161 Marines. Just what did she expect Woody to do, and where did she expect him to do it!

"Lieutenant, we will be landing on Okinawa soon. I wanted you to know that. And I wanted you to have this." Susannah handed Woody a piece of paper and returned to the galley area. Woody opened it and saw she had written the name, address, and telephone number of a hotel in Naha, Okinawa, with a note that read:

I hear Marines love hand-to-hand combat. I'd like to try that with you at this hotel. Call. It will be worth your time.

What the hell! was all Woody could think. The Corps had owned him since 30 September 1968. He would be in Okinawa for about twenty-four hours, awaiting a flight to Vietnam, and the Corps would not give him leave to get laid. He was hoping to have time to pee. He put the paper in his pocket, got up, stepped over the sleeping Captain Barkley, and walked around, getting the kinks out.

Woody's body clock was all messed up. The aircraft had crossed the international date line and several time zones, so Woody didn't know the time or even day.

The jet touched down in forty-five minutes, and Woody was directed to one of the largest buildings he had ever been in. He'd never seen so many Marines in one place in his life, and wondered if this was what Ellis Island looked like at the turn of the century—if everyone wore military green.

He found his assigned place and was bused to some building where a medical team was locked and loaded to probe every orifice of his body and stick multiple needles, taking out blood or putting in medicine of some description. Woody usually asked doctors what they were doing when they examined or treated him and was surprised that his questions ticked off some of them, as if they were too important to answer a patient's question. He was a little disappointed in himself because when he noticed a doctor got ticked off at his questions, he tried to come up with another question, just for the sport of it. His mom would not have been proud, but he reasoned the doc's mom would not have been proud of her doctor son acting like he was better than the patient who was paying him for medical services.

Every time that happened, Woody reminded himself that he would always treat his clients with respect—once he had a client. But he had learned that in the Corps, he needed to keep his mouth shut, so he didn't ask what the medical team was doing to him.

When the medical team had finished their work, Woody and Captain Barkley were bused to a barracks for officers, and Woody assumed the enlisted men were sent to their barracks. He was told he would be there for the next eighteen hours and that he could only go to the post exchange. which was within a quarter mile, the chow hall across the street, or the gym for PT. No hand-to-hand combat with the stewardess.

Reasonable Doubt

1700 Hours, Mon, 28 Jul 69
Officer's Club, Third Marine Division
Quang Tri

Kevin Ross and Mike McMurry had been sitting at a corner table in the O Club for about thirty minutes. They had finished their prosecution duties for the day and were nursing their Budweiser's. Neither said anything, which was very unusual for them.

Mike spoke up. "What's wrong with you, man? You're never quiet. What's up?"

"Well, you aren't exactly a blabbermouth yourself," Kevin replied. "But I'm having a hard time getting the Jackson case out of my mind."

"Me too," Mike admitted. "There are two things bothering me. First, the opportunity for Douglas to be certain of identifying the men running— maybe OK with Grant 'cause he was so big, but the other man—was so weak, I mean, saying you could see the men that far away well enough to ID them only when the lightning flashed is hard to believe. I can believe he saw two men running, but to have a guy be found guilty and get two consecutive ten-year sentences on the testimony of one witness who said he ID'd him from thirty yards in driving rain only when lightning occurred, well, I can't buy it. I know the panel convicted Jackson, but I wonder if we charged and convicted the right man. And to top it off, Jackson's testimony denying the charge was convincing to me. Not enough obviously for the panel, but he was convincing to me."

"I know. I've got the same concerns," Kevin said. "David did his usual masterful job in defending Jackson. I know he's rotating back next week, and that means Jackson won't have anyone in his corner. The transcript is being prepared and probably won't be ready for Suarez before he rotates back at the end of August, at least I hope it won't. His replacement will decide whether to approve the conviction and sentence. It's hard to imagine that a new SJA would do anything other than recommend the commanding general approve the conviction, assuming there were no prejudicial errors. I don't believe we committed any prejudicial errors, and in some ways, it was an easy case to prep and try, as a 'he said, he said,' case, and the panel decides."

Mike responded, "I agree. I just wonder if something was missed. That IO, was it Breckinridge? He went through the process pretty damn quickly and ended after he talked to only six witnesses. He didn't do anything else."

"Yeah," Kevin said, "but we and the NIS agents talked, or asked several questions, to everyone in the company, and at the end of the day, there was only one man who was a useful witness for the government, and that was Douglas."

Mike picked up his Budweiser and took a big swig. "Well, the bottom line is that there is no one else who can do anything about it. Everyone here knows all about the case. In one sense, it's real easy to say it's over and time to move on, but it's hard as hell for me, and I guess for you, to let it go when we have these concerns. There is absolutely nothing we could do on our own, and anyway, we're so close to the case we couldn't see the forest for the trees. It would be great if we could get someone who knows nothing about the case to take a look, but I can't think who that'd be, so I guess we're stuck. Let's finish these beers and get some chow."

Welcome to Vietnam
1700 Hours, Tues, 29 Jul 69
Officer's Club
Third Marine Division
Quang Tri

On Tuesday, 29 July, Woody left Okinawa, again on a passenger jet with stewardesses, and in a few hours landed at Da Nang Air Base. It was one busy place. F-4 Phantom jets took off and landed frequently, and every type of chopper the Corps flew was in the air at one time or another. Woody and the men on his flight were directed to a building marked "Quang Tri/ Dong Ha." He knew Headquarters Company, Third Marine Division, was in Quang Tri because his orders said so, but Dong Ha was new to him. He showed his orders to a gunnery sergeant who took one copy, returned the remaining orders to Woody, and directed him to the passenger area.

Woody placed his sea bag next to him, and it hit him for the first time that he was in a war zone and that while he would not likely be in combat, there were plenty of other ways for him to get hurt, not the least of which was from a rocket attack on the Quang Tri base. He hoped those attacks were infrequent. From his training, he knew that the bigger bases, such as Quang Tri, were targeted with rockets that were fired without any particular target in mind because those rockets did not have sophisticated guidance systems. They were fired in the direction of the base, and they hit wherever they hit. After a long wait in the terminal, seventeen officers and twenty enlisted Marines were directed to the flight deck and told to board a prop plane along with some Vietnamese, two of whom had dogs. No Susannah on board.

The plane took off, and in about an hour, Woody heard the flaps being extended for the landing as the aircraft began its descent and landed safely. Woody got off the aircraft with his sea bag and went into the wooded building marked "Transit." He was approached by a warrant officer who introduced himself as Mr. Masterson. Woody had learned at TBS that a warrant officer's rank is above the highest enlisted rank and below the lowest officer rank. The WOs were often specialists at something. Some were chopper pilots, and some were in administrative roles. Woody was not armed, and all Masterson had was a .45 caliber pistol. Woody hoped they would not encounter any bad guys on the way to the legal office.

Quang Tri was huge, at least the part Woody saw. They drove about fifteen minutes before they arrived at a hooch, Woody's home for the next thirteen months. Mr. Masterson directed Woody inside and followed him with the sea bag, which was deposited onto a bunk. There were sixteen bunks in this hooch, eight on each side. Mr. Masterson pointed out the showers, which consisted of canvas held up by ten poles, with no roof and with six shower heads. "This is the hooch for most of the defense lawyers. Come on, I'll show you the office and introduce you around."

Mr. Masterson first took Woody to a large Quonset hut with a sign reading "Division Legal," painted in the gold and scarlet colors of the Corps. The division legal hut was air conditioned, and there were about ten desks, each manned by enlisted men whom Woody assumed were legal's admin staff. Mr. Masterson asked one of the men if the colonel was available, and after getting a nod, he went to the door marked "Lt. Col. Suarez, Division SJA" and knocked. Woody heard someone say, "Enter," and he and Masterson went in.

There was only one desk in the room, and the man who sat behind it didn't stand when they entered the room. "Colonel, this is Lieutenant White, our new lawyer."

Colonel Suarez didn't look up at first but just said "Hello" as he continued to write. He finally stood up but did not extend his hand. "Lieutenant, I think you'll like this group. Someone else will decide what your specific duties will be. I'm a short-timer, twenty-nine days and a wake-up, and then I'm back to New Mexico to do something important. Mr. Masterson, has he met Major Forrest?"

"No, sir, I showed him his bunk and came straight here. Should I do that now?"

"Yes. Glad to have you here, Lieutenant."

As they exited the colonel's office, Woody spoke without thinking. "That was quick."

"Yep, not to be repeated, but the colonel is not a lot of fun, so his replacement will be welcomed with open arms, whoever he is. Let's go to Major Forrest's office. Now he is the military judge for special courts martials, and he is also the chief administrative officer for us. Normally there are two different people for those two billets, but we're short. He will decide whether you will be assigned to the prosecution or the defense team."

Woody commented, "Well, I've never tried a case before. Hope I have time to learn the ropes before I have to try a case."

"Well, if you've never tried a case before, they'll put you on the defense side."

"But I don't know jack about trying a case!"

"Exactly," Mr. Masterson said. "The government likes to have a good win-loss record."

Major Forrest's office door was open, but Masterson knocked anyway. "Major, I've got Lieutenant White, our new lawyer."

Major Forrest stood up and came from around his desk and extended his hand. "Welcome to the Third Marine Division Legal, Lieutenant White. We've got plenty of work for you." Woody thought Major Forrest had the darkest, most lifeless eyes he had ever seen. They were almost evil-looking. He was bald, and the skin on his face seemed to be pulled back tightly. The major attempted to smile as he greeted Woody but just couldn't do it.

"Sir, I am looking forward to it. I'm sure there are some good men to work with."

"There are. Lots of assault cases, some murder cases, an occasional assault on officer case, and larcenies. Pretty typical of a front-line legal office."

The major stood back a bit and looked Woody up and down. "I don't know, Mr. Masterson. Think he could take Bull?"

"Sir, my money would be on Bull. After all, he was All Big Ten defensive tackle his senior year at Iowa."

Woody was wondering what the hell was going on.

"I disagree," the major said. "I think Bull is a bit long of tooth, and I think Lieutenant White is one of those lean and mean guys. Lieutenant, are you a fan of arm wrestling? Would you like a bit of competition with our legal office champ?"

Woody knew the only answer a Marine officer could give in that situation was "yes, sir," but he sure didn't mean it.

"We can find out before chow. Lieutenant, when Mr. Masterson finishes introducing you, we go to the O Club at 1630 hours every day, and we work every day, including Sunday, 0730 to 1630, breaking for chow from 1130 to 1230. You'll be in the defense shop. I imagine they've got a few new cases for you. Did you have any trial work before coming to 'Nam?"

"No, sir, not a bit. Just some moot court at justice school."

"Well, it ain't the same, so good luck. As you know, defendants can choose to have the military panel or me hear the case."

"Yes, sir. Thank you for that information." Woody thought he'd have no trouble telling his clients to have the jury decide their case. Major Forrest looked like a man who would convict his own grandmother and give her jail time. Not a lot of the milk of human kindness flowing in that guy's veins.

"Let's go, Lieutenant," Mr. Masterson said. "You'll need to meet the men in the defense shop before you meet Bull, who is a prosecutor."

The defense shop was in a wooden building that was about fifty feet long and thirty-five feet wide with desks on both sides. Woody shook hands with all the lawyers, each of whom was very busy and didn't do much more than say "hi." The head of the defense was Captain Fred Conner, whom Woody addressed as "Captain." Fred told Woody, "We're pretty informal here. The trial and defense lawyers are on a first-name basis without regard to rank, except in the courtroom in a trial. And we don't bother with saluting other company-grade officers, OK?"

"Yes, sir. I mean, yes. I'll remember," said Woody.

Fred continued, "You'll want to advise your defendants to have their cases before the military panel, not Major Forrest. He'd convict his grandmother and give her jail time. But—and this is a big but—the military panel we presently have consists of three Marines, a couple of first lieutenants who did well in combat and are on the way back home, and a major, Judge Roy Bean."

Woody stopped him. "Wait a minute. Judge Roy Bean was a hanging judge in the Wild West around the turn of the century, wasn't he?"

"Right . That's why we gave him that well-earned nickname. His real name is Major Bullock. You can't miss him. Neck about twenty-two inches, knuckles drag the floor, a real Neanderthal-type. He finds everyone guilty. But the lieutenants on the panel are good officers who don't appear to buckle in to Major Bullock. All in all, it's a fair group. We're all busy, and we can help you out when you get started, but remember, each of us has more cases than he should have—lots of crime out here—so most of your education will be trial by fire."

Fred continued, "Let's get over to the Officer's Club. It is coming up 430—I mean 1630. I still can't remember to use military time. The drinks are twenty cents. There is some good chili, and it is air-conditioned. But before I forget, right after breakfast tomorrow, come back here. You've got your first cases. Now, let's go have a drink or two."

The O Club was packed. It was nothing fancy, but it was air-conditioned, which was more than Woody could say for the defense shop or his hooch. Woody found out at TBS and Naval Justice School, that there was a real drinking culture in the Corps. There were also rules to remember, the chief of which was to not wear your cover in the O Club because if you did, by tradition you bought a round of drinks for everybody in the club.

The bar was horseshoe shaped. It had about ten bar stools and then maybe twenty tables scattered in the room, which had a low ceiling and no windows. Woody noticed there were leather cups on the bar. He knew they contained dice, and that bets were made on the throwing of the dice, with the loser buying the drinks. Since Woody didn't know the rules of that game, he was determined to stay away from the cups. The smoke hung heavy in the air. Many of the officers sitting at the bar put their cigarette pack and lighter on the bar, along with their right elbow, and then drank, smoked, and shot the shit.

The lawyers in the defense shop gathered in a corner and gabbed about cases. Then Major Forrest came over to Woody. A Marine who looked like a Big Ten football player stood next to the major. Woody knew the major would be the ringmaster for what Woody knew would be the shortest arm-wrestling contest in the history of the Corps. "All right, I've got five bucks on Bull in fifteen seconds. Keep track of the bets, Fred. What say the rest of you?"

Bets were made, and Woody tried to look like he was not concerned—for obvious reasons. But he felt the officers who were betting on him were not people from whom he would seek financial advice.

"All the bets in? OK, outside," the major ordered. Bull and Woody sat facing each other at the end of a picnic table. Bull asked what the Third Marine Division record was, and someone said, "Three seconds." Bull boasted he would beat it by one second.

"All right, Bull, Lieutenant White, take your positions. I'll give you the 'go' signal." Bull put his right elbow on the table and held out his hand, which Woody thought was as big as a major league catcher's mitt. "OK, the combatants are in positions. Ready, go!"

Woody couldn't tell which came first, Bull releasing Woody's hand or the twenty cold beers poured on his head and back as all the officers yelled, "Welcome to Vietnam!"

Woody stood up and shook his head like a lab coming out of the bay with a mallard duck in its mouth. "Well, didn't see that coming. Anybody got a beer?" He was handed a Pabst Blue Ribbon, which he chugged in about ten seconds to the encouragement of the guys. Woody then tossed the empty into a trash can and asked, "Can I be in the front row when the next rookie gets here?" Woody had no way to see into the future, but he would be in the front row and would welcome the next new lawyer with a vengeance.

When they retreated to the bar, Woody received a standing ovation. After a few drinks and chow, Woody started back to his hooch. Fred was with him. "By the way," Woody asked, "have there been any attacks on this base, rockets, or anything like that?"

"Not in about three weeks. We're at a place on the base where the bad guys will never be around us—way too many folks to go through—and lawyers aren't high on their kill list. After all, they haven't read Shakespeare. Rockets—that's another thing. They can hit anytime, anyplace. If you hear them, and trust me, when they hit, even if they hit a mile away, you'll know it. There is a siren warning when there is incoming, so run to those sandbags." Fred pointed to a circular sandbag emplacement above ground. It didn't look like it could protect anyone from anything, but Woody kept his mouth shut.

That night at 2115 hours, thirty-five rockets hit the base in twenty-five minutes—the longest twenty-five minutes of Woody's life. As soon as Woody heard the first one explode and a siren wail, he was hauling ass to the sandbags. He ran past Jack someone, another defense lawyer, who was just sauntering to the sandbags.

Five minutes after the last rocket and the "all clear" two wails on the siren, Woody and Fred were walking back to the hooch when Woody said, "Fred, I hope you're better at giving me pointers about representing defendants than you are at guessing about rockets. If you ain't, all my clients are going up the river."

Woody's First Case
1015 Hours, Wed, 30 Jul 69
Legal Office, Third Marine Division
Quang Tri

The next morning, Woody didn't see any damage from the rocket attack. After breakfast he went to the defense shop, where Fred Conner gave him a brief explanation of Woody's first case, *The Government v. HM2 Al McArthur*, who was a Navy corpsman.

"This guy is charged with possession of 1,300 pot joints, which were found in a sea bag in his hooch. Look at his record, and you'll see he's decorated. You know, corpsmen are all a bit nuts because of all the chances they take in the field to give first aid to a jarhead who is wounded. This guy got the Bronze Star with "V" while with 1/9, which they call the 'Walking Dead' because of their high casualty rate.

"First, you need to review the spec, you know, the UCMJ specification under which he is charged and make sure you know the elements. Then talk to him and get his story. Maybe there were times he wasn't in his hooch, and someone dumped the sea bag in the hooch to be picked up later. And if you can get the officer who nominated him for the Bronze Star to testify, it may go a long way toward having Judge Roy Bean and the other panel members set him loose. But don't bet the ranch. Bean hasn't found anyone not guilty yet, and he's heard about twenty cases in a month and a half." Fred told Woody how to get up with McArthur.

Woody's interview with McArthur, his first client, was conducted later that day at Woody's desk in the defense shop. There were no walls providing confidentiality, but everyone was so busy no one had time to listen to anyone else.

McArthur was five-foot-eleven and weighed about 180 pounds. He had a handlebar mustache, which he could get away with since he was in the Navy. He was an HM2—a hospital corpsman second class, the equivalent of an E-5, a sergeant, and he wore the winged caduceus of a corpsman on his collars.

Woody addressed McArthur. "Well, Doc, you're charged with violating Article 112a, the 'wrongful possession of marijuana, a controlled substance.' I read the file. There were 1,300 joints in a sea bag in your hooch. What's your story? And by the way, whatever you tell me is confidential 'cause I'm your lawyer, but, if you testify, you can't say something in the courtroom that is different than what you tell me. You've got to shoot straight with me."

"I damn sure want to testify, Lieutenant. Those joints weren't mine, and the sea bag wasn't mine. We'd been on a three-day patrol. I came back, dirty as hell. Took off my utilities and went to take a shower. Came back, didn't notice the sea bag, which was under my rack. I hadn't been in the hooch for three damn days, and anybody could have put that sea bag there. Lots of people come through that area."

"Now, Doc, why would anyone put their joints in your hooch?"

"Well, maybe they heard there was going to be a shakedown, you know, an inspection of their own hooch, and they needed a place to hid the sea bag, and since I wasn't there, they put it way back under the rack in my hooch where I wouldn't see it but we had an inspection, the sarge found it, and next thing I know, I'm charged. And I'm innocent."

"Will the officer who recommended you for the Bronze Star testify for you?"

"Yes, sir, he said he would. His name is Fulp, and he is at our company HQ now. I'd like you to talk to him. Maybe it will help. I want to go to med school when I get back—if I get back, and I can't get in if I have a conviction and a bad conduct discharge, which they would probably give me if they convict me. There's a lot on the line."

On Monday, 4 August, Woody won his first trial when the military panel found McArthur not guilty. The doc would have a chance to apply for med school—if he made it back. Woody went to the O Club to celebrate.

"Lieutenant, come over here." The summons came from Major Bullock, aka Judge Roy Bean. He was in a corner of the O Club, sitting between the two lieutenants who were members of the court panel which acquitted McAuthur. "Take a load off." Woody sat across from them and sipped his Bud. The major spoke. "We didn't do you any favors in letting the doc go. You earned it for him. Having his CO testify about the action in the field and why he wrote him up for the Bronze Star was a nice touch, but that was not why we found him not guilty. A pot head can be a hero. You did a good job of showing that anyone could have put those joints there, and there was more than a reasonable doubt the pot was his. So—you won one."

"Yes, sir. I guess I did."

Bullock continued. "Was that your first trial over here?"

"Sir, that was my first trial anywhere."

One of the lieutenants piped in. "Well, I guess that means you've only got one way to go, and that's downhill." All laughed.

"Yes, sir. I guess that is one way to look at it."

"Well, we don't want to hobnob with you too much. You might be accused of fraternizing with the enemy if you sit over here too long."

"Yes, sir, but I would like to ask a favor. Don't know the protocol of this, but if you feel like I'm messing up in a case you are hearing, I'd appreciate your comments on my work after the trial. I want to learn from my mistakes. No way to learn better than asking someone who has experience in these things."

"We'll see, Lieutenant. Have a good day," Bullock said dismissing Woody who went to join the other defense lawyers at a table across the room.

He was observed by the lawyers who had prosecuted Jackson.

Kevin Ross said, "That's the new guy, Warren, isn't it?"

Mike McMurry corrected him. "No, it's White. Went to Wake Forest. Did you hear that today he won his first case, and Roy Bean was on the panel?"

"You're kidding, really! How the hell did he do that?"

McMurry answered, "I talked to the court reporter, Spivey, and he said White tried a real good case. Got Bean and the other guys to realize the pot the doc was charged with possessing could have been left in the doc's hooch by anybody, so they found reasonable doubt and acquitted him. I believe that is the first time Roy Bean has been on a panel that found someone not guilty."

Kevin Ross looked at McMurry. "Well, you know we said we wanted to get someone else to help us take a look at Jackson's conviction. This guy knows nothing about the fragging or the trial—he wasn't here. He would be totally unbiased. Maybe he's not real experienced, but that may be good. Not as jaded, so maybe he'll have a little messianic spirit. But in fairness, we should first talk to Fred about letting us get help from one of his defense guys. Let's see if Fred can meet with us tomorrow, OK?"

"Sounds like a plan to me," McMurry agreed.

The next evening, Woody got back to the hooch from the O Club about 1930 after drinks at the club and some surprisingly good chow—steak and baked potato. Fred was in the hooch.

"Woody, I've got a new case for you, so let's go over to the courtroom. There's nothing being tried, and we can talk there."

When they got to the empty courtroom, Fred spoke. "Well, I'm giving you your first murder case. Here's what happened. An Apache named, I kid you not, Geronimo Abaya, who is with 2/9, came in from a week-long patrol, got too much beer or booze, had a .45, got in a shouting match with a Black guy, and shot him dead in front of twenty or so witnesses. Now, have you noticed much racial tension here?"

Woody replied, "Yes, I have. Even in our area, the Blacks are giving each other the black power salutes, like those two athletes did in the Olympics in Mexico City last fall. And they wear these black, green, and red—I guess they are bracelets, which sure aren't part of the uniform, and they can seem a bit surly."

"Surly is probably an understatement. Anyway, the blacks see this murder as a 'black-white' thing, so Geronimo has been placed in solitary in the brig here, for his own safety. He will be sent to the brig in Da Nang after you interview him and give them the go-ahead to send him. Here's his SRB. Take a minute to look through it and tell me what looks helpful to you as a defense lawyer."

After examining the SRB of his first client charged with murder, Woody said to Fred, "Well, he came to the Corps because some judge gave him the choice of jail or enlisting. May have been good for the civilian world, but not the Corps because he's had five or six office hours, and every time he has made rank, he lost it because of his aggressive conduct. He dropped out of school in the eighth grade. He's had a few barracks fights, and in one of the fitness reports, his gunny sergeant noted he was a strange-acting guy. I wonder if he was in his right mind when he killed the guy, you know, either too drunk to form the intent to kill, which may keep him from the death penalty, or just off his rocker. I don't know. Some sort of defense of insanity, or something like that, could make a difference. What does that sound like?"

"Woody, I think that is *exactly* where you need to go. Good thinking. We have a form you can fill out that will start the wheels rolling on a psych eval. I'll show it to you when we get back to the office."

Woody stood up. "OK, thanks. I'd better get to work."

Fred motioned for Woody to sit down. "There's one other thing, and this is absolutely off the record, meaning you don't tell anyone, OK?

"Yes, sir."

"Here's the deal. Last June, at VCB after a big operation called Apache Snow, two Marines, Jackson and Grant, with 1/9, were ID'd running from the hooch of a lieutenant where a grenade had just exploded, killing the lieutenant. They were each charged with murder, accessory after the fact to murder, and conspiracy to commit murder.

"David Peterson in our office represented Jackson, and did a damn good job, but Jackson was convicted of the accessory and conspiracy charges and acquitted of the murder charge. He got a dishonorable discharge, reduction in rank, loss of pay in each case, and back-to-back ten-year sentences of hard labor at the federal prison at Fort Leavenworth. Grant has yet to be tried.

"The trial transcript is being prepared, and as you know, the SJA is required to make an independent review of the record and give the division commanding general, who convened the general court-martial, his recommendation as to whether to approve the conviction.

"Here's where it gets interesting. After the conviction and sentencing, the trial counsel, Mike McMurry and Kevin Ross, independently of each other, began to believe that Jackson may not have done it and that someone other than Jackson was with Grant. They told me their concerns about the conviction only because they wanted me to talk to you about helping them.

"You see, the trial was probably as close to a 'free from prejudicial error' trial as you can have. You remember from justice school that there are going to be errors in trials, but there will probably be no reversal for harmless error—an error that probably didn't change the outcome. On the other hand, reversal is probably required if the error was prejudicial, meaning something happened in the trial which was not legally acceptable, and which may, or probably did, affect the outcome. The amazing thing about this is that the two prosecutors independently came to the same conclusion in what was probably an error-free trial that the wrong man may have been convicted. They are top-notch, and their instincts mean something.

"They have been instructed by Colonel Suarez that as soon as the transcript and record have been completed and readied for submission to the CG for review, he will recommend approval of the conviction, without even reviewing the record or transcript. He wants to do that because he wants it on his record that he had something to do with the successful conviction of someone who murdered an officer, for use in his campaign material when he gets out of the Corps and runs for judge next year back in New Mexico.

"The trial transcript is being prepared but isn't finished. McMurry and Ross are hoping it will not be completed before Suarez goes back to the States in about three weeks. That way, the new SJA will have to deal with it, and they're hoping they will be able to find something that would give rise to a reversal. NIS couldn't initially investigate because a typhoon hit, so there was a very quick investigation done by a non-NIS guy, the XO of Alpha 1/9. They—McMurry and Ross—think something may have been missed. Plus, they tend to believe the defendant's testimony, and they believe the one eyewitness didn't have a good chance to see the people he ID'd as the killers even though that eyewitness testimony was good enough for the military panel to convict.

"They know you don't know anything about the case, which is an upside, because a new set of eyes can be good in this. They've lived with it since they charged Jackson and Grant. It would be a good opportunity for you, but you won't get any slack in your work. Wouldn't be fair. If you'd like to talk to them, meet them on the basketball court at 1700 hours tomorrow. If you work with them on this, don't meet in an office. Keep it among the three of you. Any questions?"

"Are Mike McMurry and Kevin Ross doing anything wrong here? I don't want to get in trouble."

"Absolutely not. They aren't willing to hurt their careers. They're just trying to do the right thing. If they told the court reporters to type the transcript slowly so Suarez won't get a chance to see it, I don't know it. They ain't telling, and I ain't asking. There is no trouble to get into here."

Woody had one more question. "Fred, what would you do?"

Fred sat back, thought a minute, and then answered. "Well, I believe it is the right thing to do. Some stone may not have been turned over in the investigation, and in practicing law you almost always do well when you go with your instincts."

Even though it was hot as hell, Marines were expected to stay in shape, even if they were not slated for combat duty. At 1700 hours on the day after Fred told him what McMurry and Ross wanted him to do, Woody was on the concrete basketball court near the O Club by himself. The two goals had chain nets. Woody was stretching and taking some jump shots when Mike and Kevin came to the court.

After introductions, McMurry started the conversation. "Fred told us he gave you the short version, enough for you to know what is going on generally. We thought we could meet here, so no one would think we were talking about the law. If you decided to help, we could meet periodically to talk about your progress or lack of it. But let's start with your questions. I know you must have some."

Woody asked, "Do you think the conviction would be overturned if it were reviewed properly?"

Mike answered, "Probably not. We think we prosecuted a trial that was free from prejudicial error, but that opinion is based on what we remember doing in prep and at trial. There may have been some error, prejudicial or harmless, but our larger concern is that the investigation was handled so quickly—understandably so given that an officer was murdered—that something, or someone, may have been overlooked. Plus, due to a typhoon, NIS couldn't get to VCB for a couple of days after the murder, so the initial investigation at VCB was handled by a first lieutenant with no investigation skills. He may have missed something. We're sure NIS did their usual top-notch job. Who knows? We hope we can have a chance to find out. That's really where we're coming from."

"So if I agree to help, what would I do?" Woody asked.

Kevin answered. "You'll want to read the transcript and record. But, you also need to look outside the trial to see if something was missed somewhere and then form your own opinions about whether Jackson may be innocent for the reason that something or somebody was overlooked. You would be free to reinterview those who testified. In fact, Kevin and I agreed that if we could get someone to help us, we did *not* want to give our opinions or reasons 'cause it may influence the person's opinion. We want you to approach this on your own as much as possible.

"The military panel was properly fulfilling its duty in believing the eyewitness and not the defendant. The word was that the victim—his name was Speight—was a poor commander. Alpha 1/9 was in some bad stuff during Dewey Canyon and Apache Snow. A lot of officers got hit and killed, and Speight's platoon had a high number of WIAs and KIAs, but that's not a reason to kill the platoon leader."

"I've got another question," Woody said. "What's the end game, the game plan, if the transcript isn't finished before Colonel Suarez rotates home?"

"Good question," Kevin answered. "When the new SJA gets here, we can make a pitch to him to let us run every rabbit we can to see if Jackson may not have done it. It is a long shot 'cause the new SJA may not let us do it. But it's the only shot we have, and we feel Jackson deserves it. Are you on board?"

Woody answered, "Yes, count me in. Where do we start?"

Geronimo and the Shrink from Everetts

0630 Hours, Wed, 6 Aug 69
Legal Office, Third Marine Division
Quang Tri

After Woody told him he was going to help McMurry and Ross, he secured the file Lieutenant David Peterson had worked on when representing Jackson. It was a large banker's box, which at first glance appeared to contain about three hundred folders. Woody began his review at 0630 hours on 6 August. Among all the folders, Woody found the trial transcript of Jackso's testimony and a file folder on which was written, "Speight murder investigation. Gov't Witnesses—prepared by 1st Lt. Donald Breckinridge IV." Woody did not carefully examine the six interview sheets in the file. The handwriting on the front of the folder and on the six interview sheets appeared to be written by the same person. Woody was told that Breckinridge had rotated back home, was stationed at Camp Lejeune in Jacksonville, North Carolina, and was scheduled to be discharged at the end of the year.

One file contained the autopsy report, but Woody didn't need to read it. The lieutenant was dead and the cause of death was not in dispute. After taking stock of the other contents of the box, Woody began reading the statements of the six witnesses, after which he planned to read the trial transcripts of their testimony. But before he could start reviewing the file in earnest, he had to first meet the Navy psychiatrist who was conducting the psych eval on Pvt. Geronimo Abaya.

The Navy medical office was located about a quarter mile from the legal building. Woody hitched a ride and walked to the front of the building.

The screen door and the wooden door behind it were both closed. Woody hoped that meant the office was air-conditioned. It was.

He saw several Navy enlisted men in the big room and asked for Lieutenant Hardison's office. He was directed to an office in the corner of the building. He went to the open door, knocked, and saw a slight, brown-haired Navy lieutenant sitting behind a desk, writing something. The nameplate on the desk read "Lt. Aaron Hardison."

A US Navy lieutenant is an O-3, the same rank as a US Marine Corps captain, so Lieutenant Hardison outranked Woody. "Sir, I'm Lieutenant White, here to discuss my client and your patient, Pvt. Abaya."

"Come on in. I'll be with you in a minute." Woody entered the office. There was a seat in front of the desk, but he didn't take it because the lieutenant had not offered it.

Woody looked around the room. There was a road map of North Carolina tacked to the wall behind the lieutenant's desk. The distinctive "Esso" gasoline logo, the white oval with red letters, was in the lower left-hand corner of the map. The lieutenant was left-handed, and Woody saw what appeared to be a college class ring with a light blue stone on his left ring finger. On his right ring finger, the lieutenant wore a gold ring with a black parallelogram in which there was a white star. Woody had seen a ring like that before.

After about five minutes, Lieutenant Hardison finished writing and looked up. "You're here about Abaya, right?"

Woody was a little pissed. Common courtesy would call for the doctor inviting him to take a seat. Woody was in no mood for military courtesy, so he decided to not refer to the higher-ranking doctor as "sir."

"I am."

"Have you met with him? "

"I have not. I wanted to meet with you first and complete my review of the file."

The doctor continued, "Lieutenant, do you know what schizophrenia is? Do you know what Thorazine is?"

"I do not."

"Well, schizophrenia is a very bad mental disorder where the afflicted can't tell the difference between right and wrong, can't think clearly, can't act normally in social situations, can't and doesn't have normal emotional responses—though I don't know how anyone can have normal emotional responses in this hellhole.

"Thorazine is the drug of choice, the best drug we have, to treat folks who are schizophrenic. It—Thorazine—is supposed to help reduce agitation and the psychotic actions of the patient. Lieutenant, have you ever seen a Shetland pony?"

Woody wondered what the hell a Shetland pony had to do with a schizophrenic Apache Indian on Thorazine. "Yes, I have."

"Well, after I received your request for the psych eval, the first thing I did was interview Abaya. It took me five minutes to diagnose the schizophrenia. I ordered Thorazine, and we are now giving that guy enough Thorazine to sedate a damn Shetland pony, yet there is no impact whatsoever. I'm ordering him to the psychiatric ward at the Naval Hospital in Philadelphia. This war is over for him. There should be an order entered that ends this murder case 'cause I'm medically discharging him because he's out of his mind. I don't guess you won the case, but you didn't lose it either. Anything else?" Hardison was ready to dismiss Woody.

"Yes, actually. Why the map of the Tar Heel state?"

"I'm from North Carolina."

"Whereabouts?" Woody asked.

"Small place, you've never heard of it—Everetts."

"In Martin County, Williamston is the county seat."

Hardison looked up, and his jaw dropped. "How the hell did you know that?"

"I'm from Greenville. I'll bet you were a Phi Gam at Carolina too?"

Hardison got up and came around his desk and extended his right hand. Woody shook it. "Damn, you are one perceptive dude. What gave it away?"

"Well, the class ring was a clue, and I know guys from Greenville who went to Carolina who joined the Phi Gams and wear that ring. One of my golf buddies, Dick Henderson, was a Phi Gam. Do you know him?"

"Know him! He was my little brother. Great guy, even better athlete. Good student. He went to dental school at Carolina. Have a seat."

For about twenty minutes, Woody and his new friend Aaron Hardison talked about eastern North Carolina, common acquaintances, and Wake Forest versus the Tar Heels. Aaron—they were now on a first-name basis—promised to come to the O Club for beers in a couple of days. As he was leaving, Woody turned and asked Aaron, "Have you ever been around or used or do you know anything about sodium pentothal, the so-called truth serum?"

"Yes. I was involved in a study program during my residency that involved administering it to defendants at Central Prison in Raleigh, of course with the permission of their lawyers and the State. We weren't trying to do anything but see how it worked. Why?"

"No reason, just wondering. Well, I'll buy you a beer when you come over."

Woody knew it was time to shoot some more hoops with Mike and Kevin and discuss his meeting with his new friend, the shrink from Everetts.

Chesty
1100 Hours, Sat, 9 Aug 69
Legal Office, Third Marine Division
Quang Tri

After Woody told Fred that Dr. Hardison had declared Geronimo unfit for trial, he prepared the form to have the murder charge dropped for medical reasons. He then resumed reviewing the trial file in the Jackson case.

He pulled out the file containing the six interviews prepared by Lieutenant Breckinridge and also examined the NIS interviews of the same six men. There was no variance in the interviews given to Breckinridge and the NIS, and what each Marine had to say didn't look good for Jackson. Each said they were in the underground bunker with Jackson, bitching about the mistakes Lieutenant Speight made on Dewey Canyon and Apache Snow, mistakes which they felt resulted in some WIAs. The notes summarizing the statements of each witness were to the effect that Speight was an inferior platoon leader who didn't know the basics of combat and who should be replaced. Each Marine said they heard Jackson say that he wished the lieutenant was dead, that he then left the bunker, and a couple of hours later each witness heard the grenade detonate.

Douglas told both Breckinridge and NIS that he saw Jackson and Grant running from the direction of the lieutenant's hooch after the grenade exploded. Douglas said that even though it was nighttime, and even though the rain and wind from the typhoon were furious at the time, he could identify each man when it lightninged. Douglas also said that Jackson and Grant were always hanging around together. Woody made a mental note to compare their trial testimony with the notes from Breckinridge and the NIS agents.

He then turned his attention to the actual transcript of Peterson's direct exam of Jackson. He had not previously seen a transcript from a trial or hearing:

Defendant was sworn in and questioned by defense counsel (DC):

DC—State your name, rank, service number, and unit.

Witness—Ricardo Jackson, Lance Corporal USMC, 6251025, 16 July 1949, first platoon, Alpha 1/9.

DC—When you were in the underground bunker during the typhoon on the night Lieutenant Speight was murdered, did you make the statement in the presence of the other Marines in the bunker who have testified in this case that you wished Lieutenant Speight was dead? (Woody thought) *Nothing like going right for the bottom line, no foreplay or anything. He wanted to remember that tactic.*

Witness—Yes sir.

DC—Why did you make that statement.

Witness—Sir, Lieutenant Speight was not a good platoon commander. He made mistakes in the field. I didn't wanna to be in his platoon and just said I wished he was dead so he won't be our platoon commander, sir.

DC: Did you mean you wanted him dead?

Woody was so engrossed reading the transcript that he didn't hear two men approach and stand by his desk, but then he sensed them and looked up and saw Warrant Officer Masterson with a captain who was wearing stateside utilities.

Masterson spoke, "Lieutenant White, I want you to meet our new lawyer, Captain Charles Brooker."

Woody stood up and extended his hand. "Hello, Charles."

Brooker did not extend his hand and looked at Woody and then said loud enough for everyone in the defense shop to hear him, "That's *Captain* Brooker to you, Lieutenant."

Woody had two thoughts at the same time. This guy was a first-class prick, and Woody wanted to embarrass the prick by being a super Marine. "Yes, sir, begging the captain's pardon, *sir*! It will not happen again, *sir*!" he said, while standing at his best straight-backed attention.

"Well, it better not. And Lieutenant, just so you know, I'm gonna be in the trial shop. I've prosecuted before, and I don't give deals, understand?"

"Yes, sir, the lieutenant understands the captain, sir!"

Masterson spoke, "Well, I guess we best meet some other officers, Captain. Lieutenant, we will see you later, maybe at the O Club."

Woody answered, "Sure thing, Mr. Masterson. By the way, Mr. Masterson, I don't think the captain can beat Bull."

Brooker took the bait. "Who is Bull?"

Masterson answered. "Sir, he is the arm-wrestling champ of Third Marine Division legal—never been beaten."

"Well," Brooker said, "we'll see about that."

As Masterson and Brooker left the legal office, Woody resumed reading the transcript, but he wanted to be sure to get a front row seat at the arm wrestling—with a mug of Pepsi. The captain needed something syrupy to go with the beer.

Woody had to hand it to Major Forrest. He played the "Brooker versus Bull" arm-wrestling match almost verbatim to Woody's experience. Woody appreciated his own initiation because it helped make him feel that he was one of the guys of Third Marine Division legal when he was hosed with the beer. He wondered how Brooker would act.

They found out that Brooker was a different breed because when twenty-two mugs of beer, and one very large mug of Pepsi, hit Brooker, he came up swinging at Bull. Major Forrest had to pull rank on Captain Brooker to get him cooled down. Brooker stormed out, and everyone else went back into the bar. In a few minutes Brooker returned, wearing his new jungle utilities and a shoulder holster holding a .45 caliber pistol. He was the only person in the bar with a firearm. No one said anything about it but just glanced at each other, thinking—*what the hell is he going to do with that thing!*

Then Brooker asked a question that stopped everyone in their tracks. "Is there any way I can go on an LP?"

Fred looked at him as if he were crazy. "What do you mean, an LP?"

"You know, a listening post, where two guys go out from the base, find a good place to hide, establish a listening post to listen for the Cong or the NVA, and report their position, so the enemy can be wiped out. We learned all about them at TBS. Don't you remember?"

Fred answered, "Yeah, we all know what an LP is, but I just wanted to know if that was what you were asking about. It's real easy to get killed in one of those LPs, 'cause if the bad guys find you, you are outnumbered and will get wasted. That's nuts."

Woody was looking at Brooker's face when he asked about the LP and noticed that his eyes were nervously darting around the room and that he had a big upper lip. Even though the O Club was air conditioned, there was sweat on his upper lip and brow, and his hands were twitching. And then it hit Woody where he had seen someone look and act like that before: Humphrey Bogart as Captain Queeg in the movie *The Caine Mutiny*, in the scene when Queeg was testifying and rolling the ball bearings in his hands. Brooker went to the bar to get a soda. The guy didn't even drink beer!

McMurry spoke up, "Who does he think he is, Chesty Puller? He wants to try to win four Navy Crosses like Puller did in WW2, and he doesn't care about his own ass, which means he doesn't care about yours either. He's a guy you need to stay away from. We need to knock him down a peg or two, and I've got just the plan." McMurry laid out his plan for the following Friday while Chesty was at the bar, ordering his Orange Crush.

As the bar crowd thinned, Woody told McMurry that he wanted him for some one-on-one basketball for five dollars tomorrow afternoon. He was ready to talk about truth serum and the shrink from Everetts.

The next day was Sunday, and Woody had a new case to prepare before he met trial counsel Mike McMurry for hoops at 1730 hours because the trial of this case was set for right trial after it was assigned to Woody.

PFC Charles Battle—Woody thought his client at least had a good name for a Marine, was charged with larceny, a violation of Article 121 of the UCMJ. The file contained to following charge:

In that PFC Charles Battle, USMC (Reserve), Second Platoon, Alpha 1/9. First Division, Service no. E07080606 did, on or about 3 August 1969, at Vandergrift Combat Base, in Quang Tri Province, the Republic of South Vietnam, steal a tape deck, of a value of approximately $125, the property of Lance Corporal Michael Pollard.

The case file contained a report from NIS disclosing that Battle was seen leaving Pollard's hooch carrying a tape deck at a time when no one was in the hooch; that Pollard reported to NIS that his tape deck was missing; that NIS found the eyewitness and obtained a search warrant for Battle's hooch, found the tape deck, and charged Battle. When Woody had finished reading the file, he arranged to have Battle report to his office.

Woody had just entered the trial lawyers' office when Chesty yelled out, "Hey. White, I bet you're here to make a deal on Battle 'cause I heard you were assigned to defend that scumbag. Well, I'm prosecuting, and there ain't no deal. I'm going for a bad conduct discharge—don't need thieves in the Corps. And one more thing—you need to pay attention at this trial, and you will learn exactly how to get a conviction with a search warrant. It's my specialty."

Woody decided to play along with the bastard. "Yes, sir, the lieutenant will pay attention and learn from the captain. Thank you, sir!"

He saw McMurry and made a hand gesture as if he were dribbling a basketball. McMurry nodded, and Woody left to put on his workout gear to shoot hoops.

"What is with this guy, Chesty?" Woody asked McMurry. "He's a nut case. First, he volunteers to go on an LP, then he is so damn unprofessional, yelling at me like that in your office. Ever met anyone like that?"

"Yep, and that guy turned out to be a psych case, busted out of the Corps. Frankly, if Chesty keeps it up, as chief trial counsel I'm going to do what I can to get him sent to another unit. I can't discuss the details with you, but he has caused a number of issues within our trial group. We were good to go before he got here, but he stirs the shit pot so much it stinks all the time. It's tough enough being here without having that kind of situation. Anyway, what's up? You got something for me?"

Woody replied. "Yes, I do. Turns out I met a Navy shrink about a psych eval in a murder case—you know, the Apache who killed the black guy. The shrink and I actually grew up thirty miles apart, if you can believe it. Small world. He acted like he was better than I before I told him we were kinda neighbors, had mutual friends, and so on. Anyway, I just casually asked him if he knew anything about truth serum, and it turns out he does—had some study work with it during med school at Carolina with some prisoners at Central Prison in Raleigh, which is near Chapel Hill. He wanted to know why, but I just told him I was curious. I have the gut feeling that he would help us by conducting a truth serum exam, assuming he can get some of that med. By the way, have you heard when Colonel Suarez rotates back home?"

McMurry smiled. "Funny you should ask. We just got the word from WO Masterson that the colonel's orders to rotate back home just came in. Going away party in a few days. His replacement comes, or is scheduled to come, in the next few days."

"Who is the replacement? What do you know about him?"

"Well, he's from Tyler, Texas, the eastern part of Texas. He's a reservist bird colonel and a county prosecutor. That's probably not good for us, you know, a 'law and order' kind of guy, 'the jury has spoken and that's that.'"

Woody asked, "So what are you going to say to the new SJA about Jackson to convince him to let us do what we can for Jackson?"

"Well, as chief trial counsel, he'll want me and Kevin to give him a stat report on all the cases. At the end of that report, I'm going to just lay it out and hope he is the kind of guy who puts a premium on taking a real good look at justice. I'll tell him what we've done and what you're doing. I hope he'll be OK with all of it and give us his blessing to move forward, not only with the truth serum but maybe also with a legit polygraph. Of course, Jackson could pass both the truth serum and a lie detector with flying colors, and the colonel could still recommend approval of the conviction and sentence to the commanding general. At the end of the day, the CG makes the legal call. Polygraphs and truth serum are not in the legal playbook."

"What did you mean by 'legit' polygraph? Has there been an illegitimate polygraph done?"

McMurry stopped dribbling. "Yep. During our trial prep, Lt. Peterson, Jackson's lawyer, came to us, told us he was convinced Jackson didn't do it in spite of Douglas's statement, and asked us to have a polygraph test run with the agreement that the results would not be disclosed to anyone, and of course they aren't admissible. He wanted Jackson to take one, and since it couldn't be used even if he passed, we had nothing to lose. I guess Peterson, who is a damn good lawyer, thought if he passed, it would sway us in some fashion. Well, from Jackson's position, it went over like a fart in a church. Showed he was lying about not being involved. But—and here's the rub—the exam was a farce. Do you know anything about the polygraph?"

"Not really. Why was it a farce?"

"Well, what I know about the polygraph can be written on a note card with space left over, but the idea behind it is that they measure the pulse, maybe blood pressure or perspiration—in other words, how the examinee's body physically reacts when he is asked, and when he answers, the questions. I guess the idea is that if his heart rate jumps or his blood pressure pops up or whatever, he may be lying. But the questions must to be correctly formulated, correctly asked, and to the point, and the examiner can't be out of control. I guess someone can get a bump in the BP if they're being yelled at, even if they are telling the truth when asked if they killed someone.

"The examiner was a gunny sergeant from Mississippi—a brownnoser admin guy. Don't know who picked him or if he had qualifications to conduct the test, but I was there, and he was terrible. Made me sick to my stomach the way the gunny conducted himself and the way he framed his questions. I couldn't have passed it, and I wasn't at VCB when the fragging took place. So we need to try a legit polygraph. After that—I don't know."

Woody thought a minute. "Well, maybe we're making some progress. But I need to finish my prep for a case Saturday. Captain 'Chesty' has bragged all over the place that he is going to kick my ass in this larceny case, and the bad news is that a first-year law school student could prosecute and win the case. I just hate losing to a blowhard like him. He needs to come down a notch or two. By the way, did you hear what we have planned for him this Friday afternoon with the siren?"

"Yes, and I'm looking forward to it."

Siren at High Noon
1130 Hours, 15 Aug 69
Legal Office, Third Marine Division
Quang Tri

The first time Woody heard the siren at HQ was about three seconds after the first rocket hit the base at Quang Tri on his first night in-country. It was the unit's way of warning the men of the HQ, Third Marine Division, to get in their foxhole or bunker during the incoming. Woody had been in-country for a couple of Fridays and knew that the siren was tested at noon every Friday to make sure it was working.

On Friday, 15 August, there was only one person at Division Legal who did not know the siren was tested every noon on Friday. That person was Captain Charles Brooker.

When the lawyers started gathering for chow at about 1130 hours on Friday, they started talking up the possibility of there being a rocket attack on the base. One trial counsel said, "You know, it has been about three weeks since rockets hit the base. Plus, it's coming up on a full moon, and they seem to like to hit us then." Another lawyer piped up. "You know, I don't know how many rockets they hit us with last time, but I thought the incoming would never stop."

This went on for about ten minutes before Chesty spoke. "Do you really think there is a chance we may get hit? You know, if you're in an area where shrapnel hits, you can get the Combat Action Ribbon." If anyone had a doubt as to whether Chesty was nuts, they no longer did.

The legal office had one hour for lunch, and since the chow hall for their area was near their bunking areas, they usually headed back to their hooch by 1145 hours to take a load off before resuming work at 1230 hours. One trial counsel again suggested it would be a good day for the bad guys to hit them.

Almost every lawyer had a fan with green blades hooked on the foot end of his rack. It was so hot that guys would lay down, take down their utility trousers (nobody wore skivvies) to their boots, and let the fans cool their private parts. There was no effort for privacy in the Corps. Most of the trial counsel had assumed this position by 1150 hours on Chesty's first Friday in Vietnam. They kept up the talk about the possibility of incoming.

The siren began with a low growl and then grew louder. At the first growl, McMurry yelled, "Incoming! I think it's gas. Get your gas masks," and then he started running for the above-ground bunker, the go-to place for legal when there was an attack. Everyone in the hooch followed him.

Chesty was on his rack with the fan blowing on his privates with his utility trousers down at his feet when the siren started its growl. He rolled out of his rack and started stumbling for the above-ground bunker. He was trying to pull up his jungle utilities as he ran but was losing that battle, in part because he was using only one hand. The other hand was holding his officer's .45 caliber pistol.

Chesty fell into the bunker with the other lawyers, all of whom were laughing at Chesty's efforts to get to the bunker. The siren stopped after about thirty seconds. Chesty had finally pulled up his utilities and was looking to the sky, holding his pistol. "Chesty, what the hell are you gonna do with your .45, shoot down the rocket?" As the lawyers made their way back to their hootches, they agreed it was pathetic that Chesty didn't even realize a joke was played on him, because all he was looking for was that Combat Action Ribbon. Chesty's reaction to the siren incident was summed up by his question: "Do you think any rocket will ever hit in our area?" He desperately wanted that CAR.

US Government vs. Battle
0800 Hours, Monday, 18 Aug 69
Courtroom, Third Marine Division
Quang Tri

Woody had entered a not guilty plea for PFC Battle. The ASJA, Major Forrest, was presiding as military judge. Chesty called his first witness, a private named Swanson.

Government Counsel: State your name, rank, serial number, and unit.

Witness: Private Sam Swanson, private first class, E2632730, Second Platoon, Alpha 1/9.

GC: Private, did you see the defendant, PFC Battle, on 3 August 1969 at Vandergrift Combat Base with a tape deck?

Witness: Yes, sir, I did. He took a tape deck into his hooch.

GC: Later that day, did you hear a tape deck had been stolen?

Witness: Yes, sir, I did. I went to my CO and reported what I saw.

GC: Did you later talk to NIS Agent Wilfong?

Witness: Yes, sir, I did. I signed a paper he typed up saying that I saw Battle go into his hooch with a tape deck.

GC: (GC approached the witness) Is this the paper you signed?

Witness: Yes, sir, it is.

GC: Your Honor, The Government moves to introduce the affidavit of Private Swanson as Government's exhibit one.

Defense Counsel: No objection, Your Honor.

Military Judge: It is received as Government's exhibit number one. Proceed Captain Brooker.

GC: Private Swanson, come down from the witness chair and look at the tape deck on this table which is marked as Government's exhibit Two. Is this the tape deck you saw the defendant with?

Witness: Yes, sir, looks like it.

GC: Your Honor, we move for the introduction of Government's exhibit two, and we have no further questions of Private Swanson.

DC: Your Honor, no objections to the introduction of the tape deck as an exhibit and no questions of Private Swanson.

MJ: Very well. "Does the government have other witnesses?

GC: Yes, sir, we call NIS Agent Wilfong (Witness was sworn in.) State your name and position.

Witness: My name is Wilson Wilfong, and I am an NIS agent assigned to I Corps.

GC: Did you have a meeting with Private Swanson, who just testified, earlier his month, at VCB?

Witness: Yes, sir, I did.

GC: Did you prepare this affidavit signed by Swanson, which has been introduced as Government's exhibit one?

Witness: Yes, sir, I did.

GC: What did you do after you prepared the affidavit?

Witness: I took the affidavit and Swanson to an officer who was assigned judicial duties at VCB, and I told him that I believed the affidavit was legally sufficient for him to issue a search warrant, which permitted me to search the hooch of PFC Battle.

GC: Agent Wilfong, did that judicial official issue a search warrant?

Witness: Yes, sir, he did.

GC: And is this document, which I have marked as Government's exhibit three the search warrant that was issued?

Witness: It is.

GC: After obtaining the search warrant, what did you do?

Witness: Sir, I left the office of the judicial official who issued it and went to the hooch of PFC Battle and executed the search warrant. PFC Battle was there, and the tape deck was there, so I secured possession of the tape deck and placed the defendant under arrest for larceny of the tape deck.

GC: Agent, has this tape deck been in your possession continuously since the day you obtained it from the defendant's hooch?

Witness: Yes, sir, it has. It has been in our evidence locker until I personally brought it to this courtroom today, and it has not been tampered with. That tape deck, exhibit two, is the tape deck I obtained from the defendant's hooch.

GC: No further questions of Agent Wilfong, Your Honor.

DC: The defense has no questions of the agent.

MJ: Very well, Agent Wilfong, you are excused. Captain Brooker, any further evidence?

GC: No, sir, the Government of the United States of America rests.

DC: Your Honor, I must say that was the best presentation of the obtaining and execution of a search warrant perhaps in the history of jurisprudence, and it was, just as advertised by Captain Brooker on number of public occasions, a veritable model of how to have the court admit the evidence seized under a search and seizure warrant. Having said that, the defense makes a motion for directed verdict of not guilty.

GC: What do you mean, directed verdict? You just said it was a perfect search and seizure.

MJ: Lieutenant White, why did you make the motion to dismiss.

DC: Well, Your Honor, the elements of the crime of larceny include the element that the property allegedly stolen belonged to someone who did not give permission for the defendant to take the property. In this charge the Government alleged that the tape deck belonged to a Marine named Pollard. Captain Brooker did not call Pollard to testify that the tape machine belonged to him.

MJ: Do you have a comment, Captain Brooker?

GC: Your Honor, the failure to call Pollard was just an oversight, and I would like to call him now. He's here in the courtroom, sitting on the second row.

DC: Your Honor, I wrote down what Captain Brooker said because he told me publicly on numerous occasions that he was going to show me how to try a case. And just a minute ago, he said, and I wrote down, 'The Government of the United States of America rests.' That means he's through with his evidence. I can show it to you, Captain Brooker. I abbreviated Government, but here it is. Here, Captain Brooker, do you want to see what I wrote when you said the government rested?

(Reporters note: GC stepped toward DC with his right fist balled up).

MJ: Gentlemen, we will take a break. I want both of you in my chambers. Captain Brooker, you go first, and then, Lieutenant White, you follow. Reporter, this meeting in chambers will not be on the record.

The judge's chambers were not much larger than a walk-in closet of a rich woman who loved dresses and shoes, but it did have a desk and chair at which Major Forrest sat. He addressed Captain Brooker first. "Captain, you made an aggressive move toward Lieutenant White in my courtroom. I want to assure you that should that occur again, I will personally obtain the appropriate specification naming you as defendant. Understood?"

Brooker was contrite. "Yes, sir."

"Now, Captain Brooker, I am giving you the opportunity to state your position as to why I should not grant Lieutenant White's motion to dismiss."

"Well, sir, it was just an oversight. We all knew whose tape deck it was. The specification listed it. I just think the ends of justice will be met if I am permitted to reopen my case to call Pollard to ID the tape deck. He's here, sitting in the second row."

The judge looked at Woody. "Lieutenant White, what do you have to say about the position of Captain Brooker?"

"Well, sir, I just don't know how freely I can talk. After all, he is a captain, and I'm just a second lieutenant—as the captain frequently reminds me. I'm afraid if I speak frankly, I could get in trouble."

Brooker spoke up. "No, no way. You speak as freely as you want, Buddy. I won't hold anything against you. We're all Marine brothers."

Woody looked at the judge. "Your Honor, then may I be assured that I can speak freely and without repercussions?"

"Absolutely, you can."

Woody turned and faced Brooker. "You know, when I first met you, I extended my hand in friendship and called you by your first name. You didn't shake my hand, and you ordered me to call you 'Captain'. You are the only officer in legal who insists that I salute you, even within our little area. You don't ask that of any other lieutenant. When this case was assigned to me, you publicly made a point, both in your office and at the chow hall, that you were the best, you were going to kick my ass, and you were going to show me how to try a case. And now that you've screwed up the Government's case, you're all buddy-buddy. But most importantly, you want me to turn my back on my responsibility to my client and let Pollard testify that it was his tape deck, and then the military panel would convict unless they are brain-dead. You want me to forget the lessons I learned from Carroll Weathers, the dean of my law school at Wake Forest—that we owed all our responsibility to our clients, no one else, and that we could not turn our back on the client, even if he were guilty. You want to be my 'good buddy,' so I can bail you out. Well, here is my answer, sir." Woody came to attention. "Hell no, sir," he said and did as crisp an about face as he could and left the room.

Brooker didn't come to the O Club that night. Woody was congratulated on winning the case, even though his client was guilty as hell, and he didn't have to buy any drinks—that was taken care of not only by the defense shop but also by the prosecutors.

As they left for the chow hall, Mike McMurry walked beside Woody. "Brooker has requested to be transferred to Division legal in Da Nang. His request has been granted. He will be someone else's problem in two days. And I've got some news about our case. We need to shoot some baskets tomorrow at 1700 hours."

There's A New Sheriff in Town

1700 Hours, Tues, 19 Aug 69
Legal Office, Third Marine Division
Quang Tri

Woody had to admit that McMurry had a decent jump shot and could handle the ball well. They played a little one-on-one and worked up a sweat, which took only five minutes, and then stood under the basket. No one else was on the court.

McMurry spoke. "Suarez is having his going-away party tomorrow night, and Masterson told me he will be on a flight from here at 0700 the next day. I guess he's going back to New Mexico to show he's a hero and run for judge. The new colonel is supposed to arrive sometime tomorrow afternoon. I doubt he will go to the party if he is here. Kevin and I plan to meet with him when he tells us he wants to see us.

"After I give him a report on pending cases, I'll tell him what's going on in the Jackson case. I'm going to tell him we think the trial may have been error free, but we nevertheless have concerns about the verdict of guilty and want some time to explore everything—even events occurring after the guilty verdict. If he doesn't give us time to check this out as far as we can go, then the transcript and record will go to him, and he'll do whatever he thinks the situation warrants in making his recommendation to the commanding general. I hope our talk with him will encourage him to tell the general the case is not yet ready for recommendation and give us time to do what we need to do to get to the bottom line."

Woody said, "Well, thanks for keeping me posted. Let me know what I can do."

"Colonel Sullivan will see you now." Warrant Officer Masterson addressed both Mike McMurry and Kevin Ross. They had prepared a list of pending cases with explanations of the status of each case in their report to their new boss. The list set out whether the investigation was complete, the anticipated date of the trial, difficulties in contacting and interviewing witnesses who were in the field, as thorough a rundown as they could prepare.

The colonel stood when they came into his office and walked around his desk to shake their hands. "Captain, Lieutenant, I'm pleased to meet you. Take a load off and sit." He talked in a flat twang. McMurry thought that at least he was cordial and not too formal, which could be unusual for a bird colonel.

Colonel Bill Sullivan sat behind his desk, which was barren. He put his feet on the corner of the desk and sat back in his seat. "Either of you men chew?" He was digging his fingers into a pack of Red Man chewing tobacco as he asked the question. He pulled out the dark brown strands of the tobacco, made it into a ball, popped the ball in his left cheek, and then offered the bag to McMurry and Ross, both of whom declined.

"Probably not a nastier or more unhealthy habit known to man, but, God, I do love it. Got started on a day when I was playing golf in early November. Either of you play golf?" They shook their heads. "In east Texas, where I'm from, the wind blows like a banshee, and if the temp is down just a bit, it can get as cold as a well-digger's ass in Alaska. One such day I was warming up, hitting some wedges, and freezing my ass. My best golfing buddy, my dentist no less, came out and started hitting shots next to me. He heard me griping about the weather, reached into his bag, pulled out a toboggan, told me to put it on—which I did—and he then handed me some Red Man. He told me to take just a small bit and put it in my left cheek and to not swallow, and he said in thirty seconds I'd think I was standing next to a fire. He was right. Been chewing ever since. They even have spittoons in our county courtroom, but I don't chew in a courtroom. That's kind of a sacred place, if you know what I mean.

"I'm told you two are the top prosecutors of the Third Marine Division and have been for several months. I guess you brought a status report on the cases, right?" They nodded.

"Well, here's the way I see it. I'm a bird colonel, an O-6. Each of you are O-3s. You work for me. I've been told that you know what you're doing, individually and jointly, that you are top-notch trial lawyers and excellent administrators, and that you keep track what is going on. Don't be falsely modest—is that an accurate assessment?"

McMurry and Ross each nodded yes.

"Good, I respect a man who is confident about his work. I don't micro-manage people who work for me. I let them do their jobs. They can come to me with a problem, and I'll fix it if it should be fixed and if it is in my power to fix. Don't come to me with a problem without at least two possible solutions. If you mess up your work by being stupid or negligent, I'll be on you like white on rice. I'm probably the most informal bird colonel in the Corps, with people I trust and like. Any questions about my MO?"

"No, sir," McMurry and Ross said.

"Good. I don't need to know about the routine stuff—you're paid to handle it, and by all accounts, you're doing a good job. Is there anything unusual you need or want to tell me about?"

McMurry answered, "Yes, sir, there is. It will take a few minutes. We prosecuted a Marine named Jackson for murder, accessory after the fact to murder, and conspiracy to murder his platoon commander, a lieutenant, who was killed by a frag grenade while he was sleeping. A Marine named Grant is also charged with the same offenses, but he hasn't been tried yet. Jackson was convicted on the accessory and conspiracy counts and acquitted on the murder charge. The record has not been completed for the SJA's review and recommendation to the CG, but frankly, the trial probably has no reversible, prejudicial error. After the trial, we each independently concluded we may have charged, tried, and the court-martial panel may have convicted, a Marine who didn't do it. And we concluded for the same reasons. The reasons we—"

Colonel Sullivan held up his hand, and McMurry stopped. "I don't need to know the facts. You tried the case. You've got a gut feeling you convicted the wrong man. What was his sentence?"

"Ten years on each count to run consecutively at Leavenworth, loss of rank and pay, and a dishonorable discharge."

"What have you done about this up to now?"

"Sir, we felt it would be good to get a different set of eyes on this 'cause we're so close to the forest we can't see the trees. After the conviction, a second lieutenant lawyer, fresh out of Justice School, reported for duty and was put in the defense shop. He appeared to know what he was doing in a couple cases, and because he knew nothing about the Jackson case, we asked him if he'd like to help, on his own time. We cleared that with the head of the defense shop."

"So to sum up," the colonel said, "you two tried a man whom you think may be innocent, based mostly on your gut instincts. You want as much time as I can give you to see if you can find something justifying your gut feelings, and you've got a rookie helping you, right?"

"Yes, sir, that sums it up perfectly," Ross replied.

The colonel was silent a few seconds and then spoke. "In my second year of practice, I represented a guy charged with stealing a car. It was found on the street in front of his house. It was stolen between ten o'clock and midnight the night before—the owner knew that time frame. My guy told me he was in an illegal poker game from nine o'clock until two in the morning, walked home, and didn't notice the car when he got to his house. But—and here's the rub—he didn't know the real names of any of the guys at the poker game who could support his alibi. He could describe them and knew their nicknames, but not their real names. His alibi was that he was at an illegal poker game with five guys he didn't know before or after the game.

"His goose was at least in the oven, even if the oven hadn't been turned on to cook it. But then a detective working another case, against whom I had a case and whom I treated fairly and with respect, heard about my case and told me that one of his witnesses in some other case had been in a poker game the night the car was stolen, didn't know the real names any of the guys he was playing poker with, but knew the game lasted from nine to two. The detective arranged a lineup for his witness in the other case to view six guys, one of whom was my man, and that guy ID'd my man as being at the poker game. The DA talked to the detective and the man in the lineup and dropped the case against my man. I understand we can't be too tight-assed with the justice system, so unless you guys did something really stupid by doing something you should not have done, and it doesn't seem like you have, I'm going to give you some time—though not a lot 'cause my boss, the commanding general, will be interested in finalizing a case because an officer was murdered. What is the name of the lieutenant helping you?"

McMurry gave the colonel Woody's name. "Both of you go get Lieutenant White and let him know he's not in any trouble. Y'all come back with him in the next thirty minutes. I've got some papers to push, and I really love doing that." McMurry and Smith Ross laughed at the sarcasm. They liked their boss.

"Lieutenant White, where'd you go to school and law school?" Woody was standing in front of Colonel Sullivan's desk. "And all of you have a seat."

Woody sat down and answered the colonel. "Sir, I went to Wake Forest College and Wake law school."

"Are you a Baptist?"

"No, sir, and if I ever thought about being a Baptist, those mandatory chapels twice weekly cured me of that."

The colonel leaned back in his chair and put his feet on his desk. He wore what Woody called "chucker boots," which he had seen before worn by Sheriff Andy Taylor on *The* Andy Griffith television show. The colonel was wearing on a cowboy hat tilted back. He reached in his pocket and pulled out his Red Man and took some to add to the chew which was already puffing out his cheek. "Lieutenant White, would you like a chew?"

"I would, sir. Thank you."

McMurry piped up. "How did you get started on chewing?"

"Well, one day during Christmas break my senior year in college, we were hitting balls to loosen up for a golf match. Our driving range faces north, and there was a cold wind blowing from the north. I told my buddy that I was cold as hell, and he said to try this and held up a pack of Red Man. He said it would warm me right up, and he was right. Don't use it a lot, but every now and then, it's OK."

Everyone laughed and looked at the colonel. Woody looked around. "What's wrong?"

Colonel Sullivan answered, "Nothing, Lieutenant, but I think you and I are gonna get along just fine. Now, what's the plan?"

"Well, I need to talk to Lance Corporal Jackson. Haven't done that yet 'cause I wanted to get familiar with the entire file. I need to go over the testimony against him and talk to him about the witnesses who testified. I need to compare their two pretrial interviews with their testimony, and I need him to trace his steps the night of the murder for me. I probably need to get out to VCB to see the area—kinda get a feel for the place. Then, I'd like to get a doctor to give him some truth serum, sodium whatever it is, and see what his answers are under that, and then give him a polygraph. And there could be some step I should take that won't show up until it shows up."

The colonel spoke up. "How are you gonna get him shot up with truth serum in Vietnam?"

"Sir, I had a murder case and met a Navy shrink—psychiatrist—who has actually done that before, and I'm pretty confidant he'd help."

The colonel put his boots back up on his desk, leaned back, and was quiet for a minute. "You know, I'll say it again. This is a long shot, but the plan sounds like a good one, given the limitations of being in a war zone and given the fact it was a good trial and an understandable verdict. You know, when I meet with the division CG, he'll for sure want a status report on this, and I can stretch it out a little bit in good professional conscience, I can tell him the transcript is being finished, and we're making sure the record is perfect for the appeal. But there will come a time when, as his SJA, I've gotta tell him to approve or reverse the conviction, and my guess is that he ain't gonna be impressed with truth serum, a polygraph, or gut reactions as reasons to free a man convicted in an up-and-up, free from prejudicial murder trial of the fragging of a Marine lieutenant while he was sleeping. But I'll give you three some rope to do some work on this. There is no need to keep me in the loop on this project. I suggest you move with dispatch 'cause I don't know when the CG will want my recommendation.

"I promise I'll tell him what you have done, but I can't recommend that he overturn the conviction unless there is some legal meat on the "free Jackson bone," so to speak, when I give my report. Unless there's something else, thanks to all of you. That's all."

It always felt hotter after leaving an air-conditioned building, and all three lawyers were sweating within minutes after leaving the colonel's office. McMurry spoke, "Well, that could not have gone better. You need to get over to the brig ASAP, introduce yourself to Jackson, and start the process. To keep control of this we need to meet daily, even if it turns out we don't have anything to discuss. Is that OK?"

Woody nodded, but his mind was elsewhere. He was wondering how his meeting with Jackson would go.

Woody's First Trip to the Brig
1300 Hours, Thurs, 21 Aug 69
The Brig
Third Marine Division
Quang Tri

Woody decided he needed to meet with Jackson sooner rather than later, even though there were parts of the trial file with which he was not totally familiar. He hoped he could form a bond with Jackson in order to maximize Jackson's opportunity to help.

Mr. Masterson drove Woody to the brig, which was about a mile from legal. "You ever been to a brig, Lieutenant?" Masterson asked. Woody shook his head. "Well, be prepared for a lot of noise—can't do much to shut up a man in prison. It will smell to high heaven—each man gets only one shower a week. The so-called interview room is secure, but you hear all the going's on like you were in a cell yourself. The guards escort your client to the room and stand outside, ready to help you if you need it. Believe it or not, some of those guys go after the very lawyers who are trying to help them. They come into the meeting without cuffs or shackles but can be restrained in seconds if they get out of line. You should be safe. What's the guy charged with?"

Woody had agreed with McMurry and Ross that no one else should know what Woody was doing, even though they had the colonel's blessing. Furthermore, Mr. Masterson would be the last person he would tell. The warrant officer was a godsend to everyone in legal—he knew where to get stuff and how to get things done better than anyone. But he dearly loved to shoot the bull, and there was no way Woody would trust him to keep quiet about what Woody was doing. "I'm seeing a corporal named Gaskins charged with larceny." It was true that Woody had a client named Gaskins who was in the brig awaiting trial for larceny, so Woody had his cover. "I expect to be with him for a couple hours."

"Well, just get someone at the brig to give me a call if you can't hitch a ride, and I'll come get you."

The brig was much bigger than Woody had envisioned. It was a square structure, constructed of cinder block walls about forty feet high, with both barbed wire and concertina wire stretched at the top of the walls. The four towers of the brig were manned by guards with M-60 machine guns, a very powerful weapon and quite the deterrent to an escape attempt. There were also spotlights positioned at each corner.

Woody entered through a steel door, went to the admin office, and told the corporal on duty who he was and who he wanted to see. The corporal told a PFC to get Jackson, and Woody was shown to a room that had one table, two chairs, and a window on the door. There were two Marines outside the door, both of whom looked like they could have played in the defensive line for the Washington Redskins. Neither wore side arms or had a rifle, so if they were overpowered the prisoners wouldn't get the weapons, but each had nightsticks about two feet long. Woody had no doubt they could handle any problem, and he hoped he would not need their help.

He knew he would not need their help when the door opened, and a Marine who was only about five and a half feet tall and weighed maybe 140 pounds came into the room. Jackson looked like he was in the ninth grade. His face was pockmarked with acne, and he had the biggest nose Woody had ever seen this side of Karl Mauldin, who had starred in one of Woody's favorite movies, *The Cincinnati Kid*. Jackson looked at Woody but just stood at the closed door.

Woody spoke, "My name is White. I'm your defense lawyer. I need to talk to you. Have a seat."

Jackson didn't move. Woody knew this part of the meeting would be difficult because the only person from legal that Jackson knew was his trial lawyer, Peterson, who had rotated back to the States. There was no one

Jackson knew who could introduce Woody to Jackson as a man he could trust. Woody knew Jackson had to be one scared guy, half a world away from family and facing twenty years at Leavenworth. Woody had given a lot of thought about how to gain Jackson's trust.

Woody spoke, "There are three people in the world who think you may be innocent and who want to try to prove it. I'm one of those people. The other two are the Marine captain and the Navy lieutenant, McMurry and Ross, who prosecuted you. You've got absolutely nothing in the world to lose by talking to me, and you've got everything in the world to lose if you *don't* talk to me because I need your help if I'm going to help you."

Jackson moved away from the door toward the table but stopped about five feet away from the empty chair. "What can you do for me?"

"Well, for starters, I can tell you that after your trial, when I got in-country, the officers who prosecuted you asked me to help find out if maybe they had charged and convicted the wrong man, that I've read some of the trial transcript, that I've got some ideas to work on that may help you, and that the staff judge advocate for the Third Marine Division, a bird colonel, knows and approves of what we are doing. You are now my client, and you and I need to talk."

Jackson moved to the table, pulled out the chair, sat down, and looked at Woody. His eyes started to fill with tears, which flowed down his cheeks. "I did *not* kill that lieutenant."

"Did you hear the grenade explode?" Woody had earlier decided to cut to the chase in the interview.

"I did, but it was thundering and lightning that night and raining like hell, so I didn't go see what was going on."

"Where were you when you heard the grenade?"

"In my hooch."

"Was there anyone else in the hooch?"

Jackson moved his head slowly back and forth. "No, sir. I don't know where everyone was then. It was late, and we'd come in from an op and were on stand-down because of the storm. Some guys got some beer from somewhere, and there was some weed some guys had they was smoking in the underground bunker. I left the guys in the bunker and was in my hooch long before the grenade exploded, sir."

"So you were in the bunker with the other guys before you went to your hooch?"

"Yes sir, in the underground bunker."

"Who was in the bunker when you left it?"

Jackson named Radcliff, Jonesy, Parker, Walters, Evans, and Douglas, who were the same men named in both the NIS and Breckinridge interviews as being in the bunker when Jackson left. "What did you say about Lieutenant Speight when you were in the bunker?"

Jackson put his hands in his face. His body heaved as he sobbed. "I was really pissed at that lieutenant. He fucked up—sorry, sir, I didn't—"

Woody held up his hand and told Jackson to not worry about cussing and to keep talking. "I—all of us—talked about the screwups he got us into on Dewey Canyon and Apache Snow. We were in the field…"

Woody spoke, "Lance Corporal, I don't care what happened in the field. That can't be changed. Whatever mistakes Lieutenant Speight may have made, he didn't deserve to be murdered. But what I want to know is what you remember saying about the lieutenant to those men in the bunker?"

"I just said that the lieutenant was a shitty officer, that he should not have been in a command position, that we tried—or the staff sergeant tried—to give him some pointers about what not to do and what to do, that he got the platoon in bad spots and got guys killed and wounded, and that I wished he was dead. Then I left the bunker. What they said in court was true—I did say I wished he was dead, but I didn't mean it."

Woody had another question. "About the Marine, Douglas, who testified he saw you and Grant running from the direction from the lieutenant's hooch after the grenade exploded, did you see him that night after you left the bunker?"

"No, sir. He was wrong. I won't ever with Grant that night."

Woody continued his questioning. "Did you get along OK with Douglas? Was there ever any trouble—anything at all—between the two of you? I'm trying to figure out any reason why he might lie about seeing you?"

"No, sir, he and I never had a problem. But he didn't see me 'cause I won't with Grant."

Woody remembered from the Mill Run Valley case that Mr. Cavanaugh asked questions about directions to the alleged victim and knew he needed to ask Jackson questions about VCB. "I haven't been to VCB yet. If I stood in the front of your hooch, where is the bunker, the lieutenant's hooch, the head, and Douglas's hooch?"

"The bunker was to the left, then next to it is a hooch, then the head, then my hooch, and about fifty yards away was Douglas's hooch, and away from that was the lieutenant's hooch. They was on the other side of the little walkway."

"When did you know the lieutenant had been killed?"

"Well, everyone…"

Woody help up his hand to have Jackson stop and said, "Lance Corporal Jackson, I did *not* ask you when everyone knew about the murder; I asked you when *you* knew about it. What's the answer to my question?"

Jackson answered, "Sorry, sir, I knew the next morning. Someone said one of the officers had been murdered and that another officer had been named the investigation officer, kinda like the detective in charge, and he was talking to people to find out what went on. The word was that Grant had done it. He was a mean guy, and he talked bad about the lieutenant all the time."

"Lance Corporal, help me with this. If Douglas was right when he said he saw a white guy running with Grant after the grenade exploded, and if wasn't you, who do you think it was?"

"Sir, I don't know. There were some other white guys in other squads in first platoon and some white guys in second and third platoons. I didn't know them well. Grant was a scary guy who could have made someone do something they didn't want to do. I don't know. I've tried to think about who might have done it, and I can't come up with a name. But it won't me!"

Jackson continued. "Lieutenant, did you know that all six of those guys who testified against me got to rotate back home right after the trial, even though none of them had pulled their tour? It's almost like they got rewarded for testifyin'."

"Jackson, that didn't happen. The Corps doesn't work that way. Never happened. Let me ask you this: Do you have a problem in taking a polygraph—a lie detector test?"

"I had one, right after I got charged. I flunked—or the gunny who gave it said I flunked. He was yelling at me and askin' stupid questions."

"Have you heard of sodium pentothal, truth serum?"

"No, sir. What's that?"

"A doctor puts a needle in your arm, and the truth serum goes into your veins. It—I think this is right—does something to your brain that causes you to lose what are called your inhibitions, which are the things you have that guard you from saying something which would get you in trouble." Woody had seen Jackson's SRB and knew he completed the tenth grade, so he hoped this basic explanation would suffice.

"Lieutenant, I'll do whatever you say to show I didn't kill that lieutenant 'cause I know that what I say after they give me that shot will be that I didn't do it."

Woody stood up. "OK, Jackson, that's all for today. I'm not sure when I'll be back. Oh, there is one other thing." Woody gave Jackson a sheet of legal pad and his pen. "Draw me a map of the area at VCB we talked about."

When Jackson had finished the drawing, Woody told Jackson to hang in there and that he was doing all he could do and would let him know what was going on as it developed. He had to report to McMurry and Ross.

Woody stopped by the prosecution shop after he left the brig, and he, McMurry, and Ross went to the empty courtroom. Woody filled them in on his meeting with Jackson and told them that he agreed with them that Jackson certainly was convincing when asserting his innocence.

Woody continued, "About the polygraph, is there a risk if we give him a legit polygraph and he still doesn't pass?"

McMurry answered, "I don't think we have anything to lose. It would not have been admissible at trial, but if he passes both the polygraph and the truth serum exam *and* if we dig up some other stuff, it may mean something to the colonel and the general, but those are big *ands*. We know a guy who can do the polygraph for us. He's with NIS and is totally honest. We deal with him as prosecutors, and he's a straight shooter. He does the testing and if he thinks the guy is innocent, he tells us, and if the evidence isn't too strong, we usually follow the recommendation that we drop, or don't take up, the prosecution. We've gotten some blowback from some commanding officers, but so far no one has pushed us too hard when we follow Graham's recommendation—that's his name, Jack Graham. I believe he'd do it for us. Want me to ask?"

Woody answered, "Yes, and by the way, should we go with the sodium pentothal too if we can find some?"

McMurry chimed in, "I think it would be a mistake not to play every card we can. This is like most murder cases in that in a way it really isn't complicated. Someone is killed. Someone is charged. There usually are no witnesses, only circumstantial evidence and not a lot of that. In this case, Jackson was convicted by Douglas's eyewitness testimony of what he said he saw when it lightninged when the typhoon was raging.

"A lot of cases like this have a big chance to have the wrong outcome. We need to present everything to the colonel, so he can present it to the general when he makes his recommendation, even if it is a long shot. I'll get up with Graham. If he will do it, he can use the courtroom where it will be quiet. I'll see him tomorrow. Woody, why don't you contact your shrink buddy to see if he can round up some truth juice in this hellhole. Time is probably running short on us, so let's move."

Woody left the courtroom feeling both elated and depressed. He was glad to be taking some action, but he was depressed because even if Jackson passed the polygraph and even if his answers while he was under the sodium pentothal were truthful that he didn't do it, those results probably would not cause the colonel to recommend to the general that the conviction be reversed. And even if the colonel recommended reversal, there was no guarantee the general would follow the recommendation.

In fact, Woody had a hard time imagining the general overturning the conviction of a Marine in an error-free trial for the murder of an officer just because the prosecutors thought he may be innocent and just because a lie detector examination and truth serum test—neither of which was admissible at trial—might indicate he was innocent. But they had nothing to lose by giving it their best shot.

Polygraph
0835 Hours, Fri, 5 Sep 69
Courtroom, Third Marine Division
Quang Tri

Jack Graham had been an NIS agent for ten years and had volunteered for his second tour of duty in Vietnam. His first tour had been in Da Nang, where he spent much of his time investigating drug traffic. He believed that of all the bad which would come from a war that was probably unwinnable, the use of drugs by servicemen might be one of the most devastating long-term consequences. No matter how good the confidential informants were and no matter how excellent the investigations were, there were just not enough people to catch the bad guys, and there were just too many bad guys. Jack was from Maine and felt the fight against drugs was like trying to sweep back a northeaster tide with a broom.

When Jack asked to return to Vietnam, he negotiated placement near the front where there was plenty of crime to be investigated, but fewer drugs than in metropolitan Da Nang. He was looking forward to dealing with and getting to know firsthand some of the Marines on the front lines.

He had seen McMurry and Ross, individually and jointly, prosecute over a dozen cases and he was very impressed with their zealous and substantial prosecutorial skills. He was also impressed with their sense of fairness and their liberal use of common sense. When they told him about the Jackson matter and that they felt a polygraph could possibly help, he readily accepted their offer to help. He wanted to know if Jackson was in the brig at Quang Tri or Da Nang.

Ross answered, "He's in the brig here. Lieutenant White, who is helping us, interviewed him at our brig."

Graham asked, "What did White say his impressions were—guilty or maybe innocent?"

Ross replied, "He thought he may be innocent. Understand, White is still wet behind the ears, but he's got a lot of common sense and is good in the courtroom."

Graham thought a minute. "Well, there is an interview room at the brig, but it is so loud—you can hear all the inmates raising hell. I need a quiet place to conduct the exam. What do you suggest?"

McMurry answered. "How about the courtroom? We can do it when no one is there. We don't get involved in the transporting of prisoners 'cause we prosecute them, but Jackson's been convicted, so we'll take care of getting him there. What else do you need other than the courtroom?"

"Get some Pepsis and some kind of snack. I want this guy to be at ease as much as possible to give us the best chance for a valid test. Let me know when you can set it up. I need about eight hours' notice."

"Lance Corporal, do you know why you are here?"

"Yes sir Mr. Graham. Lieutenant White told me I'm gonna take a lie detector test. I already done one though."

Graham leaned back in his chair. He and Jackson were alone in the courtroom. Jackson's handcuffs and ankle shackles had been removed at Graham's request, and there were guards standing outside the courtroom. "Yeah, but this one is going to be different—and done right. The other one was messed up. You with me?"

"Yes, sir."

Graham spent the next few minutes trying to get Jackson to forget where he was and what he was facing. He offered Jackson a Pepsi and Nabs, which he scarfed down. Graham took notes of Jackson's answers as he was asked about his parents, where he grew up, what sports he played in school, his first date—everything he could think of to get Jackson in a comfortable frame of mind. Graham told a story about he and some high school classmates gathering ten-thousand empty beer cans and unloading them on school property, and Jackson laughed out loud. Jack felt it was a good time to get down to business.

"Here's how this works. Before you're hooked up, I'll tell you the questions I'm gonna ask after you get hooked up, and you will give me the answers before you are hooked up, so you and I will know the questions and your answers before the test. There will be no surprises, understand?" Jackson nodded. "When you're hooked up, this machine tells me how your body reacts when questions are asked and answered. The theory is that you respond one way when you tell the truth but another way when you lie. Again, since you and I will know what I'm asking and what you're answering before we start the test, there are no surprise questions on this exam. Understand?"

"Yes, sir, but that ain't the way it happened last time. He yelled at me, and I didn't know what he was going to ask."

"Remember I told you this one will be done right. Here are the questions." Graham started with asking Jackson to answer yes or no to his date of birth, the names of his siblings, and other softball questions. When he had ten questions left, Jack looked at Jackson when asking the three most important question of the exam: "Did you throw the grenade at the lieutenant? Did you help throw the grenade? Do you know who threw a grenade into the hooch of the lieutenant?" He then asked if Jackson had gone to boot camp at Paris Island and if he had ever driven a car, and then he finished with questions about Jackson's childhood.

Graham wrote down Jackson's answers and Jackson said he was ready to be hooked up.

The application of the devices took a few minutes, during which time Graham got Jackson to talk about everything BUT the exam. When he finished hooking Jackson up to the machine, he asked him if he was ready to proceed, and when Jackson nodded yes, Graham began with the first question.

Graham's practice was to never look at the machine when administering a test. After all, the machine would record the results. He felt there were advantages to his looking at an examinee as the questions were asked and answered. The expressions on the face of the examinee could be significant to an experienced polygraph examiner such as Graham. He made mental notes of how Jackson looked as he answered questions, and Graham was very careful to look at Jackson for the several questions before the most important questions.

The exam took about twenty-five minutes, about a minute per question. Graham never rushed an exam. As he was being unhooked, Jackson asked, "How did I do, Mr. Graham?"

Graham stopped unhooking Jackson and looked him in the eyes. "I have no idea. I did not look at the machine as I was asking questions. It takes some time to interpret the results, maybe four or five hours, and then I'll report the results to Lieutenant White, who can tell you what he wants to 'cause he's your lawyer. But you could not have been more cooperative with me, which helps make the results, whatever they are, to be valid."

Graham wanted to tell Jackson that polygraph results probably never would be determinative of guilt or innocence. That was White's job, and Graham guessed White had already told Jackson that fact. He went to the door to let the guards know he was through. After Jackson was placed in shackles and handcuffs, he was escorted back to the brig.

Graham was not truthful when he told Jackson he did not look at the machine during the test. He did look at it as Jackson answered "no" to the questions about whether he killed or helped kill the lieutenant, or knew who killed the lieutenant. Graham therefore knew that Jackson's body reacted the same way during that answer as it did when Graham asked him to confirm his date of birth. Graham also knew that this data would probably not be enough to keep Jackson from going to federal prison for twenty years.

Advance Team Deployment
0800 Hours, Wed, 10 Sep 69
Office of the Staff Judge Advocate
Third Marine Division
Quang Tri

McMurry, Ross, and Woody White were in their respective cubicles when W. O Masterson told each of them that Colonel Sullivan wanted to see them in his office ASAP.

"You boys want some coffee? My wife sent it to me. She got the beans from a place outside of Texas. Hope she didn't get it from Cuba. It's strong as a mule's kick and wakes you up like an incoming rocket, but I love it. It'll put hair on your chest." The three officers declined.

"OK, boys, I normally don't like to drink alone, but since it's 0800 and I'm drinking coffee, I can handle it. Have you boys ever heard the word 'Vietnamization'?" All three lawyers stated they had never heard it. The colonel continued, "Well, this war kept one president from running for reelection, kept a candidate from winning the presidential election, and is a real albatross around the neck of the winner of that presidential election. President Nixon is desperate to find a way out of 'Nam—I guess 'cause he wants his presidency to mean more than losing a war. So, and I have this on good authority, in a couple of months, he is going to start a drawdown of US troops, called Vietnamization or something like that. What that will mean is that the South Vietnam army, the ARVN, is going to start fighting, and dying, on a larger scale for their country, and the United States is going to reduce its force, and hopefully its wounded and KIA, until all we have is a bunch of advisors, just like we started with before we got bogged down.

"What that means on a practical basis is that more Marines, and some units, are going to begin rotating back to the States, or Okinawa, or wherever, and fewer and fewer replacements will be coming to Vietnam. Of course, you can't just turn this troop flow on and off like a faucet, so we're gonna start moving our office, along with some other mainly admin offices, to Oki, and eventually the entire Third Marine Division will be gone from Vietnam and on Okinawa or other bases. One of the things happening with all of this—remember I said fewer troops will be coming into country—is that Oki is beginning to sink into the ocean 'cause Marines with orders for 'Nam via transit on Okinawa are stuck there since they ain't rotating here. And because their stay in transit has normally been short, and because the troops are normally kept on a short leash when they're in transit, they don't get in trouble and they don't normally need many lawyers, judges, etc., to deal with them. Well, they ain't on a short leash now because they are stationed there. The Marines are getting in trouble, so legal and some admin staffs there now are just undermanned to handle the increasing load.

"I'm tasked with coming up with two defense attorneys and two trial attorneys to go to Oki, kinda as an advance team, to take stock of what needs to be done for the crisis they now have and, importantly, to set up the Third Marine Division legal office, so we can be up and running when the rest of our office gets there. I don't want to be huntin' for my desk when I get there. Captain McMurry and Lieutenant Ross, y'all have been in-country a long time and deserve to get to leave early. Lieutenant White, you ain't been here very long, but I've got confidence in you, so you're deploying with McMurry and Ross, and while there are those who will take issue with my selection of you, a relative newbie, they don't have the eagles of a bird colonel on their collars, and I do. I have total confidence in the three of you. Lieutenant White, who do you recommend I name as the other defense counsel?"

"Lieutenant Ross Jefferson, Colonel. He knows his stuff. I like working with him, and it sounds like it will be important for the lawyers in the so-called advance group to get along."

"Jefferson it is then," the colonel replied. "Here's the deal. You three and Jefferson, along with Masterson, will be leaving here in one week. You're going via landing craft down the Cua Viet River, out to the Gulf of Tonkin, onto a ship, and on to Oki. There will be other personnel from other units leaving when you do.

"Once you get to Oki, you'll take charge of setting up the legal shop and dealing with the multiple issues of deciding who to charge with what and when to try them. There are two military judges on Okinawa, one who was scheduled for here and one for the First in Da Nang, but they're staying put. They do have some limited court personnel, such as reporters. You will just be a skeleton crew, but it will work for the short-term. You will set up our offices at Camp Courtney—trial shop and defense shop, admin shop, etc. Kinda along the arrangement we have here, 'cept there won't be a need for an incoming rockets siren, thank goodness. Any questions so far?"

The three lawyers were too stunned to come up with questions. They realized and appreciated the colonel putting so much trust in them. They also realized they would be out of harm's way in a week or so. It was hard to take it all in.

"Here's two other things," the colonel said. "First, our legal shop is going to know y'all are gone, so no problem in just telling them you're being deployed to Oki. If they ask you if the deployment is permanent or temporary, tell them you don't know. Do not, *do not*, tell them about Vietnamization and the pending division move, and don't communicate the phrase "Vietnamization" to your families. If you family asks, tell them you think this a temporary duty assignment move.

"Second, moving an entire division five miles is a big deal. Moving it across the ocean to another land is a much bigger deal. The CG will have this division deployment at the top of his hit parade list and will be less concerned about keeping his finger on the pulse of the review of the Jackson murder case. I can, and will in good conscience, let him know if he asks me that the deployment, and particularly moving all of you as the advance team, will result in the slowing down of that Jackson review process, giving you some extra time. I'll try to pull in some favors to get Jackson moved to the brig on Oki ASAP. Y'all got a lot to do, so get doing it. And send Jefferson here. I want to tell him this myself. And White, tell Jefferson that when you all get to Oki, he owes you at least five Kobe beef dinners and some Orion beer for selecting him. OK, dismissed."

"Is the O Club open and isn't it five o'clock somewhere so we can start celebrating?" asked McMurry. He, Ross, and Woody were walking slowly from the SJA's office back to their respective work areas. Each was lost in his own thoughts about their good fortune.

Woody realized he had to go to VCB before he shipped to Oki and was at first at a loss as to how to make it happen. Then he realized he knew just the man to handle this, so he told McMurry and Ross he'd catch up with them later.

Sinclair Wright was an E-8, a first sergeant, and first sergeants in the Corps were called "top." Wright was assigned to the admin office of the Third Marine Division, and Woody knew he could arrange a hop to VCB so Woody could see the layout where everyone slept and where the fragging was committed. He remembered that Mr. Cavanaugh's cross-exam of the alleged victim in the Mill Run Valley case centered on knowledge of the "lay of the land." He didn't think he would unearth any clues at VCB, but he just wanted to get the layout picture in his head.

"Top, can you help me get to and from VCB? Need to be there only about two hours max."

"No problem, Lieutenant. We have convoys and choppers going out every day. If you can be here at 1000 hours tomorrow, I can make that happen. By the way, I hear you're on the advance team for legal on Oki."

"That's right. Good news travels fast. What can you tell me about Okinawa?"

Woody had talked enough with First Sergeant Wright to know that he had been in the Corps for about thirty years, so he probably served in both World War II and Korea. Woody thought Top had probably made some of those horrific landings when Marines island-hopped across the Pacific as ordered by MacArthur. Although First Sergeant Wright was enlisted and

Woody was an officer—and therefore in the chain of command Woody was superior to Wright, both Woody and Wright knew that Top, with thirty years and the next-to-highest enlisted rank, was more important to the Marine Corps than Woody, so Woody deferred to him.

"Lieutenant, it is part of the Ryukyu Island chain. I can tell you that on April Fool's Day 1945, I was on a landing craft that took me to the Oki shoreline to take on the Japs. I was told we were the largest amphibious assault force in the Pacific during WW2. It took us almost three months to take the island. It was bloody as hell, lots of hand-to-hand combat. The Army was there too. We got the word that FDR had died a couple of weeks after we hit the beaches, but that didn't change anything we were doing. We'd never heard of Truman. We heard that some Japs committed hari-kari by jumping off cliffs into the sea when they knew they'd lost. Wish they'd done it before we got there. We liked Truman after he ordered those two A-bombs dropped on Japan in August 'cause we were getting ready to invade their motherland. Thank goodness he ordered that. No telling how many people would have died if we'd invaded Japan."

Woody had another question. "Top, how many island landings did you have during WW2?"

After a few seconds, First Sergeant Wright answered, "Five—Tarawa, Saipan, Guam, Iwo, and Okinawa."

"Can I ask you one more question?" Top nodded, and Woody continued. "With all that killing not only on the landings but also after you got onto an island—the Japs were so brutal—how did you keep on fighting, knowing that you could be dead the next minute?"

Top sat down and had a faraway look on his face. "Well, Lieutenant, the only way we made it was to make our minds think that we were already dead—that it had happened, so we couldn't do anything about it—so we weren't afraid of dying 'cause we already were dead. Kept us going, strange as that sounds."

Woody could not even imagine what that had been like. At OCS, the candidates were shown a film clip about the Tarawa landing, and the beaches were literally red with the blood of Marines who fell. Woody wanted to change the subject.

"Top, do you know anything about Camp Courtney, where legal will be?"

"It's a nice place. Overlooks the water. There's an air base on Oki, at Kadena, and bombers—B-52s—take off from there to hit North Vietnam and South Vietnam and I guess other places we won't talk about. The Corps has a great training area at Camp Schwab north from Courtney. Okinawa will be a good place for us. There are plenty of bars with girls for the troops, too, if you're into that kinda thing."

"Do you anything about the ship we'll be on? Are we going to climb up those cargo nets to get on board?"

"Actually no, Lieutenant. The ship is the *Dubuque*, named after a city in Iowa. It has a well deck, so you don't have to go up the ropes."

"What's a well deck?"

Top answered, "The *Dubuque* has a ballast system, and as I understand it, the stern of the ship opens up. The ballast keeps the ocean out. They drive the landing crafts into the belly of the ship the doors close, and we're done. It's a neat way to get a bunch of Marines from or onto a ship.

"There are two scary parts. You'll be going up the Cua Viet River in an LC, and the bad guys could have RPGs or small arms fire with range to hit you, and I don't imagine there will be air cover. The second problem is that if the ocean swells are high when you get to the *Dubuque*, the boat master of the LC has to time the LC going into the ship without the LC being thrown up into the roof of the stern by a swell. But those guys know what they're doing. Look at it as an adventure, Lieutenant."

Woody thanked Top and returned to the legal office to work on packing his files for the deployment before he went to VCB.

The next day, Woody took a chopper to VCB. When he looked down, he saw the rugged, battle-scared landscape of the northern area of I Corps and was thankful he wasn't assigned grunt duty. He wondered if he could have handled leading men in combat.

It was easy enough to find the area where the lieutenant was killed. Woody was pleased that Jackson's sketch was accurate. As stepped off by Woody, the lieutenant's hooch was 120 feet from Jackson's hooch, and as he faced Jackson's hooch, the head was ten feet to the left of the hooch, and there was another hooch maybe fifteen feet to the left of the head. The underground bunker was to the right of the head and Grant's hooch was past the bunker. Douglas's hooch was about seventy feet from the lieutenant's hooch and fifty feet from Jackson's. Woody wondered if there was anyone other than Douglas who saw men running after the grenade explosion.

As best he could figure, when Woody was at VCB, as best he could tell, there was no one at VCB who had been there when the lieutenant was killed, so he got on the next chopper heading back to HQ and finished packing files for deployment to Okinawa.

Deployment to Okinawa
1635 Hours, Tues, 23 Sep 69
The Cua Viet River, The Tokin Gulf, and The Pacific

On Tuesday, 23 September, Woody, McMurry, Ross, Jefferson, WO Masterson, and others from the admin staff, as well as ome Marines Woody had never seen, were transported, sea bags and files, from their hooch areas to the Cua Viet River where they loaded onto a landing craft.

Woody had no way to know if this LC had been used in WW2, but since it didn't look new and since the Corps used gear until it rotted or fell apart, Woody imagined that twenty-five or so years earlier, there had been Marines on this LC who were getting ready to land on one of those many islands in the Pacific where the Japanese army waited for them. It gave him both chills and a sense of pride that he didn't think would be replicated in his life.

Top had been right. There was no air cover—at least not that Woody could see—as the LC went down the Cua Viet River. Even though the LC stayed in what seemed to be the middle of the river, it looked to Woody like the LC was not out of the range of small arms fire or RPGs from the shoreline. There were no seats in the LC, so Woody crouched below the bulwark, which he hoped afforded some protection from any fire.

Woody could tell they left the calm of the Cua Viet River when the LC started rolling in the swells of the Gulf of Tonkin. Woody soon saw the lights of the *Dubuque* and was glad the swells weren't too high as they neared the stern of the ship. The lights from the ship then became brighter when the well deck was opened. The boat master sailed the landing craft into the ship like he was parking a Cadillac in a garage. Then it hit Woody: He was out of the war zone and probably would not be sent anywhere else until he rotated back to the States next summer.

Woody was directed to his bunk area. He took the lower bunk, and it turned out that no one else was assigned to his sleeping area, which suited him fine. The officers were shown their officers' mess and treated to a great dinner of steak, baked potato, salad, and ice cream, all served by Filipino stewards on linen tablecloths. Quite the change from the chow hall at Quang Tri.

The ship first headed south to Da Nang, where Woody saw Eisenhower's military industrial complex at work. What appeared to be the trailers, or transport parts of tractor-trailer trucks, were being off-loaded from the cargo holds of ships by huge cranes. The trailer sections were all marked "Sealand." Woody wondered if it was too late to buy stock in "Sealand," whatever that was. No one ever knew why they sailed to Da Nang, probably because there was no need for them to know. After about a half day, they lifted anchor and headed to Okinawa.

It took about five days to reach Okinawa, and they were the five easiest days Woody had in the Corps. He had no men to give orders to or to be responsible for, and he never received an order to perform a duty.

The ship had a decent library and for the first time in his life, Woody read for the pure joy of reading. He realized there was some irony in reading *The Caine Mutiny* while at sea because in that timeless classic, Herman Wouk wrote a harrowing scene of a minesweeper in the Second World War being at sea in the middle of a typhoon.

The best thing about the trip, however, was the food. Woody never regretted his decision to join the Marines, but he wished the Corps took some lessons from the Navy about chow.

The ship docked in Okinawa about 1000 hours on Monday, 29 September, and buses transported the Marines to Camp Courtney.

The legal office at Camp Courtney would be set up in a large Quonset hut sitting atop a bluff that overlooked a bay which had the most beautiful green/blue color Woody had never seen. There were a few desks and chairs in the Quonset hut, and it was large enough for both the prosecution lawyers and the defense lawyers to be in the same room positioned at opposite ends, far enough apart that each could conduct business more or less confidentially. There was plenty of room for the staff and a large office at the end of the building, which they agreed would be suitable for Colonel Sullivan. A brick building next to the hut was deemed appropriate for the courtroom.

A few hours after arriving, the Third Marine Division lawyers were joined by some of the lawyers who were posted on Okinawa. Under the ordered chain of command, McMurry was the CO of the legal office until Colonel Sullivan arrived. The lawyers met, discussed pending cases, decided who would do what, and ordered the necessary furniture to set up their offices, the courtroom, and Colonel Sullivan's office. After discussing the number of pending cases, the lawyers realized they would probably work harder on Oki than they had in Vietnam, a burden they were happy to undertake.

Woody was busy sorting the cases for trial or guilty pleas when the shrink from Everetts appeared at his door. "Well, when did you get here, and how is the shrink business on this glorious island, Doc? You look like the cat who swallowed the canary. What's up?" Woody asked as he got up to shake hands.

Aaron Hardison was happy to see Woody. "Well, I caught a flight on a C-130 and got here yesterday, and I think there will be plenty for me to do to help the mental welfare of Marines. More than enough. And I've got some good news because I found some sodium pentothal in the OR at the aid station clinic down the road. I can't get that drug for a couple of weeks, so when Jackson gets here, let me know, and I'll set it up. The sodium pentothal is a barbiturate and is kept under lock and key to minimize misuse or theft. I've got to write on the drug records exactly how much is used and why it is being used. This ol' redneck ain't willing to lose that medical degree from the greatest school in North Carolina for not being transparent, so I'm telling it like it is."

Woody replied, "While I am gratified you have what we need and have found a way to use it, I take great umbrage at your erroneous assessment of your school's standing in the Tar Heel State. I'm not even sure it is in the top three in the state, and it is definitely behind the Deacons."

Jackson continued, "I don't know if Jackson is on Oki now. Our colonel said he'd try to pull some strings to get him here ASAP. I'll check periodically with the brig and keep you posted. I can't imagine they'd prioritize transport of a prisoner, but we'll see.

"By the way are you OK with me having a court reporter at this procedure to tape-record and then transcribe everything? I think we need a record of what was said to show the colonel and maybe the general."

Aaron replied, "Absolutely, no problem. In fact, it is such a good idea I'm surprised a guy who got his law degree from that dinky school in Winston-Salem even thought of it. But I need you to tell me what you want me to ask him."

"Already taken care of, Doc. I've typed the questions, and here's a copy," Woody said as he handed the list to Aaron. "I'd like you to review them and suggest any changes you think are in order."

After glancing at the list, Doc gave it back to Woody. "It's a good idea to have some no-brainer type questions, such as his DOB, full name, mom's name, and so forth. When we had that experience at Central Prison in Raleigh, one of the things I remember is that we gave them the no-brainer questions after sticking them, listened to the answers, and watched the subjects react to get an idea when they were far enough under the influence to get to the nitty-gritty in the questioning. Does that sound OK?"

"Yes, I'll redraft with those type of questions and get them to you."

"Woody, I've got a last question," Doc said. "How big is this guy so I can be accurate on the dosage?"

"I'll find out. He's not a big guy—no more than 140 pounds, except for his nose, which is huge, but I'll get him weighed before we do this."

Truth Serum
1330 Hours, Sat, 11 Oct 69
The Aid Station
Camp Courtney, Okinawa

Aaron Hardison was nervous as he thought about sticking a needle into the antecubital vein of the right arm of Lance Corporal Jackson. The last time he stuck a person with a needle was during his first year of med school, but the entire episode of being in an OR and injecting sodium pentothal into the vein of a Marine inmate who had been convicted of accessory after the fact to murder and conspiracy to commit murder while armed guards waited outside was as surreal an experience as Aaron ever had.

Part of the process required putting Jackson at ease as much as possible. Hardison asked Jackson, "What do they call you?"

"Sir, they call me 'Nose'."

"Why in the hell do they do that?" Hardison asked, laughing, and Jackson joined in. Aaron thought that Woody was right because Jackson had one of the biggest noses he'd ever seen. It probably looked even bigger because Jackson was so skinny. Jackson was placed on his back on a gurney, and Aaron followed the standard procedure of placing a tourniquet around the bicep of Jackson's right arm as Jackson's veins popped out of his skinny arm.

Aaron continued the conversation as he swabbed the arm before the stick. "Corporal, you're going to get a little buzz on, almost like you had a few too many beers at the E Club. I'll be asking you some questions. Just answer the questions, and all will be fine. You will feel this stick, and then we'll start."

Hardison hoped Jackson didn't see his hand shaking as he placed the point of the needle in the vein, but Jackson didn't wince at all when he was stuck.

"Lance Corporal, start at 100 and count backward, please." Aaron remembered from his experience at Central Prison in Raleigh that when the patient began counting slower, or skipped numbers, it meant that the sodium pentothal was hitting the patient's system. When Jackson took about eight seconds to get to ninety-three and followed that with sixty-seven, Hardison knew he needed to adjust flow of the medicine and start asking questions.

He nodded to Woody that it was time to start the questioning. Woody had asked Corporal James Greevy, legal's senior and most-trusted court reporter, to go to the OR with him. He explained what was going to occur and obtained Greevy's word that this would remain confidential. Woody had Greevy wear a surgical gown as if he were an assistant, so the guards wouldn't be suspicious.

Greevy moved his tape recorder and stenographic machine next to the gurney in such a way that the guards could not see him or his equipment. Woody had not told Jackson that the session was to be recorded, and while he wasn't sure about the ethics of not disclosing that fact to his client, he knew a record of the interview was essential for any presentation to Colonel Sullivan and the general . Besides, he thought, Jackson would be out of it and wouldn't notice Greevy.

Aaron slowly asked all the questions Woody had given him, and Jackson's slurry answers sounded like a drunk speaking, but each time he was asked about the murder, he answered he was not at the lieutenant's hooch and did not throw, or help, or know who threw the grenade. Woody was as convinced as he could be that Jackson did not kill or know who killed the lieutenant.

After Hardison had finished the questions, Woody asked Aaron a question. He had previously instructed Greevy to record this question and Hardison's answer, but he had not told Aaron that he was going to ask him a question because he wanted Aaron's answer to be what the law called a "spontaneous utterance," a knee-jerk answer which was sometimes given more creditability than answers the witness thought about before answering. "Do you think Jackson is telling the truth, as he knows it to be under the influence of the sodium pentothal, that he did not murder or help murder the lieutenant?"

Aaron replied, "Well, I didn't know you would ask my opinion, but it is my medical opinion that this man has been given a sufficient amount of sodium pentothal to release his inhibitions so that his answers are truthful, as he knows the truth to be, and that he believes he did not kill and was not involved in the killing of Lieutenant Speight."

Aaron told Woody it would take Jackson about thirty minutes to come out of the buzz. Woody did not want Jackson to know Greevy had been recording the session, so after the session he asked Greevy to take his tape recorder and steno machine back to the office to begin transcribing the session since time was of the essence.

When Jackson came out from under the influence of the drug, Dr. Hardison helped him sit up. Jackson looked at Woody and asked, "What happened?"

"You had the truth serum. It is Dr. Hardison's opinion that you were telling the truth when you answered that you did not know who killed the lieutenant and that you were not involved in the murder. That is what I will tell my boss, the SJA. You'll be taken back to the brig. Remember you can't tell anyone what happened here. If you are asked why you were brought to the hospital, tell them it is none of their business, unless you want to be a wiseass and tell them you had a penis reduction operation."

Jackson laughed to himself and shook his head, looked at Woody, and said, "Thanks."

Woody said, "I don't know when we'll know something, but it will move as fast as I can make it move. I will keep you posted."

Woody walked over to the door and asked the guards to take Jackson back to the brig. As they were putting Jackson in handcuffs and leg irons, Dr. Hardison spoke to them. "This man will need to have some chow before he is placed back in the brig. Make that happen, and that's an order, understood?" They both came to attention, saluted, stated they understood, and removed Jackson from the OR.

Woody and Aaron were alone, and Woody spoke. "Who in hell would think two rednecks from eastern North Carolina would find themselves halfway 'round the world giving truth serum to a convicted felon trying to find enough information to convince a general to let him go?"

"It boggles the mind," Aaron responded. "When do you think you will take all this to the general?"

"Well, I don't know if the CG is back on Oki—probably not. He'll probably be among the last to leave 'Nam. Colonel Sullivan isn't here either. I guess when he gets here, and I have no way to know when that will be, we'll meet with him, and the CG will want to him to report soon. So we'll see."

Hardison was quiet for a minute. "What do you think will happen?"

"I don't think the general will be impressed either with the results from the polygraph, the truth serum, or the so-called gut reactions of the prosecutors and will ask the colonel, as the SJA, to give his legal opinion as to whether the prosecution should be upheld. The colonel has got to say that it was a trial free from prejudicial error, and since there is no legal reason to not affirm the conviction, the general will sign the paperwork, and Jackson will start his two ten-year sentences at the federal pen at Leavenworth."

Aaron replied, "Woody, you've done the best that can be done for Jackson. No one can ask for more, giving him a chance he would not have had but for you, Mike, and Kevin. Even if the conviction stands, I hope you can take some satisfaction from the efforts the three of you undertook. I know, from my training and experience, that self-esteem is critical to good mental health. Let me know if I can help."

"Thanks, Doc. That means a lot coming from you. I'll keep you posted.

Americans Oppose the War
1130 Hours, Fri, 17 Oct 69
Legal Office, Camp Courtney A

Of all the amenities offered in Okinawa, including no incoming, Woody most enjoyed the opportunity to keep up with national affairs back in the United States by reading the timeless *Stars and Stripes* military newspaper and magazines, such as *Newsweek* and *Time*.

Woody and others found out that on 15 October 69, there had been huge marches across the United States and in some European countries, protesting America's involvement in South Vietnam.

Woody, and most of the lawyers with whom he privately discussed US involvement in Vietnam, felt the war was a losing cause, but they very much resented the marches because they made them feel very unappreciated. They had put their necks on the line, and just because some of them were now safely in Okinawa, there were—Woody guessed—hundreds of thousands of American servicemen and women who were still in harm's way. Woody resented those participating in the marches who could go home after the marches, have a martini, grill a steak, and make love to their wives or girl-friends while Marines and soldiers were eating C-rats in a foxhole, wondering if it would be their last meal. Woody was trying to get better at letting go of things he could not control, as hard as that was.

The Gang's All Here
1114 Hours, Wed, 29 Oct 69
Legal Office
Camp Courtney, Okinawa

Woody was at the legal office working on the defense of a Marine charged with assaulting another Marine at the enlisted club. The office was busy as each lawyer dealt with the new cases involving restless enlisted Marines looked for fun, but instead found trouble. The office was busy as the lawyers worked quietly on their cases.

Then the noise level rose when the rest of the lawyers from the Third Marine Division arrived from Vietnam.

After many handshakes and slaps on the back, Colonel Sullivan spoke to Mike, Kevin, and Woody. "How 'bout showing me around so I can see what you've got laid out for us?"

After the tour of the lawyer and admin office space and the colonel's office, the colonel spoke. "Gentlemen, you have not disappointed me. This is a job well done. I know there's lots of organizing in assigning cases for those who just arrived, but they are ready to work out of a war zone, so don't mind loading them up. I think we'll be up and running in no time at all, due to the good work all of you have done.

"By the way, about that Jackson matter, the general sent word that he wanted to meet with me in the next two weeks—not sure when—for my recommendation. Where does that stand?"

Woody gave the colonel the results from the polygraph and sodium pentothal procedures. The colonel thought for a moment and then spoke, "Well,

I will certainly review them, but I really don't imagine those procedures, as important as they are, will carry much weight, but we'll see. I'll keep you posted on the meeting. Again, thanks for the good job in transitioning us from 'Nam to Oki. Well done."

Happy Halloween! The Corps has Screwed Up

1420 Hours, Fri, 31 Oct 69
Legal Office, Camp Courtney

Woody's mind was on Jackson, and he was having a hard time concentrating on the case of PFC Tilley, who was charged with the run-of-the-mill bar fight. He heard Mr. Masterson addressing the lawyers in the prosecution section of the building, a few cubicles away. "Gentlemen, the colonel wants to see all second lieutenant lawyers in the courtroom. Now!" Woody wondered what the hell that was about. Then Mr. Masterson came to the defense end of the shop and made the same announcement.

When all the second lieutenant lawyers in the Third Marine Division legal office were seated in the courtroom, the colonel came in, wearing his cowboy hat casually tilted back. WO Masterson, in his most formal voice, brought the group to attention. This was unusual because even though they were still Marines, the relationship between the lawyers and the colonel was more professional than military. Something was going on.

Colonel Sullivan just looked at the group for about ten seconds and then said, "Ready, seats," which was the command to sit down given at OCS and TBS. Woody was thinking of Yogi Berra: "It's déjà vu all over again."

The colonel stood at attention and addressed the attorneys under his command. "Gentlemen, the US Marine Corp was founded at Tun Tavern, on 10 November 1775, so it will be 194 years old in ten days. We are proud warriors, and we don't screw up often. But, and don't you agree, Mr. Masterson, this latest news could be the biggest screwup in the glorious history of the Corps?"

"Yes, sir, no doubt, sir."

Woody knew every other second lieutenant had the same thought—what the hell is he talking about?

"Yes, Mr. Masterson. To paraphrase Sir Winston Churchill, never in the history of the Corps have so many, who deserve so little, received so much." Now Woody was totally confused.

"Gentlemen, I have received a message from SecNav, *The* Secretary of the Navy, our boss, that defies explanation, specifically that each one of you is being promoted to the rank of O-3 captain without ever being a first lieutenant. Mr. Masterson, this means what?"

"Sir, it means the newly promoted captains must plan, execute, and pay for the promotion party to end all promotion parties."

The colonel continued. "And whom should I appoint as the commanding officer of this mission?"

"Colonel, there is only one Marine with the temperament, attitude, demeanor, and most importantly the experience, who knows the terrain, the native population, and the objective. The Bagman is your man!"

The Bagman was Cary Boudarant from New Orleans. Every day after work, Bagman would leave the legal office at Courtney and hitch a ride to the nearest bar where, it was believed, he would get to know the local females in a biblical sense and drink some brown whiskey—Bagman's words for bourbon. When the hungover Bagman dragged back to work the next day and was asked how he was doing, he'd reply, "I'm in the bag today." Woody had never heard that phrase before.

There were smiles all around. Captains in the United States Marine Corps! After discussing this good fortune, the consensus was that they must have been given credit for the three years they spent in law school, even though many of them—Woody was not the only one in this category—enlisted during, not before, law school. None of them wanted an explanation though. No reason to overturn this apple cart.

Their "commanding officer," the Bagman, was soliciting advice for the party, and there was no dearth of ideas. Woody just wished he were in a better mood for what was sure to be a once-in-a-lifetime experience.

Walleye, The Stripper, and the Snake
1830 Hours, Sat, 8 Nov 69
The Big Time Bar
Naha, Okinawa

"Tell me, who is the Bagman? I gotta thank him for this wild party," Aaron yelled in Woody's ear. The so-called band was loud as the inside of a locomotive, and about as tuneful, but no one gave a damn. The enlisted men were drinking and eating on the officers' dime, which probably made everything taste better, and all officers, except Woody, were seeing how much they could eat and drink at one time.

Woody was drinking a soft drink. He was driving back to Camp Courtney, and Kadena Air Base was between The Big Time Bar and Courtney, and he didn't want get charged on the base with driving after drinking. But there was another, more important reason he was not in a celebratory mood: He, Kevin and Mike had run out of options to keep Jackson out of Fort Leavenworth Federal Prison.

Woody pointed out the Bagman to Aaron. "He's the guy with all the gals around him, blond hair, with the shit-eating grin."

Aaron stood up to go meet Bagman. "Well, this is one hell of a party. And the beef—what the hell is it? I've never had any beef that good. What is it?"

Woody answered, "It is called Kobe beef. We heard about it as soon as we got to Okinawa. Some of us spent our first two nights here going to restaurants, eating Kobe beef, drinking Orion beer and then getting massages. What I was told is that they keep the cattle in stalls, feed them grain, and don't let them out to pasture, so there is no muscle, just good, tender beef."

Aaron sat back down and looked at Woody. "Wait a minute. Tell me about those massages. We sure didn't have them in Everetts."

Woody answered, "It wasn't a big deal. We went to these massage parlors, took a steam bath, and then went into a room. These Okinawan women who gave me massages—I had two, both women were about five feet tall and weighed about 200 pounds and were maybe fifty years old. No sex, no nothing, just a great—and I mean *great*—massage."

A roar went up, and Woody and Aaron turned to the so-called stage, which was about five feet by five feet. The band stopped playing, a sound system was turned on and was playing some slow song Woody had never heard. The spotlight hit the curtain, and out stepped an overweight, naked woman, with a real snake coiled around her neck.

Woody first saw a naked woman at the King County Fair when he was a sophomore at Wake Forest. There was nothing about that event that Woody found even remotely erotic or appealing, and he felt the same way this night.

But the stripper had one admirer. "Who the hell is that guy?" Aaron asked. Woody looked at the stage, and a man was dancing around the stripper, and like Bagman, he had the shit-eating grin of a drunk man getting drunker.

"That's Walleye, or that's what we call him. Name is Walter Francisco, a first lieutenant admin guy with our office. His eyes look like they are about to pop out of his head—they bulge. That's the way they always look, it's not just because he's been drinking. He says he can see 180 degrees without turning his head. I didn't know he was such a heavy drinker, but I'm glad he's having a good time. Looks like everybody is."

"Captain White. Kind of has a nice ring to it, doesn't it?" Woody turned and saw the colonel was speaking, and Aaron excused himself.

"Yes, sir, I guess it does. Doesn't mean I'm a better lawyer, just got some more rank."

"I thought you were a scotch drinker, but I've never seen someone mix scotch with a soft drink, which is what it looks like you're drinking. In fact, it makes me sick to even think about drinking scotch with a soft drink."

"No, sir, I'm not drinking tonight. Just not in the mood."

The colonel motioned Woody over to a corner of the bar. "Woody, I know you've got a lot on your mind about Jackson. I read the reports from the sodium pentothal administration and the polygraph. I told you boys from the git-go that I'd give you the chance to prove the wrong guy had been convicted, and I have. And you, McMurry, and Ross—particularly you—have done much more than anyone could expect to help this guy. It has always been a long shot, but if you hadn't tried, there would have been no shot at all. You didn't do this to get the experience, you did it for a much better reason—to help."

The colonel continued. "You need to learn the important lesson of taking the opportunity to have a good time every now and then. You're a captain in the greatest fighting force in the history of mankind, and you worked hard to achieve that rank. Reward yourself.

"One more thing. You will lose more cases than you'll win. You cannot, and I mean this, let a defeat in one case linger any longer than it takes for the courtroom door to hit you in the butt when you leave the courtroom, 'cause if you let a loss bother you, I guarantee you it will make you screw up your next case or not do your best in your next case. It took me too long to learn that lesson. You can and should learn from those losses, many of which you will lose because the facts weren't with you. Do not let them drag you down."

The colonel continued. "We meet with the general Tuesday, and then we'll know. I really think you should go, but we've discussed this, and I respect your decision to stay back at the office while McMurry, Ross, and I meet with him. Now, go have a good time, and thanks for the party. Bagman should get a medal for this—maybe the Bronze Star for drinking."

"Thank you, Colonel, I'll do all I can to follow your advice because I know it is good advice. It's just hard to deal with it now because I think I know where we're going to end up with Jackson, and it's not good. But thanks for reading the reports, and please let me know if you have any questions. I'll be around the office tomorrow catching up on some work."

Around 2200 hours, the Marines started leaving the bar. Woody was ready to go, so he rounded up Aaron. He also noticed that Walleye was tilting like the Leaning Tower of Pisa, so he decided to give him a ride home and let him get his car tomorrow.

"Let me give you a ride, Walleye. It'll be safer."

Walleye slurred, "Hell, no. I can drive myself. I don't need help." Walleye was having a hard time walking and talking at the same time. Woody was worried about Walleye's safety—and the safety of others—if Walleye drove himself, but Woody's efforts to get Walleye to give him his car keys only made Walleye more belligerent, so Woody backed off and decided he'd just follow Walleye back to Camp Courtney.

There wasn't much traffic, so Woody and Hardison didn't have trouble following Walleye's beat-up red with a white top 1958 Chevy Bel Air. Walleye's driving became worse when they reached the road that snaked through Kadena Air Base.

Woody said, "Would you look at him? He's moving all over the place like he was Gale Sayers in the open at Soldier Field against the Lions on Thanksgiving Day. He'll never make it home."

Woody had no sooner uttered those words when the blue light and siren from an air police jeep filled the night. "Damn, hell's bells. He's had it. I'm going to lay back a bit and see what happens. I haven't been drinking, but those air police may not like Marines, and while I'm brave, I ain't stupid."

Walleye did manage to stop the vehicle, but it didn't bode well for him that the right front and rear tires ended up over the curb. Woody and Hardison were about twenty-five yards back, and Woody cut off the engine and lights. Two air police approached Walleye's car, one on each side. Woody could hear one of the officers order the driver to get out of the car. When nothing happened, the officer on the driver's side opened the door.

Woody could not believe his eyes, because Walleye fell out of the car, landing at the officer's feet. Woody said to Aaron, "Well, I guess the officer had probable cause to stop him with that wild driving, and now, it'll be hard to say he didn't have probable cause to arrest him. I need to help him if I can. You wait here."

Woody got out of his car and walked toward the air police. Aaron heard Woody announce himself as a Marine captain named White and asked if he could speak to the air police. After about ten minutes, Woody turned toward his car and waved Aaron to join them. When Aaron got to Walleye's car, Woody said, "These kind gentlemen seem to understand that it is not unusual for someone to get too drunk at a promotion party, so they have agreed to cut Walleye some big-time slack and not arrest him. But we've got to pick up his sorry butt, put it in my car, move his car to that parking lot over there,"—Woody pointed across the street— "drive him back to Courtney, and throw his sorry ass in his rack. We thank the air force for this courtesy."

The taller of the two air police replied. "Don't worry about it, Captain. Congrats on your promotion. My brother is a grunt with the Corps' First Division, out of Da Nang, so I'm kinda kin. Drive safely." Aaron drove Walleye's car to the parking lot, and then Woody and Aaron hauled Walleye into the back seat of Woody's car and headed back to Courtney.

Time to Meet the General

0730 Hours, Tues, 11 Nov 69
Office of the SJA, Camp Courtney

Woody, McMurry, and Ross arrived at the colonel's office at 0730 hours on the Tuesday after the party. The colonel had his usual office attire—cowboy hat tilted back and wearing his chucker boots. The colonel directed the three lawyers to take seats and poured them each a cup of coffee.

"Boys, y'all remember your history? In 1918, at the eleventh hour of the eleventh day of the eleventh month, the so-called war to end all wars ended. Too bad they didn't tell that to Uncle Ho and LBJ.

"The first thing you need to know is that, except for Woody, who's not going, we aren't meeting with General Jones. Even though he is the commanding general, he is passing this off to his adjutant, General Hugh Dowda, who will be making the decision. I can fill you in about him on the drive to his office.

"I've re-read the transcript from the truth serum procedure and I reviewed the polygraph report, both of which support Jackson's claim of innocence. And I appreciate the affidavits from you two"—the colonel nodded to McMurry and Ross— "stating your feelings about Jackson's innocence. After all, the bottom line is that one witness ID'd Jackson—at night, in a storm, from about thirty yards or whatever it was, only when it lightninged. Not the strongest of cases, but strong enough for the panel to convict. All of this will certainly be considered since you were the lawyers who tried him. But at the end of the day, I'm the general's lawyer, and he wants legal advice from me about whether there were any prejudicial errors during the trial that would cause, or should cause, a reversal. I've reviewed the entire record, and there aren't any such errors. I will present all the information to the general, but I'll have to tell him that notwithstanding the post-trial efforts by you three, it's a good conviction, and he should approve it. I commend all of you. This won't make any of you feel better, but if I were charged with a serious crime, I'd want any one of you to represent me.

"Woody, I know you aren't going with us to meet the general, and I understand why. I'll tell you the same thing a judge told me in a criminal trial during a recess, and that was unless you pull a smoking gun out of your ass and put it in someone else's hand, your client is gone. I'm telling you that because once I *did* pull a smoking gun out of my ass. I stumbled onto something at the last minute and put it in the hand of the chief prosecution witness and got my man off. Do you think there are any more cards you can play?"

Woody answered, "No, sir, I'm afraid there aren't."

Woody was wrong.

There was one more card, hidden in plain sight.

The colonel concluded the meeting. "Well, Mike, Kevin, it's time for us to go. I'll drive. You boys make sure your zippers are zipped and your gig lines are right, so we can show that general how squared away Marine lawyers are."

Woody went back to his workspace. He passed by Ben Harvey, a lawyer who had reported to the Third Division a few weeks after Woody. Ben knew what Woody and the trial counsel were doing and he admired them, but he didn't hold out much hope for Jackson based on what he knew about the case. He'd heard the meeting with the general was today and thought about walking over to Woody, who was about ten feet away, to console him but figured there was nothing he could do or say that would help, so he began concentrating on case prep for a Marine charged with smoking pot, which was a very serious charge in the Marine Corps. He heard Woody once more—probably for the last time—drag out the banker's box that contained the Jackson trial folders.

"Men, have either of you ever heard of General Dowda?" The colonel was driving the vehicle assigned to the SJA office and it was a beautiful day, but McMurry and Ross feared it would be the worst of days for Jackson. They told the colonel they didn't know anything about the general.

"Well, I think he is one of the Corps up-and-comers, probably commandant material. In WW2, he was on the Canal and was awarded the Navy Cross for, basically, saving his platoon. Then, on Iwo, he was awarded the Silver Star, but it almost had to be awarded posthumously. The general, who was then a lieutenant, walked past a hidden spider hole, a Jap popped out of the hole and was about to shoot him in the back, but his platoon sergeant, who was behind him, blew the Jap away. It was almost like John Wayne as Sgt. Stryker in the movie *The Sands of Iwo Jima* when the Duke got shot in the back. The general and that sergeant have been together ever since, and the sergeant is now General Dowda's first sergeant, his top.

"He stayed in after the war and was scheduled to go to the first class at the Army War College in Carlisle, Pennsylvania, when it resumed in '50. You boys know what Carlisle is famous for? Jim Thorpe, one of the greatest athletes of all time, went to college there. At any rate, the general didn't go to the War College, he went to Korea. He got placed on the staff of God Almighty himself, Douglas MacArthur, and he helped MacArthur plan and implement the landing at Inchon in September 1950. Probably one of the greatest military maneuvers in history.

"But I believe the true mettle of General Dowda is this: MacArthur awarded Dowda the Bronze Star with the combat "V" device even though Dowda never left MacArthur's command center on the ship and was never in harm's way. I'm sure he deserved the Bronze Star—but not the combat "V" device 'cause he was never in combat. MacArthur was giving out ribbons like he was the candy man at Halloween. Dowda had to accept it, and he wore the combat "V" until Truman fired MacArthur for, among other things, being insubordinate to the president. That was the fourth best thing Truman did."

McMurry spoke up, "What were the other three good things Truman did?"

"Dropped two bombs on the Japs and ended the war. Made Israel a nation state—or led the movement—and began the process of integrating the services. Harry was one stud, in my opinion.

"Dowda is a real leader. Let me tell you about something that happened at one of his duty stations after he made general. There was a lance corporal in his office, an admin guy. Without asking, he made what was described as a beautiful wooden nameplate for the general's desk. The problem was that the general didn't like that kind of thing. He said if they didn't know who the hell he was by the time they were standing at his desk, a nameplate wouldn't help. He told his top to remove the nameplate, but Top told the general the lance corporal had busted his butt making it, was proud of his handiwork, and would be crushed if it were removed. Here's what the general did—told Top to call the lance corporal to his office right then, came out from behind his big desk when the Marine came in, shook his hand, told him to have a seat next to him, told him it was the most beautiful nameplate he had ever seen, and that he was honored to have it. Then—now remember this is a general talking to a lance corporal—the general said he'd be honored if the lance corporal would give permission to him, the general, to make a gift of it back to the lance corporal, and of course the lance corporal said yes. So the general got a pen, signed his name and something like, 'From one Marine to another—I'm proud to serve with you,' and gave it to him. Don't you know that lance corporal would run through a brick wall for General Dowda? Quite a guy.

"Now, when we go into his office, we're there to answer questions. Don't speak unless spoken to and shoot straight with him. He may ask each of you if you think it was an error-free trial and if there was sufficient evidence for the military panel to find guilt. You know there was no error, and there was sufficient evidence to convict, so I'd suggest you answer yes. Don't know if he'll ask you to give reasons for your gut feelings of innocence, but don't be afraid to look him in the eye and speak from your heart. We're here."

They parked on a horseshoe driveway in a space marked "Visitor," walked into the office, and were told to wait for the general to finish some business.

Woody didn't know why he had reopened the banker's box containing the entire Jackson file. He'd been through the five hundred documents a hundred times and thought he knew the front and back of every document. He thought there was no way he'd missed anything. He was picking up files and looking at documents but not really seeing anything. His mind was on Jackson and what he would say to him after the general approved the conviction and sentence.

General Dowda was about five feet, eight inches tall and a very unassuming man, except for the star of a brigadier general on each of his collars. He was reserved but immediately put the colonel, McMurry, and Ross at ease, asking them how they came to join the Corps. He seemed genuinely interested in their stories but after a few minutes, the colonel spoke up.

"Would the General like me to give my report on this Jackson case?"

The general replied, "Colonel, I really do appreciate your adherence to the somewhat antiquated military custom to refer to senior officers in the third person when you're in the presence of the senior officer. But to me that custom seems awkward in practice. It is almost as if one is asking questions of a corpse laid out for visitation. Let's do this on a first-name basis: My first name is General, and your first names are Colonel, Captain, and Lieutenant. I'll be more comfortable. So tell me about this case. I want to know everything there is to know."

As the colonel, McMurry, and Ross began to inform General Dowda of the facts of the case from the trial, their post-trial misgivings about the conviction, the two polygraphs, and the truth serum results, Woody was returning the investigation officer's file to the banker's box when he saw, for the first time, a card he could play.

"Son of a bitch!" Woody yelled so loudly that Ben Harvey jumped out of his chair ten feet away in his cubicle.

"What the hell happened, Woody?"

"Son of a bitch!" Woody was standing up, holding the IO's file. He looked at Ben. "You go right now and call the colonel at General Dowda's office. Tell them to tell the colonel that there is an emergency message from Captain White!"

"What the hell do you want me to tell them the message is?"

"You tell them to tell the colonel that Captain White found that smoking gun and is on the way and to not let the general sign the papers." Woody ran from the legal office to his car. Ben found the number for the general's office and placed the call.

"Colonel Sullivan, I do appreciate the report. It was concisely given. And gentlemen" ----the general nodded to Mike and Kevin—"I appreciate your candor and your efforts on behalf of this lance corporal. And Colonel, please express my appreciation to Captain White. But, at the end of the day, I've got to look at this as a legal matter, and as a legal matter, we've got a murdered lieutenant, six witnesses including an eyewitness against the defendant, a military panel who weighed the evidence and then convicted the defendant even though he testified denying the offense, in a trial that was free from prejudicial error. So, Colonel, if you'll give me the paperwork to approve the trial and conviction, I'll sign it, and we can be done."

As Colonel Sullivan was walking to the general's desk, there was a loud knock on the office door. "COME," the general ordered.

Top stuck his head in the door. "General, there is a urgent message for Colonel Sullivan from a Captain White."

General Dowda looked at Colonel Sullivan, who shrugged his shoulders as if to say he didn't know what it was about.

"Well, what's the message, Top?"

"He said to tell the colonel that a Captain White has found that gun the colonel was talking about and that he is on the way."

"Thanks, Top." The general then turned to Colonel Sullivan. "Colonel, what the hell is going on here? I've given you and your men plenty of time to go through this case and now we get a mysterious message from another member of your crew? What does that message mean?"

Colonel Sullivan came to attention. "General, when we left the legal office, I told Captain White that—well, General, may I state exactly what I said?"

"Colonel, I think you *better* do that. What the hell did you tell him!"

"General, I told him that unless he pulled a smoking gun out of his ass and put it in the hand of someone else, Jackson was on the way to Leavenworth."

The general leaned back in his chair, steppled his fingers, and nodded to Colonel Sullivan to sit back down. "So I'm supposed to believe that after all these many months and investigations and polygraphs and whatever that 'the smoking gun' to free Jackson has just now been found, right?"

Colonel Sullivan again came to attention and faced the general. "Sir, Captain White is an excellent officer and attorney. I don't believe he has it in him to waste the gen—your time with something frivolous. I would hope you'd give him a chance to tell you—to tell all of us—what he found."

"Colonel, I write your fitness report. This event and your judgment about these matters will be part of that fitness report. Are you willing to run the risk that your report may be bad if White comes up with something that falls flat?"

Colonel Sullivan seemed to stand even more erectly at attention, as if he were being inspected at OCS. "Yes, sir! Absolutely."

General Dowda looked at Sullivan for a few seconds, nodded for him to sit, and spoke to Top. "When this Captain White gets here, show him in, please."

General Dowda began reading some papers on his desk, and Colonel Sullivan, McMurry, and Ross just sat and wondered what the hell Woody had come up with. Each of them hoped this was not a wild-goose chase, but none of them could imagine what Woody found that could help Jackson.

There was a knock at the door. "COME," the general ordered.

Top opened the door. "General, Captain White is here." He stepped back, and Woody appeared in the doorway, holding a file.

"Front and center, Captain," the general ordered.

Woody crossed the room and came to attention about three feet in front of the general's desk. When he came into the building, Woody removed his cover as required, and therefore did not salute the general. General Dowda waited a few seconds before speaking.

"Captain, the colonel told me about the so-called smoking gun. I've got a second hand on my watch and you've got sixty seconds to state your case, starting now."

Woody's mind raced for about ten seconds and then he realized just how to say what the general needed to hear. "Sir, an officer named Breckinridge interviewed government witnesses who testified that Jackson said he wished the lieutenant was dead before the lieutenant was murdered. The main witness in this case said he saw two men running from the lieutenant's hooch right after the grenade exploded. He ID'd a man named Grant, who has not yet been tried, and Jackson, the convicted Marine, but given the weather conditions—that typhoon had hit and the fact it was nighttime, the opportunity for positive ID was low. The investigation file contained six interview sheets on which the investigation officer, Breckinridge, wrote what those six told him, and he wrote the names of those six Marines on the inside of the file. But on the inside of the file, where the other six names were listed, the investigation officer also wrote the name of a *seventh* Marine, but there was no interview sheet in the file for that Marine, named Jason Singletary. I don't know what Singletary said, and he may have said Jackson didn't do it. I noticed for the first time today there were the names of seven, not six, witnesses, even though I've handled this file beaucoup times since I got in-country."

The general was silent a few seconds and then spoke up. "Captain, there could be any number of explanations why the interview sheet is not in there. He may not have even interviewed this seventh person—what's his name?"

"Singletary, sir, Jason Singletary."

The general continued, "Or this Singletary may have given the same story the other witnesses gave, and the investigation officer decided it was not important to add to his witness file, or it could have fallen out of the file, who knows? You've brought me a problem you want me to deal with, without any hope that it will really help me decide this issue. I don't want folks bringing me a problem without a solution. What is your solution to the mystery of this so-called missing seventh witness?"

Woody knew from the sarcasm in General Dowda's voice that the general was running out of patience, so he needed to come up with a plan for the general that had a practical way to address the mystery.

"General, I think you should take such steps as are necessary to locate Singletary and interview him—or have him interviewed, and have that interview made available to you—and then you will know everything there is to know about whether to approve the conviction. If he's on this island, frankly I think he should immediately report to this office and speak directly to you, so you will know firsthand what, if anything, he said to the investigation officer. After all, you're the one making the decision. If he's stateside, an NIS agent can interview him and forward the interview to you. That's what I'd do."

General Dowda leaned back in his chair and again steepled his fingers. He looked at Woody, who continued to stand at attention with his eyes focused on the window behind the general's desk.

"Captain White, when you were at TBS, do you remember they had a military protocol class which dealt with the way you address superior officers when speaking to them?"

"Yes, sir."

"Captain White, don't you remember being instructed to refer to officers of superior rank in the third person when you were in their presence?"

"Yes, sir."

"You haven't done that with me today. Why not?"

"Sir, I do hope I have not offended you for several reasons. My failure to follow that protocol is certainly not a show of disrespect, but frankly I find it very awkward to speak to a person by referring to that person in the third person. It's like I'm standing next to the coffin at a visitation and talking to the deceased. I guess I didn't learn that lesson well, sir, and I hope my failure to do that right does not hurt my efforts—our efforts—to help Jackson."

When Woody gave his explanation, a small grin came across the general's face, and he chuckled. At the same time, Woody heard muffled laughs from the colonel and the trial counsel. He wondered what that was about but continued to stand at attention.

General Dowda leaned forward and picked up his phone. "Top, I need you in here, and bring a legal pad with you." He looked at Woody. "Stand at ease, Captain, and let me see the witness file."

Top came into the office and stepped next to the general's desk. "Top, drop whatever you're doing. I need you to handle this as fast as humanly possible. Find out if a Marine named Jason Singletary, a corporal, is on Okinawa, and report that to me. Thank you."

General Dowda stood up. "Captain White, I appreciate your ballsy approach to this issue. You came up with a plan of attack that made sense, can be immediately implemented, and will achieve the objective of at least finding out what Singletary knows. You've earned the opportunity for this office to follow this trail to its end. Gentlemen, let's move to that table."

Colonel Sullivan noticed that because the table was circular, there was no head of the table. The general brought the file and a legal pad with him.

"OK, let's assume we find this Singletary, and let's assume he has something to say that is exculpatory—I think that is the right word—for Jackson. We still have a murdered Marine lieutenant and a Marine named Grant waiting trial for murder. By the way, why was Grant charged?"

McMurry answered, "Sir, Grant was easy to pick out 'cause he was the tallest and biggest man in the platoon, or at least the tallest and biggest of the black Marines. And he had a cast on his left arm, which we think was caused when he intentionally broke his wrist to stay off the line. He was easy to identify when he was running from the lieutenant's hooch."

The general said, "Well, if you are right, and this Jackson was not involved with Grant, then we still have an accomplice or co-conspirator who hasn't been charged. Who might that be, and what do we do about finding and charging him? Anybody?"

McMurry spoke, "Sir, there were thirty-three men in first platoon, Alpha 1/9, on the night of the murder, eleven of which, including Jackson, were white. Singletary was one of those eleven. We and the NIS interviewed those eleven as well as the rest of the men in Alpha. Unless Grant got someone from another unit, which is unlikely, the co-conspirator is probably one of those eleven, but we don't have a clue as to which one. When we interviewed Singletary and Jackson, they denied having anything to do with the murder or knowing who did it, and except for Grant, who said nothing, the rest of the platoon said they knew nothing."

Top came back into the general's office. "General, we've located Singletary. He's a corporal with first platoon, Delta Company, and they're training at Camp Schwab."

"Top, we don't have time to go through regiment, battalion, and company to get to his platoon. We can explain jumping outside the chain of command later if anyone asks—which they won't. Right now, I want to talk to Singletary's platoon leader, and if you can, patch him through to this phone. If you can't, I'll go wherever I can to talk to him. Give the training area coordinates to the chopper pilots and tell them to immediately head up to Schwab to pick up Singletary. I need to talk to the platoon commander before the chopper picks up Singletary.

"Gentlemen, correct me if I'm wrong on this summary, and speak up, because I don't like yes-men around me. First, Singletary may not have even been interviewed by the IO. Second, if he were interviewed, the interview sheet may have simply been misplaced. Third, if he were interviewed, he'll remember what he said. Fourth, if he basically says what the other witnesses said, I have no choice from a legal perspective but to sign the approval of the conviction. Fifth, if he says something that either clears Jackson or casts doubt on the conviction, then I'll consider not approving the conviction, but no guarantee of that. Sixth, if he points a guilty finger at someone else, we can investigate that and hold the decision on whether to approve or reverse the conviction. Do any of you have anything to add or correct to those possibilities?"

Colonel Moore said, "General, you have accurately set forth the situation." Both McMurry and Ross nodded, confirming their agreement.

Top opened the door. "General, I have Singletary's platoon commander, Lieutenant Barringer, on the phone, patched through to your phone."

General Dowda picked up the phone. "Lieutenant Barringer, this is General Dowda. Can you read me? This is no joke—you understand? OK. The CG's chopper is on the way to your training area. Not sure of its ETA. It needs to bring a corporal named Singletary—Top gave you his full name—back to my office. Now, this corporal is going to be pooping in his pants when he's ordered to get on a chopper with two general's stars on the nose. You tell him, loud and clear, first, he is not in trouble; second, no one in his family has died or is in trouble; third, he has not done anything wrong; and finally, he is needed on an important administrative matter. Now Lieutenant, I'm going to ask Singletary what you told him, and I want you to know that I will be a very unhappy Marine general if he doesn't tell me exactly what I just told you to tell him. Understand? One more thing. When is your unit scheduled to return to Courtney? Well, just tell Singletary to bring his gear with him, and we'll get him a ride back to barracks since the rest of the platoon will be back later today. He can get a head start on the beer. Any questions? OK, thank you, Lieutenant. I appreciate your help."

As soon as the general put the phone in the cradle, Woody heard the "whop-whop" of the chopper's blades as it warmed up for the takeoff to the training area at Schwab, which was north. He had no idea how long it would take the chopper—he guessed it was a Huey—to make the round trip. He'd driven north to Schwab once to see a crime scene in an assault case. It was a long, beautiful drive in the hilly area north of Camp Courtney, but Woody could only imagine what it had been like to fight the tenacious Japanese army on such terrain.

The general stood up. "Gentlemen, I still have a division to help run, and since we've done all we can until these pieces of the puzzle start falling into place, would all of you please give me this office? Top will call you when we need you. Thanks."

The colonel, Mike, Kevin, and Woody went to the front yard of the HQ building. They were lost in their own thoughts, wondering what Singletary would have to say. Colonel Sullivan pulled out his ever-present Red Man and packed a chew into his jaw. "Woody, want some of this?"

"No, sir. I'm hyped up enough but thank you for offering."

Woody didn't know how long they had been out of the office when he heard, and then saw, the chopper coming from the north. It was riding a tailwind, moving like a bat out of hell. It passed over the HQ building and reversed direction, so it was heading north into the headwind, which would help the landing.

Once the blades stopped, a Marine in full combat gear jumped from the chopper. He just looked around, but then Woody saw Top walking to the landing pad to escort Singletary back to the building. The lawyers headed for the front door of the HQ building and were escorted back into the general's office. The general was seated at the conference table and directed them to take their seats.

Within a minute, Top opened the door, accompanied by Singletary, without his combat gear. Singletary looked around and saw the star of a brigadier general, the silver bird of a colonel, and the railroad tracks of three O-3s. He had a bewildered look on his face and had to be wondering—*What the hell is going on!*

The general rose from his chair and walked over to Singletary and extended his hand. "Corporal Singletary, I'm General Dowda. I'm proud to meet you. Come in and have a seat."

Singletary moved very cautiously. Just a few minutes ago, he had been training with his platoon at Schwab, then he took a ride on a general's chopper and now he was shaking hands with a general in a room with more brass than he'd seen in one place at any time in the Corps. This had to be a surreal experience for him.

After Singletary was seated, General Dowda spoke. "Corporal, I know they don't serve Pepsis in the field at Schwab, do they? Top, would you bring the corporal a Pepsi with ice?" Top said he would do so, and General Dowda spoke to Singletary.

"Where are you from, son?"

"North of Pierre, South Dakota, sir."

"Is that near Lake Oahe?"

"Yes sir, it is." Singletary broke into a grin.

"That is beautiful country. I went pheasant hunting in that area once. You ever pheasant hunt, Corporal?"

"Oh yes, sir. I love to pheasant hunt."

"What kind of shotgun did you have?"

Woody was amazed. General Dowda was talking to a Marine who initially was scared out of his skives but was now smiling and talking about shooting shotguns for fun. Singletary had inhaled the Pepsi and appeared more at ease. General Dowda was ready to get down to business.

"Corporal, your platoon leader, Lieutenant Barringer, what did he tell you when he said you'd be coming down here to meet with us?"

Singletary told General Dowda what Barringer had told him, and it was exactly what the General had ordered. *Lucky for Barringer*, Woody thought.

"We're here—these officers are lawyers—because we have some questions about the murder of Lieutenant Speight at VCB right after Apache Snow. You were with Alpha 1/9 then, weren't you?"

Woody was intently watching Singletary and noticed that when General Dowda said "murder," Singletary's body stiffened somewhat. Woody had learned that body language could sometimes tell as much or more than what a witness was said.

"Uh, yes, sir, I was."

"Did you go on Apache Snow?"

"Yes, sir."

"That was a tough operation, wasn't it?"

"Yes, sir." By now, Singletary was squirming. Woody guessed he was realizing why he had been brought to the general's office, and he didn't like the position he was in.

"Corporal, you were interviewed by a lieutenant named Breckinridge about that fragging, weren't you?"

Singletary was now becoming very uncomfortable. He rubbed his hands together and nervously looked around the room. He did not answer the general immediately.

The general leaned toward Singletary and held up the investigation officer's file. "Corporal, I believe Lieutenant Breckinridge talked to you about the fragging. Your name is written on the inside of this folder as a witness. Now I need you to tell me what you told Lieutenant Breckinridge, and remember, whatever you tell us you told him, as long as it is the truth, will not, I repeat *not*, get you in trouble. I give you my word as a general officer of the Marine Corps. Understand?"

Singletary nodded and addressed General Dowda. "Sir, Lieutenant Breckinridge had me stand at attention right there in company headquarters, and he gave me a direct order to not tell anyone else what I told him about that night. I have obeyed that order, and I didn't even tell the two lawyers and the detectives who came to VCB to talk to all of us because the lieutenant, he ordered me to not tell anyone what I told him. The order didn't sound right, but I followed it."

"Well, Corporal, my general's star outranks Lieutenant Breckinridge's first lieutenant's bar, and I'm ordering you to not follow his order and tell us what you told him about the fragging. Understand?"

"Yes, sir. This is what happened, and this is what I told the lieutenant. I'll never forget it. On the night the lieutenant was killed—I don't know what time it was 'cause I didn't keep up with time in 'Nam 'cause it don't matter. I was asleep and had to get up to go take a piss—uh, sorry, sir."

"That's all right, Corporal. I've taken a piss or two myself."

Singletary continued. "The head is right next to my hooch. I was leaving my hooch going to the head and saw Nose leaving the head and heading back to his hooch, which is on the other side of the head. He didn't look at me, and I don't think he saw me."

General Dowda looked around and asked, "Who is Nose?"

Woody answered. "Sir, Lance Corporal Jackson has a honker, a nose, that would put Jimmy Durante to shame, about like Karl Malden's nose."

"Malden, was he the actor with Steve McQueen in *Cincinnati Kid*?"

Woody replied, "Yes, sir."

"Well, I guess he would be hard to miss. So, Corporal, what did you see?"

"Sir, as soon as I went into the head, I heard the grenade explode. I looked up and saw Roosevelt Grant and Garland Greenfield running from the area of the lieutenant's hooch. They was headed right toward me and they was close to me. I saw their faces when it lightninged. Grant and Greenfield ran past the head and my hooch to their hooches, which were on the other side of the bunker, past where I was."

McMurry spoke, "General, may I ask Corporal Singletary some questions?" The general nodded. "First, Corporal, how long was it from the time you saw Jackson go into his hooch to the time the grenade exploded?"

"Sir, just a second or two."

"Once Jackson went into his hooch, did he come out when you were in the head?"

"No, sir."

"After you saw Jackson go into his hooch, was there enough time for him to run up to the lieutenant's hooch before the grenade exploded?"

"No, sir. No way."

"When you were coming out of your hooch to go to the head, how far were you from Jackson when he was coming out of the head?"

Singletary looked around the office, pointed, and said, "About as far as here to that wall over there."

"Was he facing you when he left the head?"

"No, sir, I was looking at the left side of his face. It was Nose. Can't miss him."

McMurry spoke, "General, that wall looks to be about fifteen feet away, which means Singletary was much closer to Jackson than Douglas was to the men he saw running, who he said were twenty or thirty yards from him."

General Dowda slid his legal pad to Singletary and gave him a pen. "Draw a map of the lieutenant's hooch, Jackson's hooch, the head, your hooch, and the hooches for Grant and Greenfield. Oh, and that bunker."

When Singletary had finished, Woody spoke up. "General, may I see that?" The general slid the legal pad to Woody, who examined the drawing and said, "That is *exactly* the map Jackson drew for me, except I didn't ask him to draw Grant's hooch. It's in my office if you need to see it. And I went out to VCB to see the place for myself, and that is the layout."

Everyone was quiet for a few seconds, absorbing all this information. The silence was broken by Singletary, who sobbed as his body was shaking. When he looked up, tears were running down his face. He looked at the general and said, "Sir, when I heard Jackson had been charged, I knowed he was innocent. I knowed Greenfield was with Grant. I wanted to say something to somebody, but Lieutenant Breckinridge, he give me a order. I was afraid to speak up. I didn't know what to do." He continued sobbing.

"Corporal, look at me!" General Dowda had gently grabbed Singletary's shoulders. "Son, you did exactly the right thing. All Marines are taught to follow orders, even if—make that particularly if—we don't understand them. That's just the way it is. This is not your fault. When you were talking to Lieutenant Breckinridge, was he taking notes?"

"Sir, I think he wrote some stuff down, but then he stopped. He didn't show me what he wrote."

General Dowda sat back in his chair. "Corporal, do you have any idea why Lieutenant Breckinridge gave you the order to not tell anyone Jackson was not with Grant?"

"No, sir. I didn't see much of any lieutenants, including him, sir, but he was…"

"He was what, Corporal?" the general asked.

"Well, sir, at VCB, it was like we was back in the States, the way he wanted us to look at VCB. He'd get on someone because of their hair cut or their boots being messed up—or something like that. It's like he forgot we was at a combat base and was busy cleaning our weapons after patrols and didn't have time to polish our boots. I remember, one time Lieutenant Breckinridge charged Jackson with a office hours offense, you know, Article 15. I think Jackson was filling sandbags—we did that all the time—and he was wearing a T-shirt and his utility cover, but he didn't salute the lieutenant, which normally you gotta do when you're outside with your cover on. The hearing officer tossed it out, and I heard from some guys that Lieutenant Breckinridge got razzed by other officers about his charge against Jackson being thrown out. I guess even the officers didn't like him being so tough on Jackson. Maybe the lieutenant was upset with Jackson."

General Dowda said, "Corporal, you've been a great help. You followed orders like you were supposed to even though you wanted to speak up on Jackson's behalf. You did nothing wrong. Colonel Sullivan, what is the next step?"

Colonel Sullivan answered, "General, I'd like to get the corporal to sit down with one of our court reporters, so his information can be transcribed and recorded, and the corporal can sign the statement as an affidavit."

"Good idea, Colonel. Corporal Singletary, we'll drive you down to legal, and after you give the court reporter your statement, call Top, and we'll get you and your gear back to your barracks, so you can get started on the beer. And I'll have my office give you a call, so you and I can go skeet shooting. We've got plenty shotguns for you to pick from. Thank you, Corporal, for your help. You're dismissed."

While General Dowda walked Singletary to the door, Woody called Legal, spoke to Corporal Grevey, and told him what he needed to do when Singletary arrived. The general spoke, "Well, this is something! As hard as it is to believe, it sounds like we have a rogue lieutenant who interviewed Marines who said Jackson left that bunker saying he wished the lieutenant was dead and then interviewed one Marine who ID'd Jackson as the man with Grant—at night, from thirty yards or so, when it lightninged, with a typhoon howling. Then the IO interviewed another Marine, Singletary, who said Greenfield—not Jackson—was with Grant, and then the IO didn't include that interview sheet 'cause he was pissed at Jackson. This is hard to believe. Colonel Sullivan, have I summarized this correctly?"

"Yes, sir."

The general continued, "Captain McMurry and Lieutenant Ross, if that IO, Breckinridge, had included his interview with Singletary just as Singletary told us today, even with what the other Marine said about ID'ing Jackson, what would you have done as trial counsel?"

McMurry answered, "General, eyewitness cases are tough 'cause humans are talking about what they remember they think they saw in a split second or so. To me, Singletary, not Douglas, had the better chance to see Jackson.

They were running toward him, not past him as they were with Douglas. Singletary was by far closer to Jackson than Douglas was to the guys who were running. I believe Singletary is the better, more believable witness. His reaction today is pretty good evidence of that.

"I'm not saying Douglas is lying, I'm just saying he didn't see the right man. But to your question, we'd investigate and have lawyers assigned to Jackson and Greenfield, and then see if either of them cooperated. We could not charge both of them and Grant 'cause there were only two people running. If we charged Jackson, we'd tell his attorney what Singletary said. We could talk to other Marines in Alpha 1/9 to see if we could connect dots between Jackson and Grant or Greenfield and Grant. If we decided to charge Greenfield, we'd try to squeeze him to testify against Grant. Getting the death penalty off the plate may bring him around. Of course, a conviction of the murder versus the accessory and conspiracy charges is more important to the government. And if we had both stories, we would ask the SJA to help decide, because a decision on that issue is above our pay grade."

"So," the general continued, "where the hell is Greenfield? Anyone got an idea?"

When no one knew, the general went to the office door and asked Top to come in. "Top, we need to find another Marine in Alpha 1/9 by the name of Garland Greenfield. Get right on it, and come back when you know, please."

Within five minutes, Top knocked and came into the office. "General, I've located Greenfield. That's the good news. The bad news is that he is at Kadena Air Base, or he has left Kadena to rotate back home, and when he gets to the States, he'll be discharged."

The general asked, "Does anybody have any ideas on how to locate him at Kadena, or if he's flown out, how to find out the ETA of his flight to, I guess Norton Air Base in California so we can be waiting for him? Given the twenty or so hours of flight time, we've got enough time to get NIS to Norton or wherever he lands to wait for him if he has left Kadena. Maybe we could get NIS in Hawaii to pick him up when they land to refuel."

Top spoke, "General, I believe Major Jacobs has a golf buddy—an Air Force guy—who is stationed at Kadena Air Base. That may be a place to start."

General Dowda picked up the phone on the conference room table and dialed a number. "Major Jacobs, I need you in here with a legal pad."

Tom Jacobs was a graduate of The University of the South in Sewanee, Tennessee. He enlisted his senior year of college, completed OCS and TBS, and with his intelligence rose steadily through the ranks. General Dowda handpicked Jacobs to be his aide.

Major Jacobs came into the general's office. "Tom, have a seat. I'll introduce these gentlemen later, but first I've got a job for you. I've got to locate a Marine named Greenfield, Garland Greenfield—you can get his full name and service number from Top. We need to find out if he is at Kadena. As I understand it, he has pulled his tour and will be discharged from the Corps upon reaching the States. Do you know someone at transit who can help locate this Marine for us?"

"Yes, sir, I do. Air Force Major Mike Foster is second in command of transit. He and I have played golf several times at the Kadena base course, last time last Saturday. I have his number. What shall I tell him we need him to do?"

"Tell him that there are orders on the way for this Greenfield—Top, please prepare the orders. We're changing his orders if he hasn't left, and if he has left, we need your buddy to give us the flight number and the travel itinerary of the flight. Also, he needs to do this in a way that doesn't scare off Greenfield if his flight has not left. He needs to call Captain McMurry back with his report."

"Yes, sir, I'll get right on it."

"Tom, one more thing. Did you win the match against him last Saturday?"

"Yes Sir, General, the Corps *never* loses to the Air Force."

When he was told a Major Jacobs was calling for him, Mike Foster, Major, USAF, wondered if Tom was calling him to set up another golf game or to razz him about winning the bet at their last match or both. He could not imagine any other reason for Mike to call. It never crossed his mind that he would be asked to become involved in the apprehension of a murder suspect.

Major Foster answered the call. "You were lucky as hell to sink that putt on eighteen last week. Are you calling to rub it in?"

"No, Mike, we've got a real problem to deal with and need your immediate help."

"Sure thing, what can I do?"

After Tom outlined the need to locate and hold Greenfield if he were at Kadena and to get his flight number and itinerary if his flight had already departed, Major Foster said, "There are about three hundred Marines here waiting to fly back to the States on two different flights. I can check both manifests to see if he's in that group. If he is, how can I find him? Do you have a picture? If I call out his name, he may get jumpy and bolt."

"Mike, I wish I could help you. He's probably wearing jungle utilities and would not have his name on them. A description probably wouldn't help 'cause he could see the Air Police pulling guys out and asking if their name was Greenfield. He'd know what was going on and bug out. There's got to be another way to get him without him knowing that we're looking for him."

"OK, Tom, I'll figure out something and keep you posted. What's your call-back number?"

"Mike, I just thought of something else. I know I'm loading up on you. We're gonna need a lawyer with you when you get Greenfield—if he's there. He'll need to give Greenfield his Miranda warning, you know, the right to remain silent, that what he said could or would be used against him—the lawyer will know the drill. If Greenfield says anything, we want to be able to use it. Can you make that happen?"

"Can do. The JAG office is five minutes from here, and one of my poker buddies is a lawyer there. I'll call him right now. What is your call-back number?"

After writing down Tom's number, Mike started brainstorming. How could he possibly locate Greenfield without Greenfield knowing they were looking for him?

And then he knew exactly what to do, so he got his barracks hat and a piece of paper, gave instructions to his next-in-command, and left his office.

The terminal at Kadena was large and airy. There were about three hundred Marines, plus their sea bags, ready to board two civilian aircraft for flights back to the States. Mike had checked the manifests of both flights and knew which flight Greenfield was on, but Marines from both flights were all in one place. The terminal had a sound system which worked well, and Mike knew just how to use it to get Greenfield.

When Mike got to the center of the terminal, he stood on a bench under the big clock and gave the prearranged signal to his next-in-command, who was standing in Mike's office at a window which oversaw the terminal.

Mike's next-in-command punched the key to make the announcement to all the Marines. "Marines, the Air Force very much appreciates the service you have given to our great country, and as a show of our appreciation, we are going to award a new Seiko watch to the lucky Marine whose name is drawn out of the hat of Major Foster, who is now standing on the bench under the clock. Please listen up."

Major Foster brought a hand mic which he cut on and he addressed the crowd, all of whom were looking at him. "Jarheads, you've all done a great job, at great peril, in South Vietnam. The Air Force and all Americans appreciate your service, and as a show of our appreciation, we want to award one of you a Seiko watch. We have written the names of each Marine, taken from the flight manifests of both aircrafts, and put them in my hat. I'm going to reach into my hat and select the one Marine, from all of you, who will receive a new Seiko watch, courtesy of the Air Force." Mike held his hat above his head, reached with his right hand, making a motion as if he were searching through papers with names on them, and then pulled out the one piece of paper in his hat. He looked at it, and announced, "The lucky Marine is PFC Garland Greenfield. Come forward, please."

Everyone started looking around to see who the lucky winner was. Greenfield had never won a thing in his life and smiled bashfully as he moved through the crowd. Everyone was clapping him on the back, calling him a lucky dog.

Greenfield got to the bench where Tom was standing. He didn't notice the two husky Air Police on either side of the bench, or the Air Force captain behind the major making the announcement. Foster extended his hand as if to offer a handshake, and when Greenfield did the same, the air police officer on his right snapped a handcuff on his right wrist, pulled his right arm behind him, and then pulled Greenfield's left arm behind him and cuffed his left wrist. Major Foster directed the Air Police to take Greenfield to his office, jumped from the bench, and followed them. The Air Force lawyer was one step behind Major Foster. All other Marines at the terminal were stunned and wondered what had just happened. They would never know.

"General, there is a call for Captain McMurry from a Major Foster," Top announced from the doorway. "I'll route it to the conference table phone." McMurry picked up the receiver, introduced himself, and listened. Everyone was quiet as they listened to McMurry's end of the call.

When McMurry finished the call, he placed the phone back in the receiver. "Major Foster got Greenfield, put him in handcuffs, and is transporting him to the brig. It's a good thing we had an Air Force JAG lawyer with them to warn Greenfield of his rights, 'cause Greenfield started talking as soon as they got to Mike's office. He said that he was asleep on the night of the fragging, that Grant woke him up and told him he was going to play a joke on Lieutenant Speight by tossing a smoke grenade that he—Grant—had swiped from an LZ. Greenfield said Grant said he needed Greenfield to hold open the lieutenant's hooch door since he couldn't because he had a messed-up hand and that he would toss the smoke grenade with his good hand. Greenfield said he held the door open but didn't see what Grant had in his hand or what he threw into the lieutenant's hooch. Greenfield said as they were running back to the hooch, he heard the explosion and knew Grant had fragged the lieutenant. When they got to Greenfield's hooch, he asked Grant why he'd thrown a live grenade, instead of a smoke grenade. He said Grant grabbed him, told him that he was as guilty as Grant was, and warned him that he'd better keep his mouth shut or he'd be charged too. Greenfield may not be guilty of conspiracy or murder, but he sure is guilty of accessory after the fact for helping Grant keep it quiet."

Colonel Sullivan addressed the general. "Sir, this satisfies me that Jackson didn't do anything and that Captain McMurry, Captain White,

and Lieutenant Ross were right on the money about Jackson's possible innocence. I recommend that you sign the paperwork to overturn the conviction."

General Dowda put his elbows on the table and leaned forward. "This
is so hard to get my head around it. Grant fooled Greenfield into helping,
and instead of throwing a smoke grenade, he threw a live M61 grenade—
or we think it was an M61—under the lieutenant's rack. Greenfield was
not interviewed by the IO, Lieutenant Breckinridge, but was interviewed
when NIS interviewed the company, and I guess he denied everything. An
attempt to interview Grant was made and he didn't say anything, right?"
McMurry nodded. "Corporal Singletary tells us he saw Jackson go from the
head into his hooch immediately before the grenade exploded, and he then
saw Grant and Greenfield—not Jackson—running from the lieutenant's
hooch toward their own hooches after the grenade exploded. But because
Breckinridge gave Singletary an order to not disclose that info, Singletary
told NIS he didn't know anything about it. Greenfield has volunteered he
was with Grant and that Grant tossed the grenade, and I suppose that would
be admissible as evidence, Colonel." The colonel nodded yes. "And so we've
got a rogue investigation officer who knew damn well he was not shooting
straight when he didn't make Singletary's statement part of the investigation, probably because he was pissed at Jackson. Colonel, would there be a
crime in his failure to report what Singletary said?"

Colonel Sullivan answered, "Yes, sir, it would at least be obstruction of
justice."

The general stood up. "Colonel, please prepare the documents necessary
to reverse or strike, or whatever you call it, to get rid of the dishonorable
discharge and the sentence to restore Lance Corporal Jackson to his rank,
and to return his pay, which I assume was not issued since he was convicted.
But you may think about helping him by not letting him get all that money
at once. He's been confined all these months, and I'd hate to see him blow
it all in one night on the town." He went to the door and asked Top and
Tom Jacobs to come in and have a seat at the table.

"Top, when we break up, I want you to find out the base and unit
where this Breckinridge is stationed and give that information to Colonel
Sullivan. Colonel, in a minute you and I will discuss Breckinridge. But now,

gentlemen, we have done a good day's work for the Corps, and we should reward ourselves."

The general walked over to a cabinet in the corner of the room, got a tray, put several glasses on it, and brought them to the table. He then went back to the cabinet, opened the doors, and took out a bottle of 101 proof Wild Turkey and a bottle of Old Grouse scotch which he brought to the table. "Gentlemen, pour yourself a strong belt of your preference." After each officer had followed the general's order, the general held out his glass to make a toast, and the other officers and Top stood. "Gentlemen, to the Corps! Semper fi!" The other officers repeated the toast, clinked glasses all around, and took a well-deserved drink.

"Now, gentlemen, we earned that drink. But we're not through. Here's what is going to happen next."

The Brig

0830 Hours, Thurs, 13 Nov 69
Camp Hansen, Okinawa

The brig for the Third Marine Division on Okinawa was located at Camp Hansen, north of Camp Courtney and south of Camp Schwab.

Lance Corporal Jackson was in the exercise yard of the brig when the guard told him he had visitors. All he could think about was whether he'd survive Leavenworth prison. One of the brig guards had served there, and Jackson asked him what Leavenworth was like. Jackson knew he was innocent, and he had no idea how he was mistaken for the man running with Roosevelt Grant. He thought Captain White believed him, but Jackson did not know why the military jury panel did not believe his testimony. After Jackson got the rundown on Leavenworth , he began to summon up the guts to kill himself. Captain White had told him that it was a long shot, an almost-impossible shot, that the general would overturn the conviction. He knew the visitor would be Captain White, probably with bad news.

Then he realized the guard had said he had *visitors*, more than one. Jackson couldn't imagine who, other than Captain White, would be coming to see him at this hellhole brig.

If family members visited a prisoner at the Camp Hansen brig, a thick glass partition separated the prisoner and the visitor, but lawyers were permitted to meet face-to-face with their client prisoners, sitting at tables in an open room. Several guards would remain in the room during these visits, but on this occasion, there were no guards present.

White and Jackson had met in that room several times, but this time was different. When Jackson was escorted into the room, Captain White was seated facing him, but two men in uniform were seated across from Captain White with their backs to Jackson as he cautiously approached the table.

Woody stood up. "Lance Corporal Jackson, you remember these men, don't you?' McMurry and Ross stood up and Jackson recoiled. Then he saw that they were smiling and extending their hands to shake his hand. Woody continued. "We've got good news—the best news—for you. Have a seat."

Jackson's head began to spin as he thought: *What could the good news be? Captain White said there was no chance we would win the case. I've been found guilty and am going to Leavenworth. Why are these lawyers who convicted me here?*

Jackson felt as if he were in a dream as Woody recounted the story of the witness file, Lieutenant Breckinridge, the interview with Singletary, Greenfield's confession, and the general's request that Colonel Sullivan prepare the documents overturning the conviction. There would be no trip to Fort Leavenworth!

Woody continued. "Jackson, here's what's going to happen. You're leaving here with us as a free man. Here's a power of attorney for you to sign, authorizing me to deposit and control your back pay. When you were convicted, your pay stopped until the end of the appeal, but with the conviction overturned, you are entitled to all of it. That's a lot of money, and we want to help you save as much as you can, so I'll give you money from time to time, until you get used to being on the outside. The last thing you need to do is to blow all of this on beer and women in a weekend. You'll be assigned to First Platoon, Delta Company, 2/9, and they know you are on the way. You'll have light duty for some period. Your company commander and platoon leader know your story. Any questions?"

Jackson was overcome and could not speak. He stared ahead and then bowed his head and put his head in his hands and his elbows on the table. His shoulders shook as he sobbed the cry of a free man. Woody knew Marines weren't supposed to cry, but this was the exception to that rule.

Woody, Kevin and Mike were silent and did not even glance at the sobbing Jackson. Each of them, particularly Woody, felt enormous pride, accomplishment and relief as this burden had been lifted from their shoulders. Kevin and Mike knew the conviction of Jackson was the biggest win, a huge win, of their careers as Marine lawyers, but then, through the actions of themselves and Woody and with the colonel's blessing, combined with the persistence and will to win they learned as Marines, they had undertaken the effort to overturn their greatest legal victory. They had the professional satisfaction that had they not undertaken the investigation, justice would not have been served. They had taken the moral high road and had done the right thing and therefore felt the satisfaction professionals seek to find.

Singletary Is Surprised

1245 Hours, Thurs, 20 Nov 69
Office of General Dowda
Camp Courtney

Corporal Jason Singletary had no idea that he would again visit the office of General Dowda after the meeting about the murder of Lieutenant Speight. But he was told by his platoon and company commanders that all three of them had been ordered to report to the general's office at 1300 hours on 20 November. He was not told why he was reporting. He just knew that Marines did what they were ordered to do, without questioning the order.

All three Marines changed from their utilities to their service Charlie uniform with the "piss cutter" garrison cover and arrived at the general's office at 1245 hours. They were seated in the waiting area, and Jason noted there was a lance corporal with a camera also seated in the waiting area.

Promptly at 1300 hours, the general's first sergeant invited them to come into the general's office. The lance corporal with the camera was ordered to follow them. General Dowda stood in the middle of the room.

The general extended his hand to the company commander and the platoon commander. Then he turned to Jason. "Welcome, Corporal Singletary. I know you have been a corporal in this man's Corps for only eight months, and I know that a Marine is usually a corporal for at least two years before being considered for promotion to sergeant E-5. But your service to the Corps has been so exceptional, particularly in the last few weeks, that it is my privilege and honor to promote you to the rank of sergeant, E-5. Congratulations, Sergeant Singletary." Top handed the general the three strips over crossed rifles chevrons of an E-5 which the general handed to the new sergeant. "Now, Sergeant Singletary, you get that corporal rank off your uniform and replace it as soon as possible with your new rank." The general smiled and extended his hand, and said, "And that's an order."

Singletary was so overwhelmed that he couldn't say a word. Those in attendance applauded, and the lance corporal took pictures, one with Jason shaking the general's hand.

The general continued speaking, "There is one more thing. In 1943, the Navy Commendation Medal was established to be awarded to Navy and Marine personnel who have highly distinguished themselves in their service to the country. The award can be given with the combat "V" device when authorized. Sergeant Singletary, the service you gave entitles you to the award of the Navy Commendation Medal with combat "V" device, and sergeant, it is my privilege and honor to award this medal to you, Sergeant." Top handed the general a small box, which the general opened. He then held up the green ribbon with white strips to which the medal was attached. The medal was six-sided medal and imprinted with an eagle with wings spread wide as it held three arrows. This medal could be worn when wearing dress blues or whites. The box also contained a smaller green ribbon with white stripes on which the "V" was placed, which was appropriate for wearing on the routine uniform shirt. The general nodded to Top, who then read aloud the citation detailing how Singletary had upheld the highest standards of the Corps by following orders. There was applause all around, and then the lance corporal took more pictures.

Sergeant Singletary's head was spinning as he thanked General Dowda and shook his hand. He was congratulated by his platoon commander and platoon sergeant. The new sergeant, with his new decoration, left the general's office.

As the room was clearing, General Dowda asked Top to hold back. "Top, have we taken care of that thing at Lejeune?"

Top grinned, "Yes, sir. The paperwork has arrived and will be carried out in the next four or five days."

Breckinridge Meets Harmon
0800 Hours, Wed, 26 Nov 69
Rifle Range Bravo Six
Marine Corps Base
Camp Lejeune, North Carolina

First Lieutenant Donald Breckinridge IV rotated back to the United States before the general court-martial of Lance Corporal Jackson began. He had no idea how the case was resolved, and he didn't give a damn.

For his final duty station, Donald requested assignment at the Marine Barracks at Eighth and I Streets, in Washington, DC. Such a posting would give Donald the opportunity to easily travel to Philadelphia, his home of record, so he could attend those high society gatherings on the Main Line in Philadelphia. He could also begin meeting clients of the successful family investment firm where Donald would become a highly paid associate upon his release from active duty.

But Eighth and I is a very special place, and the Marines assigned to Eighth and I are the best of the best. Donald was not close to being the best of the best. He was initially disappointed to be posted to Camp Lejeune in Jacksonville, North Carolina, in late September 1969.

His disappointment abated somewhat when he was told the duty assignment for his remaining three months. The Corps tried to assign "short-timers" to duty stations that involved minimal interaction with the command process. Why get used to a unit and have them get used to you if you're only going to be in the Corps for a short time? Breckinridge was most definitely a short-timer.

He was assigned as OIC, Officer in Charge, of a firing range. There were multiple firing ranges at Lejeune, used mainly by the graduates of boot camp at Parris Island. Those graduates were assigned to AIT—advanced infantry training—at Lejeune where, in addition to becoming proficient at firing the rifle, they learned how to take apart and reassemble the M16, hand-to-hand combat, and tactics for the squad, platoon, and company. They learned how to engage and kill the enemy.

As OIC of Rifle Range Bravo 6, all Lieutenant Donald Breckinridge IV had to do was drive to the range from his rented beach house by 0800 hours on weekdays, let the gunnery sergeant run the range, and return to his beach cottage at the end of the day. Breckinridge would bring the latest edition of *Barron's* or *Forbes* business magazines, or the occasional *Wall Street Journal*, to read after the gunny brought him coffee when he arrived at the OIC's office at the back of the range. It was the essence of easy duty, right up Breckinridge's alley.

Donald had a great run of luck with women, although he did not think of it as luck. Rather he thought of himself as a man loved by women who couldn't get enough of him. He spent time at some of the many bars in downtown Jacksonville, NC, which existed because Lejeune existed. He drove a sporty red TR-3 convertible, which he thought attracted the ladies. He would hook up with up with two, three, or four different women a week. Sometimes he and the latest "love of his life" would have dinner at his rented beach house, walk to one of the many beaches in Onslow County, and do their best imitation of Burt Lancaster and Deborah Kerr rolling in the sand.

Since the firing range would not be used on Thanksgiving Day or the Friday and weekend thereafter, Donald arranged to get leave early on the Wednesday before Thanksgiving. His clothes and gear were packed into his convertible, he had gassed up the car, and he was ready to hit the road for Philly in the early afternoon.

As Donald drove to work, he was recalling his entanglement with the beautiful, long-legged, voluptuous redhead he met earlier in the week. She was not the kind of woman he'd take home to meet Mom and Dad, but she was a great distraction.

Donald was also pissed off because even though his release date was only three months off, no one had approached him to plan the "getting out of the Corps" party traditionally given to officers receiving their DD- 214 and being released from active duty. He didn't realize that no one had approached him because no one wanted to spend time around him, and they were glad he was leaving.

But by and large, Donald Breckinridge IV was just fine with where he was. During his post-Vietnam leave, he went home and his dad bought him a wonderful garage apartment near his office, and gave Donald an unlimited budget to furnish his apartment—a budget which Donald damn near exceeded.

The life of Donald Breckinridge IV was good.

But that life was about to change.

The range was located at the end of a winding two-mile dead-end dirt road cut through the Carolina pines of Onslow County. Since there was nothing down the road except the range, there was no reason for anyone to come down the road unless they had business at the range.

No one had driven to the range after Breckinridge arrived since he became the OIC of the range.

Until today.

Breckinridge was sipping his coffee and reading the morning paper when he saw the dust from two cars coming down the road to the range. When the cars stopped, the gunny approached the cars as two men in suits wearing hats and two sergeants wearing sidearms exited the cars. Breckinridge thought that one of the Marines at the range that day must have gotten in trouble.

He was wrong.

The gunny pointed to the office, and all four men walked toward the office. As they entered, Breckinridge stood up and said, "Can I help you?"

One of the men in a suit said, "I am Special Agent Leroy Harmon. You can help if you are the First Lieutenant Donald Breckinridge the Fourth who served with First Battalion, Ninth Marine Regiment, at Vandergrift Combat Base, South Vietnam."

Donald smiled and extended his hand. "Yes, I am, one in the same."

"Well, Lieutenant, I'm with Naval Investigative Service, and I am placing you under arrest for obstruction of justice involving your so-called investigation of the fragging of Lieutenant Speight at VCB and your failure to report exculpatory evidence about Lance Corporal Jackson given to you by Corporal Singletary." Agent Harmon directed one of the sergeants to handcuff Breckinridge, who was no longer smiling, and to make sure the cuffs were on very tight. "We are not going to ask you any questions because we know you are guilty, and we can prove it. However, I'm still required to advise you that you have a right to remain silent, that anything you say can and will be used against you in a court of law, and that you have the right to have an attorney appointed to represent you if you can't afford to hire one.

"Just so you know, we are taking you back to base legal, where the articles and specifications listing your crimes will be served on you. You may be interested to know that the charges have been signed by Brigadier General Hugh Dowda of the Third Marine Division. Pretty special to get charged by a general, I'd say. Maybe you can paste them to the wall of your cell and look at them for the next few years."

The last thing Breckinridge heard as he was pushed into the back seat of the shore patrol car was the gunny ordering the Marines at the rifle range, "Ready, aim, fire!"

Epilogue

Captain Woody White thought his life would return to normal after Lieutenant Breckinridge was transferred to Camp Lejeune to stand trial for obstruction of justice, and after Grant pled guilty to murder and was sentenced to life imprisonment at Fort Leavenworth. Greenfield pled to accessory after the fact to murder, received a ten-year sentence and was sent to a federal prison in Indiana, away from Grant.

But Woody's life was anything but normal, because a bounty was placed on his head, and then an attempt was made on his life.

For his safety Woody was assigned to Marine Corps Air Station, Cherry Point, North Carolina where he soon began the investigation of the murder of a Marine who body was found in a forest, with his military ID placed between his front teeth. There was no clue to link a weapon to the murder until Woody saw a sea gull flying to its nest. And at a club, Woody caught a brief glance of his beautiful heartthrob from high school. Would he ever see her again?

After his Marine Corps tour ended unexpectedly because Woody's life was in jeopardy, Woody began civilian law practice with a senior partner who gave him guidance in litigating against an attorney Woody intensely disliked, but his senior partner did *not* give Woody critical information in the biggest criminal case of Woody's civilian career, because that was information Woody had **NO NEED TO KNOW.**

CPSIA information can be obtained
at www.ICGtesting.com
Printed in the USA
JSHW051931251022
32149JS00005B/213